W9-CHB-521

*Mary-Ann :
Wonderful
meeting you !*

JESSICA

by
Beverley Dixon Mallette

Beverley Dixon Mallette

Published by
Highway Book Shop
Cobalt, Ontario P0J 1C0

Canadian Cataloguing in Publication Data

Mallette, Beverley Dixon, 1937-

      Jessica

ISBN 0-88954-354-2

I. Title

PS8576.A55J4 1991   C 813'.54   C 91-095762-2

PR9199.3.M35J4 1991

*This novel is dedicated to my Father
Cuthbert Batten Dixon
and to his brothers, the rest of Jessica's sons —
Geoffrey Clement, Walter Glyde, Oscar Lavington,
Leonard Charles and Ernest Alfred*

Author's Foreword

Jessica is a work of fiction based on fact.

The fact is that the author's Grandmother, Jessie Selina Batten, a nurse from London (England), came to Cobalt, Ontario where she worked in a 'tent-hospital', at the turn-of-the-century. She met and married Geoffrey Walter Dixon, an Englishman who was working out of Cobalt as a topographer. She never went back to England.

The fiction part — well, that's the part that is difficult to define. Jessie, or *Jessica* told stories to the author throughout their long and close relationship, and the result of those story-telling sessions is on these pages. The author would like to apologize for any exaggerations, and would appreciate it if, while reading this novel, you keep in mind that a little girl's memory of a very grand lady, may have become a trifle magnified through the years — but not, the author believes, very much.

Contents

JESSICA

1

Beginnings

Green pine trees, tall as church steeples, grew towards
the bright blue sky, reaching as though they were endeavour-
ing to trap the small snow-white clouds in their uppermost
branches. The trees were soon replaced by peculiar rock for-
mations, both grand and small, and then quite without warning, by glistening patches of water, the brilliant northern sun
dancing off their surfaces, piercing the unprotected eye.

This unusual combination of tree, rock and water
whisked by the train window giving passengers little or no
time to commit any one thing to memory. The colourful blur
would be unforgettable, as would the immensity of it all, but
nothing specific could be viewed quite long enough to last.

Occasionally, Jessica would close her eyes and cover
them with her hand. Her eyes hurt. It was as though she
was trying to pour too much newness into her vision at one
time, and, when her eyes were filled, she had to protect them
until these visions emptied into her brain, thereby leaving
room for more new sights.

"Is this seat taken? Ma'am?" The words tore into her
solitude. She frowned, partly because she was startled, and
partly because the interior of the car was so much darker
than the luminous outdoors. Her furrowed brow must have
been interpreted by the stranger to mean that, yes, the seat

across from the girl was taken. The stranger moved on.
Jessica was too tired to feel any guilt about the slight decep-
tion, and, besides, she rationalized, glancing about the car,
there were plenty of other empty seats on the coach. She
shifted her large dark eyes back outward, squinting as she
did so, through the dusty, weather-stained window, onto the
strange landscape that was Canada. Oh, so unlike her
England!

She cleared her throat and shook her head, causing the
chignon at the nape of her neck to loosen still further, as the
pins that held it in place had been put there so very many
hours ago. She shook her head in an effort to stop the awesome memories from taking over her mind: memories of
England. She had no time, no energy for ghosts. They had to
stay hidden — for a while anyway — certainly until she was
able to settle herself in this barbaric wilderness. There
would be time enough then to dredge out the old horrors, to
go over, word by word, the painful dialogues that were forever etched in her memory. But not now. Not now!

Merciful sleep washed over her fatigue, much like the
warm, salty waves that had washed over her body at the sea-
side, and, despite her inner turmoil, she slept, dreamless.

"Dinner is being served, Ma'am." The announcement
was made by a large white-clad negro. She vaguely remembered the men back home talking over their brandy and
cigars, when she had been but a child — talking of the terrible Civil War that had raged so recently in America, and of
how so many slaves, black men and women from the sunny,
southern states, had fled north into the cold, unfamiliar,
unyielding freedom of Canada, and she wondered if the disappearing grey-haired figure, clad all in white, had once worked
the cotton fields of the south.

For what seemed to be the hundredth time, she shifted
herself in her seat, trying to inconspicuously adjust her petticoats and underthings, which had become disarrayed in her
slumber. It was not easy, and she hoped that they would,
with the aid of gravity, settle more comfortably about her
person when she stood. As she was doing this, she was surprised to note that the seat opposite her was occupied, or at

least, had been occupied, as there were bags on the cushioned seat — bags that spoke unmistakably of a man.

Irritation prickled at the very roots of her hair, and she did not know why. She had no right to expect privacy on this northbound train. 'You pays yer monies an' takes yer chances', a phrase from a comic play that she had seen in London, a few short months ago, came to her mind, and her irritation melted away leaving in its stead, resolution. This was a new emotion for Jessica — one which she had learned to cultivate only recently.

In this God-forsaken wilderness, there would be a good deal of compromise, a constant need for resolution, and Jessica would prove that she had it. She would show them all that a Baxter could persevere against all odds. She was, if nothing else, a survivor!

"The fish is good," offered one of her table companions, as Jessica perused the menu. She had long since stopped hoping for a table of her own, or even a table shared by one of the few other women aboard the train. She nodded her appreciation of the gentleman's suggestion, and then ordered the beef. Not looking at her, the man smiled, a rather derisive smile. Was she carrying her new-found independent streak a bit far? She pondered, and then she too smiled. It did not go unnoticed.

"It's pickerel," the gentleman explained, as though she might change her mind upon hearing the name of the fish. This amused her. "Wall-eyed pike," he explained further. Amusement faded to be replaced by a shuddering as Jessica imagined a fish with great round eyes staring up at her from her plate, and she was thankful that she had ordered the beef.

As was her custom during the mealtime, she occupied herself with studies of the table linens, the cutlery, the china, and only when all of this trivia had been memorized did she allow her gaze to wander furtively about the car, careful not to meet another's stare. The dining car was actually quite well appointed, which had come as a rather pleasant surprise to Jessica, but it was still not up to the standards of the British Rail. The numerous and luxurious train rides that she had taken from her beloved Kent, up along the dazzling east coast of England, to visit Grandmamma in York, came to her mind, and, because of the crowded conditions in the dining car, she felt safe unleashing of a few of the friendlier ghosts.

"Why, here's young Miss Jessica and Master Charles!" The visits to Grandmamma would invariably begin this way, with the housekeeper Martha rushing out to greet them in their carriage. Martha always made such a fuss about the grandchildren, and Grandmamma Windsor would treat the old servant doubly well for her efforts. Mrs. Abigail Windsor was a semi-invalid, her rickety old body confined most of the time to a rickety old wheel chair, and she could not manage the long stairway that led to the drive. She would send the faithful Martha in her place, hoping that the children would understand, and of course, they always did. Martha would get the first hugs and kisses, they were her due, but the biggest ones, the longest ones, the warmest ones, belonged to Grandmamma.

"My, how you've grown," the old lady would inevitably say upon her first study of her handsome young granddaughter. She was able to say this for a good many years, as the girl continued to grow until she was eighteen years of age and a full five foot ten inches in height. A bit tall for a Windsor woman, Grandmother was heard to complain more than once.

Charles, shortly after arrival, would disappear in the direction of the stables, to while away his vacation time with the magnificent hunters, the Irish groom Eric, and the many young locals who would swarm to Fairview to share his holidays with him. It always amazed and amused his Grandmother that the other young men would know exactly when to put in an appearance. It was generally about an hour after Charles had stepped from his carriage, still dressed in his stiff school uniform. They instinctively gave him time to greet his Grandmother in the appropriate manner, exit himself to his rooms, and change into the riding fashion of the day.

they would be galloping up the laneway just as he would be running towards the paddock, and there would be loud salutations, backslapping and an obvious enjoyment of one another. Charles was extremely well liked. It was impossible to imagine anyone not liking the young man. He was tall, which was quite permissible for Windsor men, exceedingly good looking, with his dark-brown curls, his dimpled chin and his broad-shouldered swagger. But, more importantly, he was fun!

Fun — a word that no one had ever applied to Jessica. Not that Jessica wasn't well liked too. She had her friends. But she had a seriousness about her that was totally lacking in her brother. Abigail Windsor would shake her head and be thankful that Charles was born to money, as he had not been blessed with much depth of character, as far as she'd been able to discern.

"Your mother and father, they are in Paris?" Grandmamma questioned Jessica.

The girl knew full well that her grandparent was aware of where her daughter Sybil and her husband Edward were at all times. But she dutifully answered, "Yes, they left two weeks ago. I think that they're going on to Rome after," she watched to see if the old woman would correct her on this point, and she did.

"Vienna, child. They're going on to Vienna for the opera season."

Try as she might, Jessica was never able to get any further comment about her parents from her Grandmother. It seemed strange that she and Charles always visited Fairview alone, and it was stranger still that these few sentences, always at the beginning of her visit, would be all that would be said about Mr. and Mrs. Edward Charles Baxter.

"I'd like to bring Katharine Singer up for the Christmas Holiday, if it pleases you, Grandmother." Almost everything that Jessica did pleased her grandparent. When Jessica received a smile and a nod, she continued. "Her parents have gone to India for some reason or other and won't be back until next spring, so

Kat's likely to be quite lonesome during the vacation."
She smiled a most engaging and sincere smile and
added, "She's not blessed with a Grandmamma like
mine." As she said this, she stroked the old woman's
arm, in a show of affection that was rare for Jessica.

The old lady beamed. Jessica was her own true love,
she made no effort to disguise this fact. "Of course! It
will be grand to have another youngster in the house
over the season. The more the merrier!" She spoke this
last sentence with such enthusiasm that her granddaughter, once again, involuntarily reached for the bony
old arm and gave it a stroke. Jessica blushed slightly
and turned away. It would forever puzzle her why it
was that it embarrassed her to touch another human
being in this manner. The instinct was always there,
but for some unfathomable reason, the message seldom
got from her heart to her head, and most caresses died
within her breast.

The waiter, another black, placed tea and sweet biscuits
in front of her, stirring her from her reverie. She wished that
he hadn't. It was the first time in weeks that Jessica had felt
warm, even safe, and she wanted to be back again, at
Fairview, back with that tiny old woman who had meant so
much to her. But the moment was gone, and when she
brought her vision back from the middle distance, she was
shocked to discover that she was staring straight into the
eyes of a man whom she had never seen before in her life.
The very warmth that her memories had evoked in her,
rushed to her face, leaving it scarlet and hot. She quickly
dropped her gaze.

"Lost in dreamland?" queried the stranger, in a soft,
rather pleasant voice. Jessica was afraid to look up and muttered, "Yes," quietly to her plate. "It's rather nice to have a
place to go when everything about you is so . . . well, so for-
eign." His perception surprised Jessica and discomfited her
even more. She did not like the thought that she was so
transparent.

The self-conscious girl murmured something that sounded like an agreement, keeping her eyes on her plate all the

while. Not to be discouraged by her quiet, the stranger continued, "If I'm not mistaken, you're from Kent?" Why was it that an Englishman could invariably pinpoint another Englishman's heritage by merely a few words spoken to a waiter? It angered her that he was correct, but there was a question mark at the end of his sentence that seemed to demand an answer. She slowly lifted her dark brown, almost black, eyes upward, noticing on the way that this man was quite well attired, and appeared to be of a sizable frame. This always interested the too-tall Jessica; she looked at a person's stature instinctively, as others might search for blemishes on one's skin, good teeth or bald spots.

"Canterbury," she answered, breaking the rather awkward silence. There were two other gentlemen at their table and they seemed to have suspended their eating clatter, awaiting her reply. "Well, just outside of Canterbury," she explained further. She was about to add Singinham, but caught herself just in time. Singinham had been the family estate. It spoke of upper class, or aristocracy, and it was no longer hers to claim. "Canterbury," she repeated. She felt that she had to say something else, it had been so obvious that she had intended to.

Her table companion raised his eyebrow and Jessica's heart sank. It was abundantly clear that this man was not a fool. His eyes twinkled and they spoke the silent words, 'So you have a secret?'. Once again she flushed and once again she was angry with herself and with this man who seemed to be able to read her mind. She excused herself hastily, despite the fact that she had not finished her tea, and went back to her car.

The bags were still on the seat opposite her and she scowled at them. What a nuisance men were, she told herself, and memories of her father and brother flooded back, bringing stinging tears to her eyes. Damn, she thought. Will they not lie still, those two? And she fairly threw herself onto her seat.

The desire to weep had been with her for longer than she liked to remember, and she had devised a simple trick to keep things in check. Every time that one of the painful

thoughts came back to her, she would quickly turn her attention to something else about her, and, failing that, she would
reach back into her memory and pull forth a thought that left
no scars. Most often these thoughts were of Grandmamma
Windsor, but even that was dangerous ground, as the most
recent memories of that dear old lady were also tinged with
sadness.

She turned her attention back out of the window. the
changing countryside passed quickly by. It was October and
the leaves were mostly off the trees, but a few remained,
causing some nearby bushes to appear almost afire in the
afternoon sunlight. There were enormous trees everywhere
now, and they almost reached to the track in some places,
causing her to inadvertently draw her head back from the
glass every once in a while. This gesture made her smile at
herself — a small, quiet smile, meant only for her soul. 'It
won't be so bad,' she promised herself, as she sighed and
thought about the future. Doctor Wilson, the director of
nursing whom she'd spoken to in Toronto had guaranteed her
that it wouldn't be too bad. Despite the fact that the hospital
was only a tent, he had assured her that there were suitable
lodgings for the townsfolk, and that arrangements had
already been made to house the nurse in one of the more rep-
utable boarding houses.

Were there other nurses on this train? she pondered.
There were only about four other women present, as near as
she could ascertain, and surely they weren't nurses! Jessica
could not be sure, of course, but she could not imagine that
these blousy females with too much rouge on, could be nurses. Her class at the Royal Victoria Hospital in London had
been filled with clean, well-scrubbed young women of
unquestionably good backgrounds, though few could have put
a claim to a heritage quite as exalted as Jessica Sybil
Baxter's. But then, hers was an unusual case and not to be
thought of just now when her defenses were down and she
was already ill at ease with the stranger at her table and his
penetrating stare.

Again she studied the passing sights, which changed
rapidly from moment to moment. There were few houses to

be seen along the railway, and those really were shacks, the like of which could not be found anywhere in the English countryside. Jessica had been disappointed to see, for the first time only a few weeks ago, the slums of London. She had been protected from that for so many years, and now it seemed she was to see a good deal more of it, if the passing log houses and wooden shacks were an indication of what one was to expect in Northern Ontario.

Even Toronto had surprised her, there were so few really grand houses with lots of land about them. There were so many tenement type dwellings reminiscent of crowded London. She knew her history. She knew that Canada was a young country, not like her England, where towns and villages would boast of being over a thousand years old. Why, York itself celebrated its eighteen hundredth birthday the very year her parents were married, she'd been told, back in eighty-one, or was it eighty? And here it was, the new century having turned, already nineteen ought five, and yet Canada was a mere thirty or forty years old - just a colonial child. She smiled again.

At that moment, there was a length of dark woods outside her window, and she was able to see her reflection in the glass for the duration of its passage. Her smile widened as she noticed her image. She was able, on occasion, to laugh at herself. It was something that Abigail Windsor had taught her and she would have ample opportunity throughout her life to be grateful for the gift. This was definitely one of those times. Here she was, Jessica Baxter, single, twenty-three, speeding north on the T&NO Railway, to a strange new life in Cobalt. She wasn't even sure if it was a town or a village. All that she knew about it was that the men there mined for silver (why not gold?) and that the men outnumbered the women anywhere from ten to one to one hundred to one, depending on the day that the count was taken.

Her dark reflection held her attention as she tried to imagine the quality of life under these unusual circumstances. she doubted that there would be electricity, as it was still so new, but was there plumbing? She'd heard horror stories of outdoor toilets, open sewers and the accompanying diseases. Surely they would have indoor plumbing, wouldn't they? And sidewalks. Would there be sidewalks? Or would there be dusty trails that turned to mud when it rained? And what of snow? That was an even more awesome thought. The tiny, rather picturesque flurries that one experienced occasionally in England were nothing compared to the snowfalls that one could expect here in Canada. That point had been made abundantly clear by just about everyone who talked with Jessica about her insane venture abroad. Snow! And lots of it!

When did it start? Soon? Part of her hoped so and her more practical side told her to pray that it was late this year, that she had enough to contend with, just getting settled. The train slowed down, as it passed through yet another small encampment. Sometimes it stopped, other times it slid pokily through these settlements, watching for a flag, and, seeing none, moved on. The arrival of the train seemed to be something of an entertainment for these people, as, invariably there would be a small crowd gathered at the makeshift platforms, all grinning and waving. Such an unusual collection of humanity, Jessica remarked to herself as she watched this group shout and wave to the train. It never once occurred to her to wave back, surely they were not greeting her!

Bushwackers, that's the word that she had heard applied to the unshaven, unkempt men who lived in this backwoods area. They were there for a variety of reasons — some were trappers and some were prospectors heading north, but somehow stalled in the mid-north, waiting for supplies, or perhaps just for the will to go on. There were settlers lured to the area by the promise of free government land, and disgruntled Americans who had moved north to escape whatever political pressures they could not bear in their own country. Of course, also, there were drifters, forever ready to head on to the next town or country, looking for the excitement they could not find in their own roots. What a strange lot!

And the Indians! There were so many Indians! They were no longer the savages of a century ago, but domesticated natives in their own land. One would expect them to be a bitter, beaten, sullen people, but the faces they offered up to the windows of the train were happy faces, with smiles that surprised and warmed. Their mode of dress was always amusing, as seldom did Jessica see a native in the stylish garb that she had imagined they would be clad in — all leather and feathers. These brown-skinned, dark-eyed people were usually in the white-man's clothing, but without the white man's sense of fashion. The men wore ill-fitting jackets over messy shirts and their pants were often tied on with bits of leather or rope. Upon their heads could often be found top hats or bowlers that perched upon their braided hair in a most comic manner. The women were usually in the background, their long black hair shiny to the point of looking greasy. They too smiled and waved, with as much enthusiasm as their men-folk. Upon the backs of the younger women could be found children of various ages, strapped there for the day, Jessica presumed. How very, very strange.

And dogs! So many dogs. There was a constant barking that seemed to attract no one's attention but her own. The animals came in all shapes and sizes and seemed to be constantly foraging for food, or quarrelling amongst themselves.

So lost in thought was Jessica, that she did not, at first, notice the stranger move his bag and sit down on the seat across from her. She was turning from the window, once more covering her eyes to rest them from the glare, when she saw her table partner smiling at her, evidently amused by the fact that they were travelling companions.

"You know, the Eskimos have a clever way of protecting their eyes from the sun." He paused, to make sure that he had her attention, and then went on, "They fashion bits of bone, whale bone usually, to make these rather unusual eye shields with tiny slits in them." He smiled broadly, showing an even row of teeth that seemed so white when contrasted with his dark moustache. "Apparently, they do your squinting for you," he added this part when he noticed that Jessica was squinting in an effort to accustom herself to the light in the car. She could not help but smile at the stranger. He certainly was doing his best to be both interesting and entertaining, and he was quite presentable, and he was speaking with an English accent.

Seeing her smile, the man continued. "You see, up in the north, the far north I mean, there is so much snow, all year round, that the sun blinds one who is not protected in some way. The white man has often lost the battle against the elements because he will not watch and learn from the native people." He seemed quite serious now and Jessica could not help but be interested in his story. He had the air about him of a man who had travelled in this far northern country, and had perhaps witnessed men, maybe even friends, suffer as a result of their own reluctance to accept help from the primitive people who inhabited this country for so many centuries before them.

"There is so much to be learned," his voice was soft now, and he was looking past Jessica, out of the window, but with unseeing eyes. She felt that she should speak, but that incredible reserve with which she had been reared, kept her from conversing with someone to whom she had not been properly introduced, so she merely smiled a cautious smile, a quiet encouragement for him to continue.

"Enough of that," his tone changed abruptly, and he focussed on Jessica and offered his hand. In the absence of someone to present this gentleman to her, Jessica took one of her first real steps towards becoming a Canadian. She placed her hand in his and shook it shyly. A slow flush rose to her cheeks as she felt the warmth of the man's hand, and the strength. "George Dickerson, topographer, at your service Ma'am," he gave a mock bow from his sitting position and she nodded her head towards him.

"Jessica Baxter, nurse," she spoke.

Before she could add another word, the gentleman's grin broadened and he said, "Well, that certainly relieves me. I've been trying in vain to imagine why a woman of your obvious breeding, would be travelling, alone, on this train, to . . . where? North Bay?"

When she corrected his assumption and said, "Cobalt," his eyes grew large and he whistled slightly through his pursed lips.

"Cobalt! Good Lord, why Cobalt?" Not waiting for an answer, he went on, "Why, it's nothing more than a mining camp. As I recall, there's not even a hospital there. Is there even a full-time doctor?" He seemed to be enjoying himself so much that Jessica did not know whether or not to believe him. "Don't tell me that old rapscallion Evans is passing himself off as a 'doctor' now?" It was now obvious that this man was teasing her, but his teasing was doing nothing to alleviate the anxiety that already existed in Jessica's heart. When he realized her concern, Mr. Dickerson quickly tried to recover his ground. "Well, of course there must be a real doctor there. Whatever am I thinking?" His voice had become serious, but his eyes still twinkled. "And a hospital too! As a matter of fact, I keep an office there, along with my partner James Coleman. Mind you, Mr. Coleman runs the office most of the time as I'm usually out in the country, doing the actual mapping myself." He spoke with some pride and Jessica, over her first annoyance with his portrait of Cobalt, warmed to the stranger's conversation.

"I've just now returned from Ottawa where I registered some maps with the government." When Jessica's eyes widened, he seemed pleased. "And a few claims as well." He added this last part rather quietly, with a quick glance about the car.

Totally unfamiliar with mining, prospecting and mapping terms, she asked, equally quietly, sensing something secret in all of this, "What do you mean, sir, claim?"

Mr. Dickerson leaned forward in his seat, touching Jessica's knees with his as he did so. She drew back with a reflex that was rooted in her upbringing. "Pardon, Miss Baxter," said the gentleman, as he adjusted his position so as not to touch her, but he remained leaning forward to enable himself to speak in an almost whisper. There was a light in his eyes, not unlike the glint that Jessica remembered seeing in her father's and her brother Charlie's eyes when they were on one of their 'adventures'. "You see, Ma'am, this is all new country, not at all like back home where every square foot of land is spoken for, owned most likely by the local gentry." If he noticed any change in Jessica's countenance, he

managed to ignore it. "Here there are untold acres of land . . .
up for grabs, so to speak. One has only to 'stake a claim' to it.
Mind you, there are a great many rules and regulations gov-
erning what you must do with the land, and how long you
have in which to do it. But that's quite alright too, as, you
see, we prospectors are staking out claims in the hopes of
finding mineral deposits. Mostly gold."

When he stopped speaking for a moment, Jessica
thought to inquire, "Why do people in Cobalt mine for silver
when gold is so much more valuable?"

Her innocence amused him and he had difficulty keeping
this amusement from showing in his expression. "Well, you
see Ma'am, it's a matter of where the deposits are. There's
silver in Cobalt, and there's no gold in Cobalt, or so very little
that it's not worthwhile mining it. Now, further to the north,
that's where the gold lies — in areas like Kirkland Lake." A
look similar to greed appeared on his face when he spoke of
the large gold deposits that surrounded the gold-rich areas to
the north of Cobalt. "That's all been staked out, of course,"
his disappointment showed in his tone. "But there are others
— there are bound to be others." His voice dropped slightly.
"Now I've just staked a few claims for myself up at Rat
Portage." A little laugh escaped Jessica's lips at the sound of
this new name. Mr. Dickerson noticed it and joined in.
"Rather a strange name, that one. It's got the makings of a
good logging town some day, but there's still some of the
shield out there and I feel there's gold." He was rubbing his
hands together, much the same way that a child would at the
promise of a shiny new penny. "Yes, there's gold out there
and some of it is to be mine!"

"I wish you good fortune, Mr. Dickerson," Jessica spoke
sincerely. "You certainly have the air about you of one who
will someday be successful." Her dark eyes twinkled. She
was enjoying this encounter. It was probably the very first
time in her life that she'd had a conversation of this nature
with a man, other than a family member. She suddenly realized that she had been engaged to Peter for almost two years
and not once had he opened up to her about his dreams and
aspirations. How peculiar that this stranger should share

such fancies with her. It made her feel good, a little less lonely, and it went a long way to help dispel the uneasiness that she had felt when he had first sat down.

"It would be most helpful sir, if someone would compose a booklet for the uninitiated, to explain some of the terms that you use in your speech." When he frowned, she added, "Not to criticize, Mr. Dickerson, it's just that I've never met a prospector before, nor, for that matter, a map-maker. You speak an unusual language, claims, shield, deposits, stakes. Perhaps some day, I will understand it all." She was about to continue when a loud commotion took their attentions away from one another.

The train was at a standstill and neither had noticed it stop. They glanced simultaneously out of the window and saw that they were in a village. Several dozens of people, as was the custom, were out at the platform, but they were not waving and smiling. They were all looking towards the front of the train, and concern was marked on most faces.

2

Next Stop - Cobalt

"Whatever can be the matter?" asked Jessica of her companion.

"It's difficult to say. Sometimes it's as simple as a cow or a horse, or even a moose on the track. I'll go up and check." He moved hastily through the car and was gone.

Jessica continued to watch out of the glass, straining to see forward, but unable to do so. She was so engrossed in the scene that she did not see Mr. Dickerson until he was at her elbow. "Miss Baxter, there's a man been injured. I was wondering, in the absence of any doctor here, if you might see to him?" Her heart thudded. She was not prepared for this!

"Yes . . . of course," she murmured, as she looked about for her bag. Thank God she never travelled without it! It was a small black leather satchel in which she kept various medical necessities. It had not occurred to her that she might need it so soon, and it was at the back of the rack above her head. Mr. Dickerson retrieved it for her and, taking her by the arm, led her quickly towards the exit. Whatever could be so urgent? Jessica wondered to herself.

Before she knew it, she was standing on the platform, looking down at a young boy whose leg was dangling from his torso. She stifled a gasp and uttered, "Why, this is not a man, he's just a young boy!"

"Old enough to be working in the mill," was Mr. Dickerson's quick comment.

She knelt down beside the unconscious boy and listened, first to his pulse and then to his heart. "He's in shock, and it's a small wonder!" Her voice was almost angry. She knew that there was nothing that she could do for the lad. He needed a competent surgeon and he needed one soon. He was sure to lose the leg, but, without a doctor, he might even lose his life. A makeshift tourniquet had been applied to the upper portion of his leg, and she checked it, tightened it slightly in an effort to stop the slow oozing of blood from his wound, and then looked up at the man who was standing next to her, "He must get to a doctor immediately!" When the onlooker made no comment, she fairly shouted, "Where is the nearest doctor?"

Mr. Dickerson's voice came from somewhere behind her, "North Bay, about sixty miles up the track." Anger and frustration brought stinging tears to her eyes, which she carefully fought back. He must get on that train and go to North Bay, that was all there was to it.

"We'll have to put him aboard, sir, and take him there. And quickly!" She added this last part as quietly as she could, as she had noticed a woman crying in the front of the crowd, and she suspected that she was the boy's mother.

"Yes, of course," agreed Mr. Dickerson and he was off to find the necessary things with which to make a stretcher. Jessica knelt beside the faintly breathing body of the boy and prayed. Oh, God, he was so young, he couldn't be more than fourteen or fifteen. Please see to it that his life is spared. She stayed in that position, afraid to look up lest she see the anguish in the woman's eyes. Mr. Dickerson was back soon with his makeshift stretcher. She learned later that it was one of his own tents, strapped across the tent poles and it worked quite well.

Jessica, not knowing any of the people, and, more importantly, not knowing their habits, relied on Mr. Dickerson to ask if there was a relative who would like to accompany the boy to the doctor in North Bay. The distraught woman from the front came forward and said that she was his mother and that she would go with her son, Danny.

As Jessica was boarding the train, behind the stretcher and the boy's mother, she turned to offer a reassuring smile to those left behind on the platform. She noticed the sign on the little brown station house, it read Burks Falls, a town that she would not soon forget.

The sixty miles from Burks Falls to North Bay were interminably long. Jessica tried to make conversation with Danny's mother, but it was virtually impossible. The woman had a sadness about her that made Jessica wonder if she'd been through this before — if she'd seen others like this, other young people, torn and bleeding, or perhaps, even dead. She seemed both anxious and resigned. It was a most uncomfortable situation, and, when the conductor announced that they were approaching North Bay, Jessica breathed a silent sigh of relief.

The hospital in North Bay was small compared to the Royal Victoria in London, where Jessica had trained and then worked. There were three doctors on staff, and one, a Doctor Steven Mason, was in charge when they arrived. He took one look at the boy and ordered his nurse to prepare for surgery.

"Miss Baxter, it's most unfortunate, but I'm afraid that we must remove his leg." He seemed genuinely sorry for the boy. His tone suggested that he would be doing his job with a heavy heart. "We see so many of these accidents," he explained. "Working conditions in this country are quite outrageous. But, I suspect that you've seen your share of this sort of thing." No, she hadn't! Even in training, she had been protected from the worst of it all. This was her 'trial by fire'.

She shook her head sadly and prepared to leave. "They're holding the train for me, Doctor. You seem well staffed — forgive me if I rush off." She turned to leave and then added over her shoulder, "I'll be at the hospital in Cobalt. Might you write to me and let me know how the lad is?"

The doctor's face registered surprise. "If you wish, Miss Baxter," and she turned again to go.

One of the hospital staff followed Jessica out of the doors and called, "Ma'am, Ma'am" and when she gave him her attention, he handed her Mr. Dickerson's tent and poles, all bound tightly together in a neat bundle. "Could you please return this to the gentleman?" She took the parcel, nodded her reply and sped towards the station — back to the train — back to the safety of her seat and the comfort of Mr.

Dickerson's company.

She was so hurried and excited when she first sat down that she wasn't aware that Mr. Dickerson's things were gone. She assumed, when he was not sitting there, that he had merely gone off for a smoke, but, after several minutes, she realized that she was quite alone. A melancholy swept over her and she was at a loss to explain it away. It was just a chance encounter — a table companion, nothing more. But you would have thought that he would have said goodbye. Bother! I'll think of him no more! It was like a command that she gave herself and it worked. Her mind immediately searched for more pleasant thoughts and Grandmamma Windsor came drifting back on the clouds of her memory.

"You girls have been invited to Lord Thompson's to a party!" Abigail Windsor's whispery old voice fairly sang with excitement. `Jessica and her friend Katharine Singer had barely settled into the parlour after their long trip up from Kent when Grandmamma made her announcement. It was as though she had been waiting for weeks to share this wonderful news. And wonderful it was! Lord Thompson, his wife and four children lived in Falconridge Castle, just north of Fairview. An invitation to one of the Thompson parties was a treasured thing, and even though Katharine did not yet realize its importance, Jessica certainly did.

"Grandmamma! You old dear. However did you manage that?" The girl gave full credit to her grandparent for the invitation and she was really quite right in doing so. Abigail Windsor had worked very carefully finagling the invitations. The old girl's eyes twinkled. She was not about to give away her secrets. She fluttered a wrinkled old hand in the direction of Jessica, as if to dismiss the question.

"The party's on Saturday evening, so you've two full days to prepare yourselves." She spoke in a teasing voice, obviously enjoying the entire situation. "William will take you over in the carriage for dinner about eight, and then there's to be a ball." William was Abigail's driver and he was also the one who took care of the car-

riages, wagons, harnesses and so on. "Now off with you.
Mildred will help you unpack. Katharine is in the room
next to yours, my dear. Go, search your things and
decide what it is that you're going to wear to dazzle the
young swains hereabouts. Come back quickly and show
me, though." Her eyes were bright with excitement.
She could not have been happier if she herself were sixteen again and preparing for a ball.

It was a difficult decision. This was no ordinary
party. Each girl was certain that her dresses were
unfit, too plain, too out of fashion, too old. They totally
enjoyed the agony with which they made their decisions
and soon they were back downstairs to show off their
gowns.

They were tip-toeing across the grand foyer, wanting
to surprise Mrs. Windsor. Their silent approach made it
impossible for the women in the sitting room to hear
their arrival and the girls were able to hear the conversation that was obviously not meant for their ears.

"You really should tell the girl, Ma'am," Jessica recognized the voice of Martha, the housekeeper. There
was a mumbled response and then Martha continued,
"But she must know. It's not fair to make it a surprise,
or a shock, if you will. Begging your pardon, Ma'am."
Jessica and Katharine were now close enough to hear
the second voice, that of Abigail Windsor.

"But you see, Martha, Jessica is too dear. I feel as
though I could tell anyone else, the world even, but not
my Jessica. She's, well . . . she's me. she's me as a child.
How can I tell her that I'm dying, it's like telling her
she's dying. Oh Martha, it's all too cruel . . ." The fragile
old voice drifted off and the girls could hear movement
that suggested to them that the women were embrac-
ing. What to do? Jessica stood there in the big hall, in
her pretty pale green ball gown, paralyzed. It was as
though she had been struck, the pain that flashed
through her body could not have been more intense if
she'd been hit by a speeding carriage. The pain moved
to her head, and, for the very first time in her life, she

was threatened with fainting. Her hand went out to
Katharine and she leaned against the girl to steady herself. It was a fleeting moment, as it was unlike Jessica
to show this much emotion. She wheeled suddenly
about and went quietly up the stairs.

"She's expecting us, Jesse," Katharine pleaded with
Jessica to return to the parlour. "We must show up soon
or she'll know that something is amiss. She did beg us
to be quick. Oh, come, Jesse, please." The unfortunate
house guest was wishing now that she had stayed on at
school for the vacation. This was a most impossible situation and she did not know how to handle it.

"Wait!" Jessica's voice was sharp. "We'll both go
down in a moment. I mustn't let Grandmamma see me
like this. In a moment, please." She was sitting at the
dressing table, staring into the mirror, but not seeing
her own reflection, only that of the old lady, so thin, so
wrinkled, so very frail. Grandmamma was the one who
made it all worthwhile, the long hours at school, the
even longer hours with her parents - strained hours
where nothing important was ever said. How could she
face the death of this dear old soul? Where would she,
Jessica, be without this gentle person? What would
Jessica Baxter be, if not Abigail Windsor's granddaughter? She felt that she had no other identity, that her
only importance on this earth stemmed from the fact
that this old lady loved her above all else. It was the
only love that she had ever known — the only true love.
It was a love that demanded nothing but love in return,
and, because it demanded nothing, Jessica endeavored
to give her everything. She lived only to please Abigail
Windsor, to make her smile, to make her laugh, to hear
her say that she was proud of her — of her schooling,
her piano, her horsemanship, even her appearance. No
one else seemed ever to care, except Grandmamma, and
now she was going. Where would the girl who lived
only in the light from the old woman's eyes go? When
those tired brown eyes closed for the last time, taking
with them the gleam that was her life force, what would

happen to her?

Jessica made herself look at her own reflection in the mirror and she was startled. Abigail's eyes were her eyes! They were such a dark brown that the pupil was seldom visible. It was as though the entire eye was pupil, giving such a depth to her gaze that it frightened her. She had always thought that her Grandmother was all-seeing because of these enormous black pools, and, for the first time, she realized that she had that look also. It was part of her heritage. What else did the woman give to her? Did she give her the strength to face this awful fact? Yes, Jessica decided that she did.

"I'm alright now, Katharine," she turned slowly about and her friend was shocked by the change in her expression. It was as though Jessica had aged ten years. No longer was she the sixteen year old, excited about the prospect of a party, but a grown woman, resigned to this horrible news, and somehow, able to deal with it. "Let us go and see Grandmamma."

The memory of that moment brought tears to Jessica's eyes. They leaked out of the corners and her handkerchief smelled dusty as she drew it to her face to brush them away. Suddenly she was no longer concerned that others in the car might see her anguish. Pain and fear were too much and she succumbed to them, letting quiet sobs rack her body, as she rocked to and fro in her seat, much like she did as a child.

"Don't cry dearie," a timid female voice could be heard through the sniffing and hiccoughing that the tears had brought about. Jessica looked up through the blur and saw a woman sitting across from her. She was actually perched, in an attitude of one who is not quite certain of being welcome. "There, there, you mustn't cry. You did such a splendid job, takin' care of that poor lad and all." This unusual woman must think that Jessica was crying for the wounded boy in the hospital. Jessica decided not to correct her.

"I'm . . . I'm alright. Thank you, Miss . . .?" Jessica asked, genuinely pleased to see and talk with another female, despite the fact that this female was rather commonly attired.

"Beauville. Rosina Beauville's my name, Ma'am," she held out her hand. When Jessica hesitated to take it and offer her name in return, the woman withdrew slightly and a rather hurt expression crossed her pretty face. Jessica quickly reached forward and shook Miss Beauville's hand and said, "Miss Baxter, er, Jessica," she offered shyly and added, "You are French?"

Miss Beauville was still perched on the edge of her seat, as though she was waiting for either a dismissal, or an invitation to stay. Jessica proffered neither. "Yes, at least my pa was French. Mom was Scottish. But me, I'm Canadian. Born right here in Ontario." She seemed to stall for a moment, as though she were trying to ascertain if her listener was really interested or not. When Jessica raised her eyebrows in an inquisitive gesture, the Canadian hurried on. "Born in a town down near Toronto. Brantford." Another pause. She shuffled in her seat and made a movement as if to leave.

"Please, have a seat," Jessica finally asked and the warm smile that she was given in return made her instantly glad that she had asked Miss Beauville to join her. The woman was quite attractive, in a sort of theatrical way. Jessica couldn't help but wonder what her business was on this northbound train. She could have been one of the women from the theatres of London, whom Jessica had seen loitering about the cafes that the theatre crowd was known to frequent. But surely, there were not theatres in Cobalt? And what if this woman wasn't an actress? What other profession could possibly lure her up to the wilderness? Jessica remembered being warned by Doctor Wilson in Toronto about 'camp followers'. Women, he explained, often followed the men into these remote mining camps and, well, replaced the comfort of a wife — for a price, of course. A slow flush came to Jessica's innocent cheeks as she thought of the possibility that she was conversing with one of 'those' women. But then, she didn't really want to know, as she was enjoying the soft features of the woman, her gently curved chin, which was perhaps the first chin that she had seen in days that did not require a shave. The woman had sparkling blue eyes that twinkled mischievously when she spoke or smiled, which she did often.

She gestured frequently, with small, dainty hands, and her voice had a curious mixture of accents to it.

"There are a lot of Indians down where I come from, but they mostly stay on their reservation. I wonder if we'll see many up north? Do you know?" Miss Beauville cocked her head to one side when she asked the question and Jessica thought how young she looked. She reminded her of a young pup that she had had when just a girl. It had a habit of cocking its head to one side whenever Jessica gave it a command. The dog had been a Spaniel, and its colouring was so like this fair haired young woman's that Jessica smiled a soft smile at the girl.

"I really don't know, Miss Beauville. You see, it's my first time up North. As a matter of fact, it's my first time in Canada. I've been here only a few weeks, and I've seen nothing of the Indians, but what I've noticed out my window. They do seem a comical bunch, with their strange ways of dress. I must confess, I quite expected them to be attired all in their leathers and feathers." Both women gave a little laugh at Jessica's accidental rhyming.

"They do dress like that on special days," Miss Beauville explained. "Some times, back home, when I was just a little girl, we'd see them in a group, come into town for some reason or other. They would all be dressed in their Indian dress, the chief with a big feathered headdress, the rest of the men all in leathers. The women, they seldom came, but when they did, they all seemed to have babies on their backs. Papooses, I think they're called. Quiet, those babies, I remember. Mom used to say that they were strapped in so tight that they couldn't cry, but I don't know. they all seemed happy enough to me. And their horses, they were so well behaved too. Just stood there, with no one to hold their reins when an Indian got off. Just stood there 'til he got back on. That always surprised me. My Pa's horse was always running off. I hated going chasing after it down the street. Always felt like the town folks was laughing at us 'cause we couldn't keep old Rifle tied still . . . My, how I do run on." She looked quite apologetically at Jessica, who had remained quiet and fascinated while the young woman spoke. Jessica was not with-

out imagination, and she quite enjoyed Miss Beauville's conversation. It conjured up interesting pictures in her mind, of
what life in Canada was like.

"Please go on, Miss Beauville. I find your accounts most
interesting. You must keep in mind, that I am so new to your
country, that whatever you tell me can only educate me."

This seemed to please the young woman and on she
went. Brantford was a small town about forty miles west of
Toronto. The Beauville family often went into the city to sell
Mr. Beauville's goods. He was a harness maker. There were
three girls and four boys in the Beauville family — not a
large family by some local standards. Most of the children
had ended up in Toronto, as there were only so many things
that a person could do in Brantford, and Miss Beauville's oldest brother Thomas had taken over her father's business.
Miss Beauville had lived in the big city for a few years, but
she did not like it, and had gone back to her home town. She
had stayed there with her mother, helping about the house
and shop, but her mother had died, and, when her father had
remarried, there was no room for her in the new matrimonial
house, so once again, she moved back to Toronto. Unskilled,
except for housework, she got a job at the Royal York Hotel,
'the biggest in Canada', she said quite proudly to Jessica.
While working there, she met Samuel Hobson, a prospec-
tor/miner from the north. They had courted, and he had
asked her to marry him. She was on her way to Cobalt to
meet him there, to be married. And that, the breathless girl
said, was the story of her life.

Jessica felt a sudden relief when she realized that Miss
Beauville was not a 'professional' woman. She sighed, and
then, worried lest her relief show in her face, she rushed into
conversation herself. "I am from London," she smiled,
adding, "England," when she remembered that the Canadians
had a London of their own. "I am a nurse." That was rather
redundant, she thought to herself. It had already been estab-
lished that she was a nurse. "I'm on my way to Cobalt
because they are so short of trained personnel there." She
silently hoped that she didn't sound pompous. Miss Beauville
did not react to her statement in any way, but sat there

almost mesmerized by Jessica's speech and accent. "I've
come to Canada because I, too, had to leave home and make a
way for myself." She suddenly saw a similarity between Miss
Beauville's story and her own. Although Jessica's mother
was not yet dead, she was institutionalized for life, and there
was really no other place for her to go.

Jessica fervently wished that she could tell her story to
this eager girl who had so openly told hers. But the shame of
it all! The sorrow! Perhaps someday, she would share this
girl's confidence, but not yet. She wasn't ready to share it
yet. "So you've never been to Cobalt either?" she changed
the subject. When the young woman shook her head, Jessica
continued, "I understand that it is still quite primitive. Did
Mr. Hobson tell you anything about the living conditions?
I'm really curious to know what we are to expect. Dr. Wilson
did promise that the nurses would have suitable accommodation, but I'm not quite sure just what that means up here."

"Oh, Sammy . . . er, Mr. Hobson, did say that there were
lots of houses there. Mind you, he also said that they were
pretty shabby and rough, considering what you're probably
used to." She said this with no sarcasm, just stating the obvious. "But he did say that there were lots of 'boarding houses'.
Seems that's where most of the married folk live 'til they get
into houses of their own. I guess that's where you and me'll
be. Mr. Hobson, he stays at the mine most of the time. They
have these big 'bunk' houses where the men all sleep, and a
big dining room where they all eat together. Mr. Hobson says
it's really pretty good there, the grub I mean. The men play
cards and drink a little I guess. But mostly they're tired
'cause they work ten to fifteen hours a day, so they sleep a
lot. Once, when this big guy named Burke was trying to get
some 'shut-eye', Sam calls it, and the fellows were making too
much noise with their cards and all, he went berserk. Just
went crazy." She made a little circular gesture with her fore-
finger about her temple. "He beat up a couple of the men and
sorta tore the place up. Took six fellows to stop him and now
he's in Toronto at some hospital, you know, for the mental
people." How very well Jessica knew, as the dreadful memories of her mother came rushing over her and she so dearly

wanted to change the conversation in case her intimate knowledge of the insane showed in her face. Fortunately her young companion continued, quite caught up in her story. "Mr. Hobson, he stays out at the mine most of the time himself. Says it keeps him out of trouble in town. I'm not sure what kinda trouble he's talking about, maybe drinking and gambling and such. And sometimes he goes out to his own claim. Stays there for long periods of time — says he has to protect it, as there's lots of claim jumping going on up there in the bush — lots of claim jumping, drinking, stealing and even some murdering." This last part was spoken in a whisper, accompanied by a shudder. Her blue eyes were widened now, and, once again, Jessica thought of her spaniel, Nipper.

"Surely there are police up there?" she asked, trying to keep the surprise and horror from her voice.

"Oh, yes, there's some law, but then there's so much bush, Sammy says," she bit her lip, thinking that Miss Baxter might not approve of her being on first name basis with her intended.

"But, in the town itself? Surely there must be protection?" Jessica was thinking of her English Bobbies and of how comforting it was to see them walking two by two through the streets of London. Surely they would have Bobbies of some sort in Cobalt. It couldn't be safe for a woman on the streets, with the men outnumbering the women so greatly. Surely there would be protection!

Her concern was so obvious on her face that Miss Beauville reached out to comfort her. "Oh, Miss Baxter, don't fret. There's bound to be some kind of police. You'll ... we'll be quite safe. I'm sure." Her very positive tone made Jessica relax a bit, but she couldn't help but wonder how it was that she had not thought of this before. In her anxiety to start a new life, to make a new beginning in this new country, it had not once occurred to her to think of her own personal safety. She had always realized that the living conditions would be pretty basic, but to have to worry about her safety on top of all else, that seemed just too much!

"I think I'd best be getting back to my things, Miss Baxter. I overheard one of the chaps say that we're nearing

Latchford, which is the stop before Cobalt." She stood up,
weaving slightly with the motion of the train. Jessica looked
up into her soft blue eyes and thought how innocent she
appeared. Perhaps they could be friends in this new town.
She hoped so. "See you, Miss Baxter," Rosina smiled a broad,
warm smile, turned and began to walk down the aisle.

Jessica realized that she should say something, anything, lest she not see this nice young woman again, "Miss
Beauville," and when the woman turned Jessica gestured to
her to return. She made her way back to Jessica's seat with a
look of inquiry on her face. "Please look me up in Cobalt. I . .
. well, I expect I'll be quite lonely there. It's so nice to know
another woman." Jessica found herself blushing again, not
the hot frustrated blush that the presence of a man might
bring about, but the embarrassed flush of one who has
stepped so out of character as she was now doing. Never
before in the English woman's life had she felt such a desperate need for another human being. Not even through her
Grandmother's death, her father's death, nor her mother's
confinement. Suddenly she needed the warmth of this young
woman, and she was willing to pay the price of embarrassment to have it known.

"Oh, Miss Baxter. I'd be mighty pleased to visit with
you," Miss Beauville, in her own discomfiture at witnessing
the bowing of such a dignified person, found herself in a
slight curtsy. She did it quite involuntarily and she hoped
that it had not offended her new friend. When Jessica held
out her hand once again, Rosina Beauville took it and
squeezed it as one might the hand of a child, in an effort to
reassure it of her presence. "I'd be mighty pleased," she
repeated, looking Jessica directly in the eye and there was an
honesty there that Jessica had not seen since the death of
Abigail Windsor.

Her new friend lurched down the aisle on her way to the
next car where her belongings were and Jessica slowly sat
back down, enveloped in a warmth that was quite new to her.
Things in this frontier town could not be so very bad if there
were people like Miss Beauville there, she mused.

The train chugged to a stop and Jessica looked out of

the window to find that she was on a bridge. Up ahead could be seen a small station with the name Latchford painted in white on its side. There were stacks of wood everywhere, on either side of the narrow river that the bridge straddled. It was a low bridge and the girl wondered if the angry water ever got high enough to endanger the foundations of the bridge. There couldn't be more than five or six feet of clearance, surely after a heavy rain, there would be a possibility of that occurring? She wished that Mr. Dickerson was back, sitting in the seat across from her so that she might educate herself further by asking questions of him, but, alas, she was quite alone again. She sighed, a deep, weary sigh, and allowed her mind to slip backwards for a moment. The rushing water could be heard throughout the car, and its very sound brought back the sound of other waters...

It was summer. Grandmamma Windsor had lasted until March, and then finally succumbed, but not without a fight, to the cancer within her. The doctors had assured Jessica that she had not suffered a great deal, but what did they know of suffering? Knowing that she was going to die was the greatest pain of all. But that was March. June was warm, death was past and Jessica was sailing with Peter Thompson. He had been such a strong arm throughout the terrible spring and Jessica found herself growing fonder and fonder of the man. She knew too that Abigail approved of him, so her feelings were not just those of the heart, but of the head as well.

"Are you going back to school?" Peter asked this question of Jessica as he expertly manoeuvred his small boat amongst the other boats lazily sharing the bay with him.

"I'm not really sure, Peter. I know that Grandmamma had her heart set on my going abroad, and I feel that I should follow her wishes, but it's such a big decision, I'm not quite ready for it just now. It may well be that I'll stay at home with Mother and Father for a season." She smiled a wry smile. "That would be unusual," she added.

"I always thought that you didn't get on so well with them?" It was really more of a statement than a ques-

tion. Jessica felt that she should defend her position
with her parents.

"It's not really just a matter of getting on, Peter. We
. . . well, we're just like strangers, that's all. Perhaps I
should take this opportunity to get to know them.
Watch it!" She was loath to give Peter directions, as he
did not take kindly to them and she knew that, but it
had appeared, just for a second, that he was going to
upset a small craft that was in his path.

He gave her a stern look and moved out of the other
boat's way with considerable ease. Jessica bit her
tongue. She wished that she did not find it necessary to
do that, but she seemed to have absolutely no control
over her speech at times.

"Sorry, Peter," she murmured. He threw her a
glance of forgiveness, but she did notice that he began
to pay just a bit more attention to the heavy traffic in
the bay. "I would really prefer to live here, at Fairview,"
she spoke shyly, watching for signs that he might enjoy
that, but he was busy with his navigating. Receiving no
encouragement from him, she went on, "But Mother
thinks that I should go abroad, so, I guess it will be
Switzerland for me."

Peter manoeuvred the sailboat out further into the
sea, where it required less concentration from him and
then he turned to Jessica, "I don't really know how to
say this, Jesse," he spoke her pet name with a fondness
that made Jessica's heartbeat quicken. Surely he was
going to declare his intentions? Even though she was
but seventeen years of age, she was old enough to be
betrothed. She was extremely fond of Peter, and of all
that Peter stood for — the good life, the comfortable life
here in York, where Abigail Windsor had lived out her
lifespan. What more could a girl ask for? She looked at
Peter with her heart in her eyes and he turned away,
and spoke to the wind. The words were thrown back to
her with a harshness that might have knocked her out of
the boat had she not been sitting so securely against the
side. "I've heard . . .", he cleared his throat and began

again, "I've heard that your mother intends to sell Fairview." He turned about, not certain that Jessica had heard his wind-torn words, but one glance at her stricken face and he knew.

Sell Fairview! Sell Fairview! Why, how could she? Was it even hers to sell? Yes, it was, Jessica remembered. The lawyers had made it quite clear at the reading of the will, that Abigail Windsor had left her estate, Fairview, to her only daughter, Sybil. Her monies had gone to her sons, Jessica's uncles, John, Geoffrey, and William. But Fairview, it was Sybil's. So in shock was the girl that she did not even realize that Peter had put his arm about her and was holding her close against him with one arm, while he attended the tiller with the other. Her brain pounded with fury, the pounding of the waves echoing her thoughts. The water rushed by the side of the boat with a roar that suited her mood. She wanted to roar! She wanted to scream out to the sea, to the sky, to the world, that her mother had no right to sell Fairview. No right at all!

"Take me back, Peter," she managed, but she could not look at him. The ugliness that she felt in her heart was written on her face and she could not let him be witness to it. She stared at the sea, the brown-blue water, coursing past, gurgling against the wooden side of the Gallant Lady, as Peter's boat was called. When the man did not respond immediately, she hissed, "Now!"

He turned from her to give full attention to coming about and heading for shore. He was a kind young man, not insensitive to Jessica's plight. And he was very fond of the girl. She had about her, a certain strength that he recognized and respected. So unlike the rest of the young ladies hereabouts. They were all so empty-headed, so flighty. It was difficult to imagine any one of them showing this much emotion. It excited him. The anger that was emanating from Jessica at this moment was almost sensual, and Peter was physically moved by it. Her anger and determination were like a third presence aboard his Gallant Lady — a presence that could be felt as clearly as he could feel the salty spray, as clearly as he could feel Jessica's body so close to his just a moment before. He trembled with the newness of it all, and mistook it for love.

They became engaged that day. He asked out of a mixture of admiration and pity, and she accepted out of frustration and insecurity. It was destined never to be.

The water that flowed under the Latchford bridge came back into focus, and the North Sea vanished, slowly, in a grayish haze. Jessica sighed once again. That old expression, 'water under the bridge' came to her mind and she smiled at her reflection in the glass. That's all that it was, water under the bridge.

"Cobalt, next stop Cobalt," announced the conductor. It was dark. Darkness had settled on the countryside somewhere between Latchford and Cobalt. It mattered not. Jessica's fatigue was such that new sights were not welcome just now. To have a bath and a bed were all that she wanted. Tomorrow she would have time for the grand tour. She would be ready tomorrow.

3

Settling In

The porter helped her off the train with her baggage, and there she stood, on the strange platform waiting for someone to rescue her from the noise and the smell, and the cold. If she had thought that the crowds at the other stations had been large, this one was monumental. It seemed that everyone aboard got off here, and each and everyone of them was met by at least ten others. She glanced about in desperation for Miss Beauville, but to no avail. Most probably she was rescued by her Sammy and whisked off to safety in some nice, warm, clean boarding house.

Strange men pushed against her, some bothering to apologize, most just careening on, in search of a familiar face. The smell of tobacco was strong, and, at times, the smell of liquor was even stronger. There was a dustiness everywhere, despite the fact that they were standing on a wooden platform. the dustiness apparently was on the people, and, when she looked about, she saw that most of them were dressed in dirty bush clothes, and when she looked even more closely, they all seemed in need of both baths and shaves. She wanted to reach for her scented handkerchief to protect her nose from this assault, but she daren't put down her bag. It was not that she expected it to be stolen — these men did not look like thieves — she was just afraid that she might be physically jostled away from it, never to see it again. The wait was so long that eventually she, in very unladylike fashion, put a foot on either side of her large bag, to keep it from being pushed out of sight, and she began to pray silently that someone from the hospital would find her and take her away.

"Miss Baxter?" her prayers were finally answered, but not until she had been nearly knocked off her feet by one exuberant drunk. There were tears of frustration in her eyes when she turned about to see who it was who knew her name. "Jim Coleman's my name, Ma'am." The name did not ring a bell instantly, as Jessica was not expecting help from this quarter. She looked puzzled and he added, "George Dickerson sent me."

The surprise with which Jessica received this information was so evident on her face that kindly Mr. Coleman smiled a wide smile, causing his rather formidable moustache to curl up towards his eyes. "Yes, he telegraphed me to look out after you," he further explained. This was neither the time nor the place for conversation, so she followed Mr. Coleman, who took her large bag and one of her smaller ones and headed out into the blackness. So afraid of being abandoned in this strange, excited crowd, Jessica fairly flew after the man. She found him at the bottom of the short flight of stairs that led to the platform and handed him her medical bag.

"Oh, thank you, Mr. Coleman. I was feeling so very alone out there." She glanced back towards the melee on the wooden stage and smiled, that comfortable smile of relief that one gets when finally removed from a mob. "Is it always like that? So, well, so crazy?" she asked of her saviour.

"Yes, Ma'am. Specially on the Saturday train. See, no one works on the Sabbath hereabouts, so it's kind of like a holiday Saturday nights. There'll be a dance and party later, you'll see." Jessica hoped that she would not see — or hear, for that matter. She'd had quite enough noise for one night.

"You say that Mr. Dickerson sent you to fetch me? I'm puzzled about that, Mr. Coleman. I haven't seen him since lunch today." Was it only that short a time? thought Jessica. So very much had happened in just one day that she would not believe that it was a mere eight hours since she last saw Mr. Dickerson.

Telegraphed me from the Bay, he did, Ma'am. Said to pick you up and take you to Mrs. Carson's. That's about our best boarding house. I went to see old Meg — that's Mrs. Carson — and she'd got a room for you. Where'd you meet old George?" He raised an eyebrow in a rather suggestive fashion and Jessica began to realize that this man thought that she was Mr. Dickerson's 'friend'.

"I met your good old George on the train, just this noon, sir, and, well, that's it!" She was poor at this sort of thing. She'd never had to defend her reputation before and she was afraid of saying too much, or too little.

"Begging your pardon, Ma'am," Mr. Coleman said quickly. "Honest mistake. George, er, Mr. Dickerson has been known to have his 'lady friends' visit him before." He smiled an apologetic smile at the rear end of his horse and Jessica thought it best to let the conversation end. Mr. Coleman was not of the same mind. "If you'll forgive me for asking, Ma'am, what is a lady like yourself doing in Cobalt? Seems an unlikely place for a person of such - refinement, shall I say?" These words were spoken with the greatest of respect, so Jessica decided to forgive Mr. Coleman his original thoughts and answer him.

"I am a nurse. I answered an advertisement in England, about the need for nurses up in the Northern woods of Canada, or should I say, Ontario." Her host stole a sidewards glance at her and she noticed a touch of approval in his eyes. Finally! Someone who appreciated her arrival. "I was expecting someone from the hospital to meet me. I hope that they are not back there amongst that terrible crowd," she peered over her shoulder in the direction of the station house and there was a strange orange glow, and a low rumble of excitement still settled about the track. "Do you think that's possible, Mr. Coleman? Maybe the Doctor's looking for me?" She had not thought of this in her anxiety to be away from the noisy throng.

"Doc Evans's up the way a bit, up near Liskeard. There was a fight up at one of the camps and he's mending bodies." These words were spoken with such ease that Jessica wondered if it might be a common occurrence, this fighting and wounding. As if in answer to her silent inquiry, Mr. Coleman added, "nothing much. No one killed or anything. It's just that sometimes tempers get short when a man's worked all week and there's not much to show for it. A few drinks and he's like a firecracker. First match that's lit too close to him and boom, he's off. Happens all the time. Guess you'll be seeing a lot of it, being a nurse and all." He smiled still another smile of approval at Jessica and she thanked him for it with her very soul.

Mrs. Carson proved to be a friendly sort. A rather large woman with a great shock of red hair, she reminded Jessica of a servant that they'd once had in Singinham — a servant that she'd liked a great deal. It would be easy taking to her, and Jessica breathed a sigh of relief when she settled into her lodgings. She had one large room. Mrs. Carson assured her that it was the largest in the house. In the room were all the things necessary to survive, with the possible exception of a toilet and a kitchen. The bed was big and comfortable, and, Jessica discovered after turning down the covers and examining them closely, they were clean. There were ample quilts provided, and three pillows which Jessica was to be very thankful for, as she liked her tea in bed. There was a small desk at a window, and the light would probably be good, once day came. She was mildly curious about the view, but tomorrow would tell. A settee nestled against one wall, and behind it hung a somewhat attractive tapestry depicting a sea scape. She tried the settee and found it rather coarse, but otherwise comfortable. She would remember to place a quilt on it whenever she chose to sit there. Very old carpets covered the wooden floor, but the carpets were clean and not too badly worn. They had the appearance of rugs that had witnessed many beatings at the hand of the red-head below.

A dry sink stood in one corner, with a massive pitcher and basin on it, and several other china pieces that matched. Jessica bent down and looked under the bed, there was the matching chamber pot. She grinned and reminded herself that she was in the wild north. A handsome armoire stood tall and wide on another wall, and, upon investigation, she discovered that it too was impeccably clean. Mrs. Carson was living up to her reputation, Jessica could see. A bonnet chest sat beside the armoire and there were several chairs placed about the room. Pictures hung on the walls, and an oval mirror hung above the sink. Two small tables sat at either side of the bed, and on each was a coal oil lamp. There was also a candle holder, complete with candle on a shelf near the door. It was quite complete, and, while not quite as elaborate as Jessica was accustomed to, suitable.

It was obvious that no bath was to be offered tonight, but she did discover that there was hot water in the large pitcher on her sink and cold water in the smaller one.

Too tired to put her belongings away, Jessica slipped out of her dress, her petticoats and her under garments and washed quickly, knowing that it would take many washings to get all of the travelling grime from off her body. She hastened into her nightdress. It was made of thick, flannel material, quite unlike any nightdress that the girl had ever worn before, but she had purchased it in London, after hearing about the awesome cold that one could expect in Canada. She was glad of its coziness tonight, as there was a chill in the room. She missed a fireplace of her own, but there was a large black pipe running up a wall adjacent to the bed and she surmised that it would supply heat from some stove below. She nestled into the covers, blew out her candle and slept the sleep of a weary child.

It was quite late at night that she was awakened by the noise of the party-goers on the street below. Once she realized where she was, and what the clamor was, she reached for still another coverlet, to ward off the cold, and was quickly off to sleep again.

Sunday dawned, a dreary day. The brilliant sunshine that had been such a treat on the train ride had abandoned her, and, in its stead, a quiet drizzle beat unheard against her windowpane. She should go to church, she thought, as she buried herself even more deeply into the bed that smelled vaguely of lavender. She'd discovered that when she poked her head out from under the wool and feathers, a brisk, cold draught met her nose. Her window was open. She had not noticed that the night before. As soon as she placed her bare foot onto the floor, the need to go to the washroom came over her, and, even though the night before she had resolved never to use the thing, she reached under the bed for the chamber pot. It had been her plan to get to the toilet first thing in the morning, thereby avoiding this exceedingly unladylike apparatus. So much for that resolution, she laughed to herself. Back in bed, she began to plan her day. A walk about town was in order, if, of course, the rain ceased. It couldn't be very big, the town that is, could it? And, perhaps she would visit the hospital. Remembering that she had been pressed into medical service in Burks Falls, before she was actually ready, she decided to forget the hospital for today, and concentrate on the town. Was there a school? An opera house? What of a post office? A newspaper? A saloon? Not that she was interested in alcohol, but it was her impression that all of the frontier towns had a saloon or two. She had read several novels about the taming of the Americas while she was in training, having to hide the unsavory books from the sisters, and she had quite a clear picture in her mind of what to expect. It would be fun to see how right, or how wrong she was.

Was that heat? A faint feeling of warmth crept across from the pipe and she jumped up to test. Sure enough, it was radiating warmth. She could get dressed now. Wisely, she took all pieces of apparel that she intended to don and hung them over chairs next to the black stove pipe. In short order they were toasty warm, and what a pleasure they were to draw over her shivering body. With the warmth of her heated clothes still encasing her, Jessica left her room to go down the stairs and find her landlady.

"I don't really expect people in my kitchen, Miss Baxter," Mrs. Carson said as Jessica entered the cheery, warm room. The girl stopped mid-stride and was about to exit, when the kind lady added, "Oh, it's all right, I guess, I don't mean you, Ma'am. It's the men folk I don't allow in here. Anything I can't abide is a man telling me what to do in my own kitchen. Cup of tea?" Jessica smiled and answered, "Yes, please." "I'm telling you, you let one man into your kitchen and all hell breaks loose, begging your pardon Ma'am, but my language has suffered a wee bit since moving here. You'll see, you'll probably get like me too." She hoped that she hadn't overstepped her mark by suggesting that a woman of Jessica's obvious breeding might learn to curse like the men, but Jessica set her mind at ease and said that she expected so. This earned her a hearty grin from the massive red head, and a steaming hot cup of tea.

"Breakfast is at eight sharp. 'Tis now a quarter of, so I guess that'll tide you over. Might make an exception for you, Miss Baxter, but if the men don't get to the table on time, I don't serve." She smiled a rather apologetic smile and explained, "Did in the beginning. Course I had Mr. Carson here to help me then, but soon I was feeding them rascals all hours of the day and night. Once Mr. Carson went, I just didn't have the time. Got a young girl that comes in to help now and again, but that's not enough. I got a bad reputation for talking too much, so any time you got something to say I just jump right in."

Mrs. Carson stopped talking just long enough to put a tin of biscuits into the oven and Jessica took the opportunity to inquire about a church. "Yes, the Church of England has a spot here in Cobalt, not much though. The R.C.'s, now they got the best church hereabouts. Damn near a cathedral, compared to the rest. Me, I go to the Methodist church, when I get a notion, but Sunday's no day of rest for me, so I don't go often. The Anglican Church is on top of the hill. I'll show you after breakfast. You can see it from here — the hill, I mean. As a matter of fact, bet you can even see the little steeple, now that the leaves are gone. We'll see." She busied herself with breakfast preparations and Jessica thought she'd best let her be. It had occurred to her, to offer to help, but it had just as quickly occurred to her that she wasn't sure how. Kitchen duties had never been assigned to her and she admitted to herself that she would be quite lost.

Breakfast was served in the rather spacious diningroom, which was the biggest room downstairs. Jessica realized that she had the room directly above, and she saw the old black stove in the corner that must serve her room, as the pipe ran across the ceiling and then up through the floor above. The table was big and full. There was plenty to eat and she shared her meal with five men. The men were strangely quiet, and even a bit awkward, Jessica thought. They were all clean shaven under their moustaches, and fairly presentable. The girl finally realized that they were shy of her and she found that she enjoyed that. How awful, she reprimanded herself, and looked at Mrs. Carson who presided over the meal from the head of the table. She too was enjoying the discomfiture of the men, and it was obvious in her smile. She and Jessica exchanged a few sentences and the men continued eating in silence, their quiet now taking on a rather sullen air. Mrs. Carson, when her honest good nature won out, announced, "This here's Miss Baxter. You might just as well get accustomed to her being here at the table with you fellows, 'cause she's staying quite a while." The men appeared to relax a bit, and a low murmur began to circle the table.

"You're wondering why she's here? So fine a lady and all?" Each pair of eyes was upon Mrs. Carson's mouth as she offered an explanation to Jessica's presence. "Miss Baxter here's a nurse and she's going to be working at the hospital, so you fellows had better be good and polite to her, as you never can tell when one've you'll be needing nursing." She laughed a raucous laugh and the men all smiled, first at her, and then at Jessica. Jessica smiled at each one in turn, spending just a moment to study their features and, hopefully, remember their names, as Mrs. Carson introduced them. They were all miners, miners and part-time prospectors. There was the look of the hard worker about each of them, but there was also a haunted look that suggested to the girl that they too had a dream, like Mr. Dickerson, that they would some day stake a claim that would make them rich. It lent a bit of excitement and mystery to the bunch. Sitting here was so unlike sitting amongst the menfolk back home, where the most exciting thing they could aspire to was winning the next cricket match. These men were doing something! Something big! They were shaping a new country, taking chances, dreaming dreams. Suddenly the Peter Thompsons back home paled in comparison.

"I certainly hope that you'll not be needing my services, gentlemen," Jessica spoke, meaning every word. These men were to be her surrogate family and she did not wish to see any of them hurt or sick. She engaged in a conversation with them, becoming slowly aware as she did so, that they were easy to talk to, interesting to listen to and fascinating to watch. Mr. Mason — Henry Mason — he was the oldest of the lot, a wiry, almost toothless old man with an incredible glint in his eye, evidencing that he had not yet lost sight of his particular dream. He had a curious habit of popping little bits of biscuit into his cavernous mouth and swishing them about with his tongue. Instead of horrifying Jessica, it amused her, and her very amusement surprised her. Was she, after all, the survivor that she claimed to be? Not to be repelled by this coarse new life, but amused and entertained by it. Could be.

Mr. Tofler seemed to have difficulty sitting still. Even as he spoke to Jessica, he squirmed about in his chair. Jessica wasn't sure whether the man had a medical problem, or was simply anxious to be off. She did notice that he was the first away from the table and the first out of the front door. Mr. Bidding was the quiet one — almost foppish in his manners — and apparently not well liked by the others. He did not have the appearance of a miner, but he assured her in a rather nasal twang that indeed, he was. Mr. Rogers had the air of a rogue about him. His manner of dress was a cut above the others and he seemed to be aware of the difference. He stared boldly at Jessica, while the others stole glances. Finally, Mr. Simmons rounded out the table. He was a heavy-set, affable sort who reminded Jessica of her brother Charles, even though they bore no physical resemblance to one another. There must be some common thread that runs through people like Mr. Simmons and Charles, thought Jessica, something about their smile, their quiet eyes that pleaded for peace at all costs.

"I'd be pleased to escort you about town, Miss Baxter," Mr. Simmons spoke as they left the table and headed for the parlour.

"I'd like to attend church, Mr. Simmons." She saw him shudder slightly and cough into his fist. "But of course, I don't expect you to attend with me, good sir. If you could just show me where it is, I'd be much obliged." She thought again of Charles and smiled a gracious smile at the large, awkward man.

"Go on, Pete, take the lady to church. Won't hurt you a bit." It was Mr. Roger's teasing voice that Jessica heard.

She hastened to Mr. Simmons' rescue. "As a matter of fact, Mr. Simmons, I might just miss the service today, and spend the time familiarizing myself with the town." The man gave her a grateful smile. "And thank you, sir," she added loudly.

The rain had ceased, but there was damp chill in the air. Jessica had dressed against the possibility of cold weather, but perhaps not quite well enough. "You're shivering, Ma'am," stated her escort. "It's kinda worn, Ma'am, but would you accept my coat?" He began to unbutton his large woolen jacket, and, as much as Jessica would have appreciated the added warmth, she declined.

"Are there sidewalks anywhere about town?" asked the girl, tiring of catching her skirts up in her weary hands. The mud was not thick, it had not been a heavy rain, but she could tell that there must be times when it was a foot deep or so. She looked at Mr. Simmons.

"Well, I reckon there's not, Ma'am." He spoke apologetically. "I never thought of it before. But I guess there's not." He seemed to regret this oversight, but she smiled and looked away. Mud, mud everywhere. And dog dirt, and some garbage. Nothing in her background had prepared her for this.

Careful not to hurt this gentle man's feelings further, she sought to ask questions of a more pleasant nature. "Is there a post office?" She knew that this was to be her link with the outside world. When he answered that there was one just around the corner, they headed in that direction. That brought them to within sight of the railway station. How different it looked in the daylight! There was no one about, only the odd dog, sniffing around for some forgotten bite. That there had been so many excited people on that platform just the night before, mystified her. That the arrival of a train could cause such a furor was always to remain a mystery to Jessica.

The post office proved to be one room in a building that

housed many other businesses. The telegraph office occupied another room, and that made her think of Mr. Dickerson and Mr. Coleman. She was about to inquire about these two gentlemen when she noticed a sign in front of a window, just next door. Geo. Dickerson & James Coleman, Topographers. She must remember to return the tent one of these days.

There was an opera house, of sorts. It was a low slung building made of logs. To compare it with the opera houses of Britain and Europe was absurd, and Jessica, realizing so, refrained from any comment at all. There was one school, a 'public' one, as they were called. It consisted of two large rooms. A student could be taken from forms one to eight, but there was no further schooling here. Plans were in the wind for a senior school in the area, but no decision as to where it would be built had been arrived at, as yet. Some Catholic children took their schooling in the basement of the Catholic Church, the Catholic Church being one of the few buildings that had a basement. Most of Cobalt sat on the surface of the hard rock that encompassed most of the country, making it virtually impossible to have basements without extensive dynamiting of the rock. A Priest and a Nun conducted school for the Catholic children, and most of the town disapproved of this practice. Mr. Simmons echoed the feelings of the Protestant townsfolk, that the Catholics were not highly thought of and should remain on the east side of Lake Temiskaming. Jessica had no opinion on the subject. Her family and all of her friends had always been Church of England, and, even though she knew that Ireland was constantly in a turmoil because of the friction between her church and the Catholic Church, the problem had always seemed so remote that she had given it little or no thought.

"Are there always this many dogs about?" she inquired of her new friend as she side-stepped another dog dropping.

"Never noticed, Ma'am. Guess so. Strays, mostly. See lots of them out by the dump all the time. Indians eat them, I heard tell." A nervous shudder ran through Jessica. The dogs were dirty and unkempt looking, so different from the pets back home. Of course, at home there had always been servants to tend to them and keep them clean and fed. Also, the breeds in England were easily recognizable, but here, they were all mongrels and not very attractive cross breeds at that.

When they turned a corner, a large sign told them that there was indeed a newspaper in Cobalt. Bold and fancy letters painted across a wide window read THE NUGGET, Joseph T. Barlow, Publisher. She was instantly curious about the local news coverage and made a mental note to ask Mrs. Carson if she had a copy of the paper when she got back home.

Shortly after they passed the newspaper office and several other store fronts and hotels, they came to the base of a hill. Mr. Simmons pointed out the Anglican Church to Jessica, tipped his hat and left her to climb the steep grade by herself. It was not a lack of chivalry on his part, but a fear of being coerced into the building that made him hurry away.

There were logs that looked like they might be railway ties imbedded in the ground to assist in the climbing of the hill. There was a narrow road that the horses and carriages used, but it was rocky and muddy, so Jessica took the path that led to the street above.

As she neared the tiny white church she could hear organ music, and a hymn that she favoured, and she felt a small measure of security in it. There were about sixty seats in the building and it was full when she arrived, rather breathless from her climb. She stood at the back, away from the drafty door. "Hymn number thirty-eight," the hard voice of the preacher spoke out and everyone opened their hymnals and began to sing. Jessica knew the hymn by heart, and closed her eyes as she joined in. She was surprised into opening her eyes by a slight poke in the shoulder. It was Miss Beauville, and Jessica, so very happy to see her friend, spoke aloud, "Oh, Miss Beauville, it's so good to see you." She was instantly aware that all eyes were on her, including the Minister's . She turned red to the roots of her dark hair and Miss Beauville giggled. Jessica managed a weak smile.

"We'll see you after the service," whispered the younger girl, and she turned her attention back to her hymn book. Good Lord, worried Jessica, to have made such a spectacle of herself in church! What would the Minister think of her?

She was thankful that she was at the back of the church when the service ended. She hurried out the door and stood to one side, to await her friend.

"Miss Baxter, I'm so glad to see you." Miss Beauville's sweet voice was full of affection. "This here's Mr. Hobson, Sam, my fiancee," she beamed. Mr. Hobson extended a shy hand to Jessica and withdrew it quickly after they shook. He was not at all what Jessica had expected. She was somewhat embarrassed to have to admit to herself that she had guessed him to be a bit of a ne'er-do-well, probably because the couple had met at a hotel. It was silly of her, but she had formed that opinion and was now slowly eating her own unspoken words.

"I was going to find you out tomorrow, Miss Baxter. I, er, Sammy and me, we'd be so pleased if you could attend our wedding. It's just three weeks from now, the first bans were read today." Jessica vaguely remembered hearing wedding bans read out in church, but her acute embarrassment with herself had left her almost blind and deaf.

"I'd be honoured, Miss Beauville." She was about to ask where the girl was staying, when it became apparent that there was something else on the younger girl's mind.

"I was wondering too, Miss Baxter," the girl spoke in a whisper, "If you might, well, sort of act as my maid of honour. I don't have any kin here, and Sam here doesn't either, so it would be so good of you if you could."

"Why, I'd be pleased and proud to, Miss Beauville," answered Jessica, with enthusiasm. Her tour of the grimy town had left her slightly depressed, and the promise of a wedding did a great deal to raise her spirits. Sam edged away from the two women and stood nervously beside the road. "You'd best go," spoke Jessica kindly. "I think your fellow is anxious to be off."

They parted promising to see each other the following week and then Jessica too hurried away, hoping that the Minister, who was shaking hands with his parishioners at the door of the little church, had not noticed her. The climb down the hill was so much easier than the one up, and the sun had begun to shine, so Jessica arrived at Mrs. Carson's with a song in her heart.

"Mrs. Carson," Jessica began, quietly, as this was not a conversation to be overheard by the men, "I was curious about the bathing arrangements." When the big woman offered no information, she continued. "I'm, well, I'm accustomed to bathing daily, and, while I know that's probably quite impossible," she raised her eyebrows in a question and when Mrs. Carson did not disagree, she went on, "I was wondering just how often I might expect to bathe, and where?" Her innate shyness was momentarily gone. This business was just too serious to be kittenish about.

"Well now, Miss Baxter, we have a tub. It's out back in the shed. On bath nights, I generally get it in here, fill it with warm water, and bathe. Mind you, it only happens once in a while, special occasions and the like. But, as you say, you're 'accustomed' to more, so maybe we'll have to make some arrangements." Jessica could not tell if the woman was being slightly sarcastic or not. "Tell you what, it's a lot of water carrying, and my back's not what it used to be, but maybe we could leave the tub in your room, that is until the mood strikes one of the men folk, and I wouldn't be betting any money on that 'til at least Christmas come. But you'd have to fetch the water, or maybe get Hazel to help. Hazel's the youngun from next door that helps out once in a while. I'd have to ask you to pay her yourself though. Not fair me spending out my hard earned money so you can bath daily." There was just a trace of sarcasm obvious now, but Jessica refused to be dissuaded by it.

"That's quite alright, Mrs. Carson. And I'll not expect a bath every day, but several times a week, even twice, would be nice. That's if you don't mind?"

"Got a good well, lots of water. I don't mind, long's you do the carrying. My back, you know," she emphasized her problem by leaning forward slightly and massaging the small of her back to show where the pain was located.

"I'd be happy to give you some liniment for your back, Mrs. Carson, and even a massage now and again." And so it was that Jessica settled into her lodgings. A clean bed, the promise of a bath at least twice a week, good food and interesting company. She was ready for the hospital.

4

The Hospital

There was a dusting of snow swirling about the frozen mounds of mud along the road that Jessica took to the hospital. The dainty white flakes seemed loath to land on the horse-manure-dog-dirt-mud-mixture and they flitted back and forth, before eventually landing when the slight wind that propelled them moved on to tease other flakes. It was cold. Jessica had dressed very warmly against the prospect of freezing weather. She did not have far to walk and so it was pleasurable, especially since there was no immediate danger of sinking up to her ankles in the brown goo of yesterday.

It was rather fun to see the surprised glances she received from the people she passed on the street. Despite the early hour, the town had a bustle about it that spelled excitement. The cold, fresh air and the drama of a frontier town heightened Jessica's colour and she arrived at the hospital quite breathless.

True to the warnings that she had received both in England and Toronto, and most recently, by Mr. Dickerson on the train, the hospital was but a tent — a very large, rambling tent. Every effort had been made to keep the wind out, but it was still chilly inside.

Doctor Evans proved to be a rather interesting gentleman. And he was, indeed, a doctor. He was probably in his mid-fifties, but it was difficult for the girl to be certain, as he had a rather ageless appearance about him suggesting that he could be a great deal older, or, perhaps, even a few years younger. He had a large red nose that Jessica worried about, lest it mean that the good man had a penchant for the demon rum. He was always busy, reminding her a bit of Mr. Tofler, back at Mrs. Carson's. Even as he stood with Jessica, talking and smoking his pipe, he fussed about, shuffling piles of papers on a make-shift desk, or constantly tapping his pipe against a pole, or refilling it. The floor was wooden, but it was apparent that the cleaning staff had long since given up on their efforts to keep it clean. The ashes and tobacco from the Doctor's pipe were barely noticeable as they dropped to mingle with the dirt and dust of so many feet.

There were wood-burning stoves scattered throughout the tent, their chimneys rising up through the irregular roof that was stained with the smoke and soot of many cold nights. Beds were arranged in what seemed a rather haphazard fashion, and Jessica was to learn later that the patients were not above moving them about themselves, jockeying for a space nearer one of the stoves for a little extra warmth. There were two other nurses already in attendance, both tired looking young women who seemed too young for the demands made upon them in this harsh environment. One girl, a Miss Pamela Watson, was from the Maritimes and had a rather unusual accent. She was wearing a stained uniform and her hair was disheveled. Jessica was at once sorry for the girl and angry with her for allowing her appearance to be less than professional.

The other girl was from North Bay. She had trained at the very hospital Jessica had delivered the young Danny to. Her name was Gloria Reynolds and she too had the air of one who had seen more than her youth would normally dictate.

The essential introductions over with, the doctor indulged in a bit of gossip. "Hear you're from the Royal Victoria?" he queried. His head was tilted to one side, the better to see Jessica in the light from the hanging oil lamp. His eyebrows were bushy and they were arched in question.

"Yes, sir, I took my training there, and then worked at the hospital for several years." She spoke slowly, trying to imagine what exactly it was that the doctor wanted to know, as it was apparent that he was not through questioning her.

"I know a chap from Royal Vic." Jessica recognized the pet name that most of the staff used when referring to the hospital. "He was a doctor there, name of . . ." he scratched his graying head, never taking his eyes off the girl. She made no effort to help him recall, as there were dozens of doctors on staff, and it would be quite senseless to try to guess which one it might be. She stood there in the half light, meeting the doctor's gaze with her own straightforward eyes.

"Fairley. His name was Fairley." He smiled, quite pleased with himself for remembering. Jessica could not control her surprise, and this pleased the doctor even more. She had trained under Doctor Fairley, and he had been one of her very favourite people at the hospital. She forced herself to seem calm and replied that yes, she did know a Doctor Fairley. "Thought you might," was the doctor's comment, and he had a twinkle in his eye.

Darn it, thought Jessica, I wish that I could read this man's mind!

When it became obvious that he was not going to explain where he had met this doctor, she curbed her curiosity and began, once again, to ask questions about the hospital. "And the medicines, where are they kept?" The answer was in a lock-up at the back of the tent. When she looked through the haze, caused by the smoke from many pipes and the odd cigarette, she noticed a wooden cupboard with a padlock on it, at the far end of the room. "And where is the . . . well, the sanitary disposal?" She hated to ask this question, but it was necessary.

"The slop pails are emptied every few hours, by the orderlies, out back, in the 'out houses'." She had been afraid of that answer. The orderlies she discovered were a couple of youngsters in their teens, who worked for the hospital because they had finished with the public school, and were not able to afford further schooling, and, by their parents' standards, were too young to go to the mines. They were a rather surly twosome, constantly teasing the patients and squabbling between themselves. They wore white uniforms, but that did little to improve their general demeanor.

The entire morning was taken up with questions and

answers, and it was quite exhausting for poor Jessica. She found the air foul, but could think of no immediate remedy, as it was quite out of the question to ask the men to refrain from smoking, as there was precious little else for them to do while they lay on their cots, mending or dying.

If there was better light, at least they could read, thought the girl. She decided to make that one of her priorities, as she walked about, meeting the patients and talking about their sickness or injury. There were twenty-eight men in the tent at present, she was told by Gloria, who took over when the doctor was called away. Three men would be leaving in the next few days, as they had recovered from their maladies. There were five more that would be leaving, not because they would be getting better, but because they were going to die. These five were grouped together around one of the pot-bellied stoves and Jessica admired the doctor for trying to ease their last days with at least a little bit of heat. Two were unable to appreciate the gesture, Jessica discovered upon touring the 'terminal' area. They were unconscious and were unlikely to regain their sensibilities before the end.

Jessica leaned over one of them and thought that he could not be more than twenty, or twenty-one. His face was peaceful, almost as though he'd been drugged. She found herself wondering if the kind doctor had eased his way even further by giving him a massive dose of morphine. It could be. She knew that sort of thing did happen, even at her beloved Royal Vic.

How very far away she was from that hospital, she thought. She glanced slowly and sadly about the room, comparing. The Royal Vic had shining walls, painted either startling white or pale green. Here, the walls were canvas, and they were constantly in motion, swaying in response to the winds outside. They were discoloured, a rather musty gray-brown, and there were patches of darker colours that may even represent blood, she wasn't sure. The marble floor that she used to watch the cleaning staff polish every day, twice a day, had been replaced by a wooden floor that was uneven, and soiled. Again, there were suspicious dark stains that made her feel a bit uneasy.

She sighed deeply. The air! It made her want to go out of doors and get a good clean lung full of fresh air. Surely this couldn't be sanitary? The air was visible. It hung like a fog about three or four feet above the beds, or cots, and she had to fight the urge to fan the haze away as she moved about. She was accustomed to the smell of disinfectant, of clean linen, and of medication. But not here. Not in this God-forsaken spot. Her eyes stung, and she wasn't sure whether it was because of the smoke or the sadness in her heart as she looked about the dismal room. Her eyes rested upon Miss Watson, and, before she could arrest the impulse, she was back in England, back at the Royal Vic, and it was Heather that she was looking at and her heart ached.

"Oh, there you are Jessica," Heather's lilting Scottish accent greeted Jessica, who had just come on duty. The girl rushed over to her and there was a mischievous look on her freckled face. "There was a fellow here looking for you just an hour ago." She smiled broadly, displaying large, straight teeth, whitened by the contrast with her ruddy complexion and her freckles. "A verrrry nice looking fellow too, I might add." She was enjoying herself. "I told him you'd be coming in this noon, but he couldn't wait. Left this for you," she added, almost as an afterthought. She handed Jessica an envelope with 'Jesse' written on it, and Jessica shivered. It could only be from Peter. Her concern must have shown on her face, as Heather reached out for her arm and asked if there was anything the matter. Jessica drew back as was her custom when anyone touched her in this manner. But Heather was not offended. She knew Jessica and her desperate need for privacy. She smiled and discreetly moved away so that Jessica might read her letter.

It took but a moment. Peter was going abroad. He'd get in touch with her when he returned. Short. But it said so much.

Poor Peter, mused the girl. He's so helpless when it comes to uncomfortable scenes. He's rather go off to Europe indefinitely, than explain to her that he could no

longer marry her. Jessica understood. She'd even
rehearsed the encounter they would have when he told
her, but now she'd been robbed of even that.

She looked up from Peter's note into the stare of Dr.
Fairley. He was standing just a few feet away, leaning
against the doorway into the nurses' station, smiling a
little half smile of encouragement. Jessica shrugged her
shoulders, held her head up and walked over to the man.

"Good day, Miss Baxter," spoke the tall man, still
smiling. His eyes were blue, and soft, and they obviously liked looking at Jessica. She knew this and it usually
made her uncomfortable, but not today. Peter's note
was a final thing. An ending of sorts. And she was in
the mood for beginnings.

"Good afternoon, Doctor Fairley." She smiled her
widest smile, her black eyes shining. "I thought that
today was your day off." She wasn't even embarrassed
that she should know his schedule. "Surely you've better things to do with your time than hold up the walls of
the Vic?" She was almost flirting and it made her smile
even wider.

The doctor sensed a change in Jessica and was obviously pleased. "Perhaps I just couldn't stand to be away
from . . . my patients for a whole day." There was an
invitation in his voice to substitute 'you' for 'patients' in
that sentence and she took the cue.

"It's always nice to be missed," she replied vaguely,
still not flinching under his appreciative gaze.

This was easily the most encouragement that Doctor
Fairley had ever received from the aloof Miss Baxter,
and he was visibly upset when he was summoned by one
of the other doctors. He grinned sheepishly over his
shoulder at Jessica as he hurried down the hall to the
operating theatre.

It wasn't until Jessica was checking the daily procedures at the stations that she realized that she was
blushing. Her face fairly throbbed with colour and it
was not lost on Heather, as she approached the desk.
Heather had not seen Jessica's encounter with the

Doctor so she assumed that Jessica's flush had something to do with Peter's letter and she gestured to the
crumpled note in her friend's hand. "Is he coming
back?" She looked eager for some romantic gossip.

"No. Never," was Jessica's reply.

It was Miss Watson's hand on her arm that brought
Jessica back to the present. "Would you like a cup of tea,
Miss Baxter?" was the girl's question and Jessica realized
that she very much wanted a nice warm cup of tea.

The conversation around the tea pot was one that would
be repeated hundreds of times in the future. The weather
was remarked on first, then some reference to the dying and
the recently dead, and then, mercifully, it would switch to the
private lives of the nurses. Jessica was disadvantaged as she
did not know any of the people that the younger girls were
talking about, but she tried her best to sound interested. She
had made her bed, and she was quite prepared to lie in it. If
gossiping with her co-workers was to be a daily ritual, she
would join in, but, as was Jessica's nature, she would come
away from any conversation of that sort with more information about the others than they were able to glean about her.

"Well, I understand that the fellows are coming back
this week." Gloria was saying. "Wonder if any of them has
'struck it rich'?" she smiled and allowed her eyes to become
large circles as though punctuating the question.
"Remember that fellow, what was his name? Murray or something?" she waited to see if her friend remembered and then
continued, more for Jessica's benefit than anyone else's.
"Anyway, he came back from up near Timmins somewhere,
with more money than you could shake a stick at! Sold one of
his claims to some big outfit up there, right next to a strike of
theirs and they sure paid him a handsome amount just
because he was 'next door' so to speak." Jessica was interested in this story. She knew precious little of prospecting and
mining and was anxious to learn more. She encouraged the
young lady to continue. "He stopped here on his way to
Toronto and was showing off for all his buddies at the hotel.
Buying beer for everyone. They say he must have spent a
small fortune. The he left the next day on the train." She

sounded sad and Jessica couldn't help but wonder if perhaps
the girl had fancied the lad and his 'fortune'.

Jessica asked the girls where the fellows were coming
back from and who they were. The girls exchanged silly
glances and then described how the men went out, those who
weren't working full time in one of the mines, and prospect-
ed. They were usually quite secretive about their where-
abouts, as it was a sort of 'first come, first served' kind of
business. There was a fierce rivalry amongst the men, but,
fortunately, also a strange kind of loyalty. Jessica heard stories of men carrying their rival prospecting friends out of the
bush on their backs — men who had been hurt, or had taken
ill with one of the many unexplained illnesses that took some
of the men who lived in the bush. Jessica was terribly interested now and was sorry when one of the girls looked at her
timepiece and announced that they should be starting the
midday meal preparations.

It had not occurred to the Englishwoman that she
would be responsible for delivering meals. In her hospital,
there had been staff for that sort of thing, and she smiled as
she wondered why it hadn't occurred to her before that it
would be a part of her job. The food was delivered to the
tent by a wagon operated by Gus Menzies, who worked at the
hotel. Gus was a 'jack-of-all-trades', turning up in the most
unexpected places. Just now, he was skillfully passing out
trays of food covered with clean white napkins, cleaner than
anything Jessica had noticed in the hospital.

The men that could, sat up in their cots, eagerly looking
forward to the meal. There were several who needed help,
and then, of course, there were the very sick who would have
to be force-fed by the nurses. It was a time-consuming ritual
that was to be repeated three times daily, but it certainly
helped to make the workday pass quickly.

The workday, for the nurses, began at 8:00 a.m. and
ended at 7:00 p.m. It was a long, gruelling day and they took
turns working on Saturdays and Sundays. It was not
unheard of for a girl to work fourteen or fifteen days without
a break. There were male volunteers who sat with the
patients throughout the night. These men were not responsi-

ble for the care of the sick, it was just their job to see that they were comfortable and to fetch the doctor or a nurse if something of a serious nature arose.

Jessica discovered that Doctor Evans often worked late into the night, yet he was always there when she arrived in the early morning. She tried to imagine when the good man slept, but she had to conclude that he was one of those who needed little sleep to function.

Jessica, on the other hand, was accustomed to eight hours a night and had difficulty operating on less. She would slowly get used to less, but it was a very long struggle and one that she did not give up easily.

The evening meal at Mrs. Carson's was served promptly at 7:15 and that gave Jessica precious little time to get back and get cleaned up for the table. Her life seemed to take on the appearance of a race. She raced through her morning wash, her breakfast and then hurried through the dirty streets to the hospital every morning. The days were a blur of activity, the only quiet periods being the tea time that she found herself looking forward to more and more each day. Sometimes they were robbed of this break because of some emergency or other, and it made Jessica a bit cross when it happened.

Jessica would scurry home to dinner, then fall into bed totally exhausted, only to dream tiresome dreams in which she was racing up and down the streets of Cobalt, looking for 'God knows what!' Her bath nights, as important as they were to her, were even more tiresome than ordinary nights, as she had to help carry the water upstairs and then assist Hazel in the removal of the same water. She wondered sometimes if the men thought her a bit strange, insisting on a bath so often, but none of them commented, so she went about her schedule as though it were the most natural thing in the world.

Jessica had been working at the hospital just over a week when Doctor Evans came up to her with a letter. He looked puzzled as he handed it to her. It was postmarked North Bay and the girl immediately thought of the young Danny. She tore open the letter and was so shocked by its contents that she let out an involuntary gasp. The Doctor stood in front of her, sucking on his pipe that was, once again, out, and he sensed the sorrow in the girl. She tried to fold the letter neatly and put it in her pocket, but her hand shook and her vision blurred. Doctor Evans put his hand on her shoulder and said, "Out with it, girl. You can't keep it bottled up inside you!" When Jessica did not respond, his voice rose sharply, "Miss Baxter!"

"It's . . . Danny," she spoke the boy's name as she would a loved one. Her voice was soft and hoarse and her eyes welled with hot tears that she struggled to keep back. "He's dead." The finality of that word shook her body with such intensity that her watch rose and fell on her bosom and the note fell from her hand.

The doctor stooped to pick it up and then read it. It was short and to the point. Miss Baxter had requested that she be told about Danny Pinks' case and Doctor Mason was complying. Danny had died two days after he was operated on, loss of blood and shock being listed as the causes.

Doctor Evans had heard about the incident at the station at Burks Falls, and he remembered George Dickerson's account of Miss Baxter's bravery and tenderness, a very good combination in a frontier nurse. He was genuinely sorry for her. He was no stranger to grief, and he also knew that this was worse because it was the girl's 'first' loss here in Canada. He was about to suggest that the nurse take some time to herself, but before he could speak, Jessica snatched the letter from his hand, shoved it in her apron pocket and wheeled about, busying herself with a patient. Everyone had their own way of shouldering sorrow and the good doctor was not about to intrude on Jessica's way. He too moved aside, and, if someone had cared to look, a tiny glistening tear could be seen in the corner of his eye, picked up by the light of the swaying lamp that hung nearby.

That very lamp was a warning. It stopped moving to and fro, but only for a few seconds and then resumed its motion with such fury that it had to be removed along with the other lamps that hung about the tent. "It's a bad wind," one of the young orderlies explained to Jessica as she stood bewildered at the sudden rush of activity in the hospital.

Even some of the patients were helping to secure things against the mighty wind. "Happens every once in a while. Probably a blizzard. We hafta keep the lanterns from falling down because of the fire." He was busily moving about, placing the lanterns in holders especially designed for them at the base of the poles. "Had a fire here onct," he explained further to Jessica who was following him about, helping and learning. "The whole hospital nearly went. My uncle Nels was killed, along with some others. Started when the lanterns were knocked down, and then went like wildfire. I don't remember it much, but me Mum tells the story every onct in a while. Some fire!" His eyes were round and shiny and he was licking his lips like someone with an even bigger story to tell, but time would not allow.

There was a crash at the far end of the tent and Jessica went running. One of the outside poles had bent to the force of the wind, knocking over a tray with metal spit bowls and bedpans on it. They went clattering to the floor and the post swung back and forth as it was no longer secured at the base. Jessica instinctively began moving the patients closest to the danger away from the spot. She was helped by the other nurses and the young orderlies. When everyone seemed out of danger, they began picking up the mess, careful not to be hit by the swinging pole. There was an air of silly comedy about the whole thing and it was difficult not to laugh as they squatted on the floor, ducking the post and picking up the bedpans. If Grandmamma could see me now, thought Jessica, and she smiled a bizarre smile at her reflection in a bedpan.

When the local workmen had fixed the post and it was nearly time to leave, Jessica went to the front of the tent and peeked out. There was snow everywhere. It was not the soft, easy kind that melted when it hit the ground, but deep, white snow that piled in little mountains against the sides of the tent and obscured the walkway.

It's here, she thought. All that winter and snow that everyone had warned her about, was finally here. It was as though the enemy had been recognized and now she could fight it. She was ready! So she thought!

She secured her scarf carefully about her neck and

tucked it in her heavy coat before she left for home. Her
boots were laced up to the top and she wore warm gloves.
The adventure was about to begin. The trip up the street
and around the corner to Mrs. Carson's generally took the
girl about eight minutes. Today, twenty-five minutes were
spent, picking her foot steps, turning about to catch her
breath and rest, after a particularly difficult passage. She fell
twice, and the added weight of the snow that clung to her
coat as a result slowed her down even further. She was within sight of her boarding house when she fell the second time.
She was struggling to get up when she felt strong hands
grasp her under the arms. She did not try to turn about to
identify her saviour, but kept her head down against the
wind, and, using his strong hold, lifted herself once again to
her feet. Only then did she see Mr. Dickerson. He was barely recognizable in his furry outfit. Only his moustache, which
was edged in white, and his laughing eyes were clearly visible, and Jessica smiled her thanks to him.

Conversation was quite out of the question, as the wind
was howling louder than either of them could speak, so he
just continued to hold her, and assisted her to the steps of
Mrs. Carson's. Once on the porch, and out of the worst of the
wind, she turned to thank him, expecting him to leave, but he
was opening the front door and leading her in. The dry
warmth of the boarding house engulfed Jessica and her
cheeks reddened much like two ripe apples. It was most
becoming. "I'm quite alright now, Mr. Dickerson," she began,
once again assuming he'd turn and leave. She wanted to take
him to task for his teasing about Doctor Evans and Cobalt
conditions in general, but she thought that this was not the
right time or place.

"You're not to be rid of me quite that easily, Miss
Baxter," he smiled at her and she flushed even deeper. "Mrs.
Carson sent me out to fetch you, and I'm going to deliver you
right to her, in her kitchen, next to that great hot stove she's
busy keeping your supper warm on." He held her arm and
led her deftly through the house, and into the bright kitchen
where Mrs. Carson was indeed fussing about the stove.

"Why, you must be near froze, Miss Baxter," said the

older woman as she helped Jessica off with her hat and coat. "Bet you never saw anything like that before, back in England?" she teased, gesturing with her head towards the window and the howling wind. But she was quite right, Jessica had not seen anything to compare with this Northern Ontario blizzard and she was not shy to admit it.

"Mr. George here came calling on you, so I sent him out when you weren't here the usual time." Mrs. Carson grinned at Mr. Dickerson and it was quite obvious that these two were not strangers. Jessica vaguely remembered Mr. Coleman saying that it was Mr. Dickerson who had arranged for her to stay at Mrs. Carson's, and, had she not been so cold and tired at this moment, she might have endeavoured to find out the connection between these two. "He was pleased as anything to go out and save you. Said saving damsels in distress was his favourite pastime." She giggled like a schoolgirl at this and turned to tend the stove.

Jessica looked up into Mr. Dickerson's eyes and there was a warmth there that matched the woodstove in comfort. She wondered if it was for her, or for the round lady at the stove who was so obviously pleased with his presence.

5

Rosina's Wedding

"Sam Hobson and his young lady were asking after you," Mr. Dickerson said, by way of explaining his presence at Mrs. Carson's boarding house. "Seems you promised to stand up for Rosina at their wedding?" He tilted his head to one side and smiled an inquisitive smile.

Jessica was sipping a hot cup of tea, trying to keep her teeth from chattering. She nodded and Mr. Dickerson went on, "The wedding's to be a week Saturday at the Church of England. I was speaking with Doctor Evans and he assured me that you'd be able to attend."

Jessica's need for control brought a cold glint to her eyes, that did not go unnoticed by the handsome messenger. The young lady was not accustomed to being told when she might or might not do something. It smarted. But it, too, was something that she recognized as being an integral part of her new life, and her eyes softened. She could not resist a sarcastic, "That's nice," though.

"I volunteered to take you 'round to Rosina's lodgings tonight so that you ladies might make your necessary plans, but if this blizzard keeps up, none of us will be moving from here."

That statement brought a chuckle from Mrs. Carson who was ladling out a healthy portion of steaming stew on Jessica's plate. The girl noticed that Mr. Dickerson was to join her for the meal and that somehow pleased her. That he had waited for her, when it was obvious that the others had all had their evening meal, indicated a politeness that reminded her of her upbringing.

She made her decision then not to berate him for his teasing and asked, "Surely the snow will subside soon, Mr. Dickerson?" Her voice was still a bit shaky. "I mean, how long can this go on?" She too looked towards the window that let in the howl of the wind.

"It being the first of the season, just might quit soon, Miss Baxter, but rest assured, my dear," he had a tease in his voice, "that there'll be storms that last for days, even weeks, before winter's end."

Even though she had decided not to believe everything that this man told her, ever again, she shivered.

The storm did not end in time for the pair to go to Rosina's, so they made plans to go the following night. Jessica wended her way wearily to her room. Her wintry escapade, coupled with the incident at the hospital, had left her totally exhausted. She was quickly in bed, but not quickly asleep. She lay there wondering if Mr. Dickerson was spending the night. She listened for the front door closing, but there was still enough noise from the storm to obscure all other sounds. Why the possibility of Mr. Dickerson's spending the night in this house, her house, should keep her awake when she was, oh, so tired, was a mystery to her.

The front walk was shovelled by the time Jessica headed for the hospital the next morning. The brilliant sunshine was doubly hard to bear, as it reflected off the clean white snow. She remembered her train companion's explanation of how the Eskimos protected themselves from snow blindness and she wondered once again, where he had spent the night. He'd not been at the breakfast table and she'd been reluctant to ask after him.

The horses were making their way with much difficulty as the snow on the road had not yet been cleared away. Jessica was wondering how this chore would be handled when she turned a corner and encountered a team of horses pulling a plow. There were four strong animals dragging a wooden contraption behind them, that directed the snow to the sides of the roadway. The newcomer was surprised when she recognized Mr. Menzies directing the horses. He nodded his head to her as he passed and she turned and finished her walk to work.

There was a flurry of excitement in the hospital when she arrived. Jessica was to discover that blizzards generally brought with them a series of mishaps, both major and minor. A snow-laden tree had fallen on a young boy whose shoulder was broken in the incident. Several people had already been treated for frostbite and an elderly gent had suffered a heart attack while shovelling a path out to his 'convenience' in the back yard.

Miss Watson and Miss Reynolds explained about these usual winter occurrences as they went about their morning tasks of feeding and caring for the ill. At tea time, they entertained Jessica with stories of incredible blizzards of years gone by. It was a busy, exciting day and Jessica wondered on her trek home if it was really so special, or if the prospect of seeing Mr. Dickerson again that evening was what stimulated her.

She was doomed to disappointment.

It was not the handsome George Dickerson who came to fetch her, but the very shy Sam Hobson.

Mr. Dickerson had been called away — up to the Kirkland Lake area, and wouldn't be back for several days. Jessica tried to conceal her disappointment and her job was made easier when she met with Rosina Beauville and her enthusiastic joy.

"I can't thank you enough, Jessica, for doing this for me . . . for us," she added as she glanced coyly at Mr. Hobson, who sat quietly in a corner of the parlour at the Walker Boarding House where Rosina was billeted until the forthcoming marriage. "There'll be a dinner afterward at the Hotel . . . hope you don't mind," she added quickly, probably fearing her new friend's reaction to 'hotel'.

"I'd be more than pleased to attend, Rosina," Jessica spoke with sincerity. She was quite in the mood for some fun, and was not averse to attending a meal at a respectable hotel and she knew that there were several in town. The girls were on a first name basis now and they were both a bit reticent and awkward about it.

The times and wedding roles were agreed upon and then the girls shook hands and Jessica headed home. She was accompanied by Mr. Hobson who remained quiet the whole way. This did not bother Jessica, as she was in a pensive mood.

Her thoughts flew back to England and to her own plans for marriage, and she had difficulty shaking off her melancholy as she said good night to the quiet young groom.

Before Jessica knew it, Rosina's wedding day arrived. She had not seen Mr. Dickerson since the night of the blizzard and had actually stopped wondering about him. Then, suddenly, there he was, standing at Mrs. Carson's front doorway, all 'gussied up' in his 'Sunday-go-to-meeting' clothes, as fine looking a figure of a man as any Jessica had ever seen. She struggled to conceal her pleasure, but it was obvious that some of it had shown, as Mr. Dickerson doffed his hat, bowed his head and then gave her a very engaging and knowing smile. It was impossible not to smile back.

This was going to be a very special day!

The service at the church was solemn. The minister cautioned the young couple about their obligations to one another and to the church. His voice droned on and on, but Rosina seemed not to notice. She gazed up at her intended with such adoration that Jessica's breath caught in her throat. It was a truly holy moment for Jessica, one that she would never forget!

The small wedding party moved to a dining room at the Frazer House, where a delightful supper was served them. Mr. Dickerson seemed to know Sam Hobson quite well and he acted as spokesman for the party, offering toasts first to the beautiful, blushing bride, and then to the nervous groom.

He turned then to Jessica and lifted his glass in a gallant gesture. Jessica had been caught up in the mood of the occasion and had indulged in several glasses of champagne that had been especially imported, by Mr. Dickerson, for the ceremony. Her cheeks glowed and her black eyes shone.

"And to Miss Jessica Baxter, who lent such a serious touch of class to these festivities," he spoke softly, sensuously.

"Hear! Hear!" echoed the rest of the party, tapping

their glasses on the table.

Mr. Dickerson continued, "And all of us here —" he motioned with his arm to include the entire table and then finally pointed to himself, "Hope to be with her to celebrate her nuptials."

Jessica's heart skipped a beat. She felt as though she'd just been proposed to. She tried with all her might to withdraw from his gaze, but her eyes were locked into his. The combination of the wine and the memory of Rosina's look of love made her want to cry out 'yes' to this stranger. This man whom she barely knew, and yet who seemed to know her so well.

It was Mr. Dickerson who broke the spell. He reluctantly released her from his grip and looked again about the table as everyone raised their glasses to Jessica.

She was uncharacteristically shy as she returned their homage. Something about the moment subdued her and her need for total control, and she relaxed ever so slightly as she smiled about the table, careful not to look directly at Mr. Dickerson again.

Before she had a chance to wonder what might happen next, a loud alarm sounded, followed by the words, "FIRE! FIRE!"

Everyone at the table stood up suddenly and the glasses went flying. Mr. Dickerson seemed to naturally take charge - ordering the women to grab their wraps from the clothes trees at the doorway and to exit the building as quickly as possible. Jessica's training as a nurse compelled her to search about, looking for something useful to do. But the need for help was not apparent. The fire seemed not to be at the Frazer House.

The alarm had been set up so that all volunteers would hurry to the streets, where they would be met by the fire wagon. And that was precisely how things happened. Mr. Dickerson, Sam Hobson and the other men jumped on the wagon as it slowed down to pick them up and then they were gone into the black night.

Jessica left the others to follow in its wake, knowing that the presence of a medical person might be necessary.

She regretted that she'd not brought her bag, but there was no time to go back to Mrs. Carson's to fetch it.

Her chest hurt as she took in great lungfuls of cold air, but she kept up her hurried pace. The fire was not far away and the orange glow in the night sky was like a beacon for her.

She saw when she arrived at the site that it was a small, private home that was ablaze. The fire wagon was pouring water on the adjacent buildings, trying to keep the fire from spreading. The men at the hand pumps were glistening with sweat, despite the bitter cold, as they pumped up and down in a definite rhythm that was such a contrast to the chaos about them.

Mr. Dickerson spotted the nurse and grabbed her arm, leading her to a woman huddled in a snow bank. The woman was blackened with smoke and soot and it was obvious that her shawl had been on fire. Jessica held her, soothing her with strokes and words. The woman rocked back and forth in Jessica's arms, whispering, "My baby, my baby."

The true terror of it all struck Jessica. She glanced about, not loosening her hold on the woman. She saw Mr. Dickerson in the thick of things, and noticed a look of horror on his face. She overheard, "The men have gone in," then some loud noises. "The baby's up there," and more noises and then the hissing of water and fire as they met. "For God's sake, watch out!" then a loud crash.

The woman stiffened in Jessica's arms, and then fainted.

She stayed unconscious until Jessica had her back at the hospital. And even awake, she was in a semi-conscious state. She didn't seem to need anyone to explain to her that her child was dead. Some mysterious bond had snapped within her and only time would help her now.

Jessica made the woman as comfortable as possible and then stood up to stretch her back. She was tired and sad. It had been an incredible night and she was so glad that it was over.

The men filtered back from the ruins, to be treated for minor burns and scratches, happy to report that 'it' had not spread. It was as though the fire was alive, an animal that was in hiding, coming out only occasionally, to eat up as much of the town as it could, only to go into hiding again, 'til the next time. It could have been worse, they murmured with awesome respect.

It was as Jessica was tidying up that she saw the stretcher come in. The body on it was blackened and the face was covered with a soiled handkerchief.

She was confused. She was prepared for the body of a child, but not for this. This was a man's body. She walked over to the stretcher that the quiet bearers had placed upon the floor and reached down to remove the piece of linen.

"Oh, my God! No!" she cried. "Not Sam!" Her knees went out from under her, and the only thing she could remember as she blacked out was Rosina's face as she looked up at Sam and said "I do."

Jessica would never know for sure just what it was that brought her to this dark abyss, where thoughts floated about as though they'd been chipped off her memory, anchorless. Certainly Sam's death was a part of it, and perhaps even young Danny's. But the darkness went beyond that — deeper into her core. It went deeper even than the recent and dramatic changes in her lifestyle. The blackness crossed the Atlantic to that misty isle, England, and to her roots. She had a terrible fear that she would have to come to grips with some or all of these black memories before she woke and began to function again in her new environment.

"Oh, Jessica, there you are, darling," Sybil Baxter greeted her daughter cheerfully, and her very sunniness brought a cold shiver to Jessica. Abigail Windsor was not six months in her grave and Jessica's mourning was so total that she could not bear her mother's good humour. The girl had been fairly successful at avoiding Sybil the past few weeks. Fairview was a large estate and the two women varied greatly in their choices of pastimes. The mother would flit about the house, not bothering to disguise her greed, as she fondled the artifacts that her parents and grandparents before her had admired enough to collect. On the other hand the girl would walk or ride horseback for hours on end, stopping only when her energies were spent. She would then sleep the deep sleep of the exhausted — dreamless.

"The appraisers are coming this afternoon, dear. Do try to be civil." Sybil smiled a forced smile, but her eyes betrayed her feelings. She knew how much her daughter disapproved of her selling Fairview, and all of its treasures, but it was hers and Edward's to sell. She would do whatever she wanted with it, whatever it took to maintain the lifestyle that she and her husband so enjoyed.

Sybil Windsor Baxter always did what she wanted.

Rather than answer, Jessica turned and exited the room, and the house. She walked for hours in the fields that she used to call hers. She stopped to pick wildflowers. She gulped the clean, fresh air. She smelled the damp earth as she sat upon it, tucking her long skirts about her ankles, lifting her knees to her chin. In that little-girl attitude, she cried her only tears. They were not just tears of sorrow, but tears of frustration. Jessica was not in control, and that exasperated her. She wept quietly into her skirt, until the cool dampness of her own tears cooled her hot cheeks.

It was a time for turning about. A time for slipping back into command. Blast her mother! And her father! They chose their lifestyles. Why could she not hers?

She decided that independence was the only form of existence she could tolerate. To rely upon her parents' largess was more than she could bear. She considered the monies that Sybil and Edward would realize from the sale of Abigail Windsor's estate to be 'ill-gotten-gains' and she would have no part of them.

She loved her brother dearly, but somehow, she knew that he would not agree. As long as he had his fun with the 'chaps' and the 'hunts' and the 'clubs' and all of the other niceties that went with the aristocracy, he would not question the source. And yet, Jessica loved him no less for his lack of character. She looked upon Charles as a young boy, desirous of a sweet, and not caring much who gave it to him. He'd been brought up that way. Sybil and Edward were good teachers. It had not been easy for her heart to fault her brother. She felt only a sadness and a pity, and a deep, deep love.

But Sybil had not been Jessica's teacher. It was as though, from the very beginning, the mother did not know what to do with her 'girl-child'. It was as though her daughter was a potential rival. She resented the very few attentions that Edward paid the child, and was openly thankful when Abigail slowly took over her 'motherly' chores. The two grew apart, mother and daughter, never to merge again. Gradually the branch became stronger that the tree and the weaker Sybil's resentment only deepened.

Edward, a totally shallow man, saw none of this, and, if he had, it's doubtful that he would have cared. His self-centredness was matched only by his wife's. Children represented responsibility and that was a trait completely lacking in his make-up. His decadent youth led to an even more decadent adulthood.

London was the obvious place for Jessica to go. She had school friends in Croydon, and she would go to them. From their home she would travel up to London and carve out a new life for herself. She would get a job, or perhaps go to the University. Yes, she would go to London.

She stood up, shaking the grass and twigs from her dress. She felt suddenly lighter, younger. The decision having been made, she felt a great burden lifted from off her slender young shoulders and she strode quickly back to the house.

Her attitude was so positive that not even the carriages in the big circular drive bothered her. They represented her mother's frivolous friends and, of course, the appraisers and the collectors. Vultures, all of them. She walked through the big house, oblivious to all. Sybil tried to get her attention, but the girl sailed by as though in a trance. She went up to her room, where she folded everything that she owned neatly into piles on the furniture. She rang for a servant whom she dispatched for travelling bags.

When the servant girl returned, she had Martha in

tow. Dear Martha, how she was suffering. Jessica immediately felt guilty that she had not realized up until now just how terrible this whole thing was for Martha. The old woman had aged ten years in the last few months.

How could Jessica not have seen it?

"Martha, are you ill?" Jessica exclaimed. The housekeeper's hand shook as she reached out to touch the girl, in much the same manner as she would when Jessica returned to Fairview from school. The girl backed away, and was instantly sorry. An even deeper sadness clouded Martha's eyes. Jessica reached for her this time and the woman moved into her arms. "You are ill, Martha," Jessica declared as she felt the feeble old body shiver against her.

"No, Miss Jessie, I'm just tired," but her voice made her a liar. It was raspy and it was apparent that she was having difficulty breathing. In a flash Jessica realized she could not leave this old lady here to watch the destruction of everything that she'd ever loved. Martha had been with Abigail Windsor here at Fairview for over fifty years. To lose both all at once was too much for her. She was giving up and Jessica was not one to recognize surrender.

"I'm leaving here tomorrow, Martha, and you're coming with me." Her voice was authoritative. "I'm going to London and I'm going to need you." The word 'need' was the magic one. Martha smiled a very weak smile, and surprised Jessica by nodding her consent. There was nothing here for her. Miss Jessie had always been a favourite of Mrs. Windsor's — what better than to go with the girl? The sense of purpose rallied her and she moved slowly about, helping to pack Jessica's things in her bags.

And so it was that Jessica Sybil Baxter left Fairview. She moved with Martha to London where they took a small flat. Jessica spent her days looking for work, Martha spent hers waiting for the girl to return. Jessica did not go to Croydon. She did not tell anyone where

they were. It was her most fervent wish to remain
anonymous in the vast city. And it worked.

One day, when Jessica returned with her usual discouraging news regarding employment, she found
Martha in bed. The old lady had gone back to bed when
Jessica had gone out in the morning and had been
unable to get up since. Jessica called a carriage and
took the told woman to the hospital. It was there that
Jessica was introduced to hospital life. She spent three
weeks sitting and watching Martha die. But as she sat,
she learned. She learned that she liked the cleanliness
of the hospital. She liked the caring. And so, when
Martha died, Jessica enrolled in the student nursing
program and stayed there at the Royal Victoria for
three long years, living off a small inheritance bestowed
upon her by her housekeeper Miss Martha Cockersell.

Her connection with her family all but severed,
Jessica formed a new life. When she did feel the need
for closeness, she visited with her old friends in
Croydon. It was in her third year at the hospital that
she learned her father had died. Cirrhosis of the liver.
Jessica was not surprised.

News flashes of her mother filtered through to her
from her friends and the odd bit in the papers. Sybil
was not aging well. She had become somewhat of a
laugh to the elite. Edward had successfully frittered
away the entire estate on bad investments and high living before he died, leaving his wife to live off the gen-
erosity of others. Jessica could not bear to think of this,
so she avoided all conversations about her mother. And
then, one quiet afternoon, Sybil Baxter was brought
into the hospital, and Jessica could no longer evade the
issue. Her mother was losing her mind!

"She's coming about," Jessica heard someone say. She
tried desperately to recognize the voice, but it was strained,
as though someone was calling to her through a tunnel. She
tried to move, but it was as though a great weight had been
placed upon her and the effort was too much. She drifted off.

It was a while later that she heard, "Ah, ha, here she is,"

and this time she knew the voice. It was Pamela Watson's unusual Maritime accent and it sounded so good. The ghosts of the past were once again relegated to the back of her mind. And she was so very glad to be here, in this dingy old tent-hospital, in primitive Cobalt.

She was helped to a sitting position by both nurses and when she looked about she was astonished at her audience. Doctor Evans was there. The two orderlies were there and so was George Dickerson. She flushed when she realized what a sight she must be, lying on a cot, her dress wrinkled and soiled, her hair disheveled. But they did not seem to notice or care.

"You gave us quite a start, Miss Baxter." It was George Dickerson's mellow voice that broke the anxious silence. His appearance matched her own. His hair was messy, his clothes in disarray and there were black streaks of soot across his face. Suddenly Jessica remembered what had happened just before she had fainted and she glanced quickly for the stretcher that had borne Sam's body. Mercifully, it had been removed. But the tightness in her heart could not be removed that easily.

"I must go to Rosina," were her first words.

6

The Peters' Baby

The bleak, cold winter days that followed matched Jessica's heart. It was as though everything that could go wrong, did, including bone-chilling fifty-degree-below-zero days and even colder nights. There was little to lift her spirits as the cold weather prophesied by one and all descended upon the town in the form of a large, white blanket.

Rosina Beauville Hobson left Cobalt at the first available moment, not giving Jessica an opportunity to express her sorrow. Jessica felt that she had failed her new friend, and that saddened her. Doctor Evans was called away for days at a time, his departures creating more work and responsibility for the nurses. The tent was harder than ever to heat and the spectre of fire was ever present. One of the orderlies developed pneumonia and became a patient and, there was no one to replace him. Also George Dickerson went away without so much as a goodbye.

If ever Jessica was going to doubt her decision to leave England, this was the time. And she almost did ... but, ever so slowly, she began to find purpose in her spartan existence. More and more she was called upon to tend difficult cases in the doctor's absence. The other nurses bowed to her obviously better training, and then, one day, something happened that endeared her to Cobalt and the northern wilderness forever.

There was a flurry of excitement at the entrance to the tent as Jessica was making her 'rounds'. She turned to see a prospector in a state of anxiety, talking to Miss Reynolds.

The young nurse came over to Jessica and explained in a hopeless tone, "Pete Peters' squaw's in a bad way. She's having a baby, but something's gone wrong. He couldn't get her here in the deep snow, so he wants Doc. What'll we do?" Doctor Evans was up at New Liskeard and wasn't expected back for several days. Jessica considered sending for him, but at best, that would take twelve to sixteen hours, and the look on Mr. Peters' face suggested that they did not have that much time.

"I'll go," she announced, much to the surprise of both Gloria and herself. "Do you know if it's far?" she asked, as she went to the back of the tent to fetch her bag and some medication.

"A couple of miles west, I think," replied the girl.

Jessica hurried to the front of the hospital and was pleased to see the relief on the man's face when she announced that she would accompany him back to his house and his troubled woman.

They trudged along a path that was barely wide enough for one person. Mr. Peters explained that he had no horse and sometimes used his dogs to pull a sled. But several of his bitches had had pups and he was afraid of their milk freezing in the extremely cold weather.

Jessica marvelled that this man could walk and talk at the same time. She was having a great deal of trouble breathing and her lungs hurt. She warmed the air entering her chest through a thick woolen muffler, but still it stung. Mr. Peters had a thin scarf wrapped about his face and his speech made snowy crystals form on the outside. Jessica found the agile man hard to keep up with and the more she hurried, the more she feared the searing sensation in her chest.

It was just as she was about to plead for a rest that she saw the shack that was obviously Mr. Peters' home. It had log walls and a canvas roof. Smoke rose straight up out of a metal chimney, and light was spilling out a tiny window. A sled leaned against the side of the house and there were small wooden dog houses scattered about the yard. As they approached, the animals set up a howl, but quieted quickly after a threat from their master.

The wooden plank door was thrown open by a young boy of five or six, whose eyes were round with fright. "Pa, she's worse," was his only greeting. Then, upon seeing the strange woman, his mouth closed in a tight line.

There was a low moan from the far corner of the room and Jessica headed towards it. There was an alcove sectioned off by a blanket that hung from a rope that was supported by poles stuck in the dirt floor. She went to pull the old gray blanket aside, when Mr. Peters gently took her arm and said, "Jeannie's not used to white folk much, 'cept me of course. I'd best prepare her." His eyes were soft and there was compassion written there.

Jessica stepped back, allowing the man to pass. She felt like an eavesdropper as a mixture of Cree and English filtered over the top of the blanket wall. She turned to walk away, and came face to face with the young boy who had opened the door.

His look was hostile.

"I'm a nurse," Jessica began to explain, lifting up her black bag as though it were proof.

"Pa went to fetch Doc." His look indicated that he thought she was somehow responsible for the fact that the doctor wasn't there. He stood with his legs apart and his arms folded across his chest, much in the same manner as the pictures that Jessica remembered in her school text books — pictures of the Savage Indian in the New World.

"Well, Doctor Evans is away, up north. But I'll be able to help your mother," she tried to reassure the boy.

He eyed her up and down and she felt more than a little uneasy. He could have been taking her measure for a pine box, his look was so menacing. She tried to maintain her dignity, but it was becoming more and more difficult as the minutes ticked by. Fortunately, Mr. Peters called from the corner and she turned and went quickly to him.

"She don't speak no English, only a few words," he explained of the woman who lay on the floor on a mound of blankets. "She's mighty scared. Had no trouble birthing that one," he gestured back towards where the boy would be standing outside the blanket wall. "She wants her mother, or her grandmother, or the medicine man from her old tribe. But they're long gone. I told her you were a kind of medicine woman and she says it'll be alright if you help." He started to leave, then turned back and added, "You need me?"

"I'm not sure, Mr. Peters. Will she let me examine her without your presence?" Jessica was praying to God that the answer would be yes. She was not prepared to give a pelvic examination to this strange woman with a male audience. She was nervous enough already, having only attended births in the past, never actually acting as midwife. How she wished now that she'd taken that course. But she hadn't, so her innate common sense would have to be her guide.

"I think so," he turned and whispered a few words in Cree to Jeannie and then nodded, "She says it's alright," and then he was quickly gone.

The next two hours would be indelibly etched in Jessica's memory for the rest of her life. In some miraculous manner, a terrified Indian woman and an equally frightened English woman worked together to bring a boy-child into the world, who would surely have died without their co-operation.

Jessica quickly ascertained that the mother was in the late stages of labour, and that she'd probably been in that condition for twelve or more hours. Jeannie was in a state of exhaustion, but the contractions would not let her rest. The baby lay upside-down in the womb and Jessica gestured with her hands to the woman that the baby was the wrong way in her belly. She made a ball of her fist and pointed to her head, explaining in their silently agreed upon sign language that the head had to be born first. Jeannie nodded her own head in understanding. She was glistening with perspiration and her jet black hair was damp and it matted where she'd been rubbing it against the blankets behind her.

The entire procedure took on the appearance of a parlour game, as the women spoke to one another without words. Jessica tried turning the baby, but he would slip back into the wrong position before she could pull. It would happen again and again. Just when the nurse thought that she had things under control, a severe contraction would jerk the baby back to the incorrect position, often trapping Jessica's

hand in the violence of the motion. The woman seemed to
sense that she should push when Jessica almost had the head
in place and that she should ease back when the nurse's
weary expression indicated that she'd lost it. Jessica was
thankful for her patient's instinctive co-operation.

In the brief moments that they had between contractions, Jessica marvelled at the woman's calm. Of course
Jeannie was frightened, and so she should be. A birth of this
nature often ended in the death of one or both of the partici-
pants. But at no time did she scream or get in Jessica's way by
grabbing at her the way the nurse had seen other mothers do.

Jessica's struggle to keep her own panic under control
was no less heroic. She was wet with perspiration and at
times, the salty moisture fell into her eyes, causing her vision
to blur. She'd snatch a piece of her skirt or petticoat and wipe
her eyes, just in time to assist Jeannie with her next pain.

An hour went by, and everyone's nerves were beginning
to fray. Mr. Peters stood outside the blanket wall and
inquired, "Is, is she alright?" Jessica, in a voice that betrayed
her, assured the husband that things were fine. The nurse's
body ached from kneeling in such an awkward position on the
dirt floor. She was constantly reaching up to help the pregnant woman and her back was at a most unusual angle. She
would like to have straightened up, walked about the room
for a moment or two, but she daren't leave her patient.

Once Jessica exclaimed, "Oh, there it is!" but quickly had
to indicate that things were not just right when she recognized a foot, not a head, begin to protrude. She was quick
and efficient as she moved to try and right the baby. If only
she could turn it completely about before the next major contraction. She worked feverishly towards this end, and could
only pray during the next pain that the head was in a downward thrust.

Their corner was now almost misty with the sweat of
both women. There was no window and the enclosure was
small. Jessica leaned back briefly to massage her own aching
muscles and gulp a breath of air. Horrible thoughts came to
her head, thoughts of babies being taken by surgery and she
knew that they had no chance if this proved to be necessary.

It was then that Jessica remembered something that she'd read in the maternity section of a medical book at her old hospital. She got the woman on her side and slowly rotated her body, bringing her up to her hands and knees on the rotation. As she did this, she massaged the woman's abdomen in a circular motion, always finishing with a downward press. It was a most awkward and back-breaking position for both females. The Indian woman's centre of balance was greatly misplaced as she moved to her side. But she never questioned her midwife with so much as a raised eyebrow. She would just struggle to her knees and slowly back to her side, and then her back again, stopping only when the pain was so intense that she was immobilized by it. The nurse, on the other hand, her knees numb from the long time in the kneeling position, had quite a time to reach and massage wherever the large maternal mass was. The object of the exercise was to force the baby down into the birth canal. And finally, it worked! Suddenly, as if a miracle had occurred, the baby's head appeared. Jessica managed to carefully slip her hand about it and finally she had something to hold on to. And hold on she did! She hoped that she was not hurting the baby's tiny ears as she grasped and pulled, but she daren't let go. With a heavy sigh, Jeannie pushed with all of her might and the little boy was delivered into Jessica's waiting hands.

The two women looked at one another, tears shining in their eyes. There was a mutual respect written there for one another to see. "You have a son," Jessica managed to utter, as she lifted the boy onto his mother's bosom.

Jeannie crooned some native words in a thick voice that was most attractive. Jessica busied herself with the cord and the afterbirth and then called Mr. Peters to come. The child was crying fiercely and his wee head was floundering about, looking for somewhere to nurse, when the father appeared. Jessica took the soiled covers away and went to fetch some warm water, leaving the new parents to marvel over their newborn.

There was a majesty about the moment that even the young boy's unpleasant looks could not dull. Jessica Sybil

Baxter had delivered a child into this world against all odds and she was justifiably proud of herself. The glow she felt transcended itself to the one room shack that she sat in and it became a beautiful home. The soft warm glow from the oil lamps made one forget the bitter cold whiteness outside.

The strange odours that had offended her upon entering the home, now had meaning. There was a drum cut in half lengthwise that served as a stove, upon which a thick piece of metal supported a boiling pot and kettle. The cracks around the edges of the surface released smoke into the air. And the steaming pot gave off a most pungent and unusual odour. The walls were lined with assorted clothing, mostly leather and plaid wool. The beds were simply mounds of blankets and such on the floor that, surprisingly enough, looked comfortable to the exhausted Jessica. The musty odour that she'd noticed was explained by the beaver pelts that were stretched on boards and leaning against the walls to dry. All in all, it was a most 'native' habitat and Jessica felt privileged to be there.

"Begging your pardon, Ma'am, but Jeannie would like to know your name," Mr. Peters smiled from around the edge of the make-shift wall. "Your first name, I guess," he added.

"Jessica. My name is Jessica," she replied.

He disappeared and she could hear that funny mixture of Cree and English spoken in soft, musical tones.

"We'd like to call the boy Jesse, after you, Ma'am, if you don't mind." Mr. Peters came out to stand in front of Jessica, his eyes shining.

Jessica was quick to recognize the honour and she blushed. "Of course, Mr. Peters, I'd be proud."

Much to the nurse's surprise, Jeannie appeared from around the curtain. She was walking gingerly, but other than that, no one would have guessed that this woman had spent the past twenty-four hours in labour. Jessica remembered back to the hospital in England and of how the noble ladies there were molly-coddled for weeks after even the simplest delivery. Her admiration for the native woman rose even further.

"Your wife should rest," she spoke to Mr. Peters but

watched Jeannie as she shuffled about, setting the small wooden table with bowls and spoons.

The prospector reddened and Jessica realized that she'd called Jeannie his 'wife' and he seemed so pleased. As though reading her mind, Mr. Peters said, "She is my wife, true and proper, you know. We was married all legal like when the preacher came through her village years ago. But some folks don't count marrying Indians, so we keep pretty much to ourselves." Jessica couldn't help but think that that was the white community's loss. Racial prejudice was new to her. She'd read about it, but had never really been exposed to it. She hadn't expected to encounter it up here in the wilderness, but now that she knew of its existence, she realized that she did not like it at all.

She would like to have suggested that Mr. Peters stay with his family, but it was getting dusk, and she was afraid to head back to town on her own. They walked in silence, both deep in their own thoughts about what had just transpired. At the entrance to the hospital, Jessica turned and thanked the new father for allowing her to deliver his child. He insisted that he was the one that should be thanking her and they parted, each one the richer for their encounter.

The birth of Jesse was to mark the beginning of a new era for Jessica, an era decidedly happier. Her pride in herself made her an even better nurse and Doctor Evans was constantly praising her work to the others, even in her presence. She was modest enough to blush on these occasions, but her self-esteem would not let her drop her head down in the usual demure and ladylike fashion. She would stand straight, her shoulders back, her head up and her dark eyes shining. She was Abigail Windsor's granddaughter!

The Indians of the town treated Jessica as special. It was really a thing of mannerisms, nothing overt, but the respect was there in their eyes as they'd nod to her as she passed. The white people could be heard to whisper about her in the shops or at the post office . . . "That's the one. . ." or "Saved the boy and the squaw . . ." She was flattered by all of the attention, but wise enough not to let her head be turned by it.

The weather showed signs of warming ever so slightly and the blizzards were fewer. There were not as many patients at the hospital and Jessica seemed to have a bit of time for herself. All in all, the latter part of the year proved much better than the first for Jessica Baxter.

7

Christmas

Christmas snuck up on the young woman. There were none of the familiar mementos of the festive season to prepare her for the sudden realization that Christmas was only days away. Upon inquiring, she discovered that special presents were sent away for, and gifts of a not-too-important nature were purchased locally.

Jessica busied herself with her small list. She wished to give something to her co-workers, and that meant the nurses, Doctor Evans and the two orderlies. Mrs. Carson had been especially good to her of late. It may have been that she was just thankful for the liniment that her boarder had given her, along with a few back rubs, or it may have had something to do with the fact that Mr. Dickerson's attentions were like an endorsement of the young Englishwoman. In any case, their relationship was pleasant. Hazel, still helping Jessica with her bath water, deserved a present, but the other boarders at Mrs. Carson's were quite another matter. She'd ask her landlady what was expected in that quarter.

Wee Jesse Peters would be first on her list. The boy had been brought into the hospital by his father one fairly mild day and Jessica had been pleased as punch to see her namesake again. Even at only a few weeks of age, he was a fine, robust boy, whose thick, black hair was reminiscent of his mother's. When Jessica asked about Jeannie, Mr. Peters mumbled that she was waiting outside. This angered Jessica, but she could not, just then, go out and ask Jeannie in, as she was quite busy. She scolded Mr. Peters and insisted that his wife be brought in, on the next visit. He made no promises, but his broad smile indicated that he was pleased with the invitation.

Yes, she'd get something special for the boy, and perhaps some token for Jeannie, too.

She began to get into the spirit of Christmas, and, even though her shopping was limited to the small local stores, she did well. When she came home one evening after visiting the shops, she went to put her parcels in her wardrobe and found it difficult to find enough room. When she moved her dresses aside, there was Mr. Dickerson's tent, all bundled together, just as the man at the hospital in North Bay had handed it to her. She brought it out, sat down on the bed, and remembered the occasion. A little spasm caused pain around her heart when she thought of Danny, but she smiled when she remembered her travelling companion, and what good company he was. She thought about each time she'd seen him, and that brought her to the memory of Rosina, and, once again, her heart shuddered. She wondered where the girl was, and more importantly, how the girl was. If she'd only left word . . .

There was a soft knock at her door and she went to open it, thankful for an interruption in thought. It was Mrs. Carson and she had post for Jessica. Mail was not necessarily a pleasant thing for Jessica of late, so she took the letter reluctantly and put it down on her washstand.

"Before you go, Mrs. Carson, I thought I might ask a few questions about Christmas, and how it's celebrated here." She held the door open and finally Mrs. Carson shuffled in, murmuring that she could only stay a moment.

Christmas dinner would be served at six sharp. There would be breakfast laid out at nine in the morning, but it had been her experience that the men boarders often did not get down Christmas morning. Making too merry the night before, was her supposition. Some exchanged gifts, she explained, but mostly they did not, so nothing was expected of the young girl. Jessica opened the door to let her leave when she began to fidget about, obviously not comfortable in the room.

She went back to her Christmas business and it was quite a while before she remembered the letter. She had half a mind to ignore it, things were going so well for her just now. However, open it she must, so over she went and took it from the washstand. It was then that she recognized Charles' handwriting. Good old Charles, it was probably a Christmas greeting. She tore it open.

Dearest Jessie:
How very much this old thing misses you!
Why in blazes Canada? You couldn't get much farther from Mum and me than that, except possibly Australia. You are a silly goose, you know. But how I do love you, and miss you, and, dear sister, need you. There are so many decisions to be made, and, of course, Mum is no help whatsoever, so here's poor old Charles, stuck with all this bother. It's not quite fair, you know."

Jessica put the letter down for a moment, as she was having difficulty seeing the lines. She reached for her handkerchief and dried her eyes, muttering and shaking her head, "Poor old Charles."

"I visit the old girl every week. Aren't I just grand? She doesn't always know it's me. She just rambles on and on. The whole thing is such a dreadful bore. Wish you were here to spell me. But there you are, all those miles away. Oh well, you've heard all of that before.
I've come up with a smashing idea, but I know you're going to not like it, so I've half a mind not to tell you, but of course I must. I'm entering into Her Majesty's Service. I've been guaranteed a commission because of our family and all, so baby brother's off to Africa, or some other weary place. I know it's not really fair to Mum, but, as I said, she hardly knows me, and she's well attended at the hospital. It's a good thing that Doctor Fairley is a friend of yours, or Mum might not be that well off, there not being so much money anymore, and all.

Well, no one need worry about Charlie anymore. I'll earn my keep and probably have a bloody good time doing it. I always thought I'd look agreeable in a uniform. What do you think, Sweets?

Oh, do write and tell me all about the Indians and so on. It must be so primitive over there.

Here's hoping I'll wind up in some lazy civilized little city with all the comforts of home. I understand everyone's got at least a dozen servants down there, black fellows all. It'll be different, I'll say."

Forever concerned with his own creature comforts, Charles' letter was true to form. But, once again, she could not fault him for his selfish ways, and it bothered her not a bit that he was leaving Sybil alone in England. It was as much as she deserved. A shiver of guilt ran through her body as she said this to herself. It upset her that Sybil could reach out across the ocean and make her feel delinquent. Perhaps it would forever be this way, she wondered . . .

"As soon as I get settled in my new life, I will write, I promise. In the meantime, any post to me can be sent in care of Uncle John.

Ta for now, Love. Happy Christmas time. Sorry there's no gift, but then, there's no money.

Your loving brother
Charles"

Jessica held the letter to her bosom and closed her eyes. She sighed deeply, but she did not cry.

Poor old Charlie. Contrary to what he thought, she was quite pleased that he was entering the service. Perhaps they'd do what his society had been unable to and make a man of him. She was pleased that he'd go in as an officer. She really felt that he'd never make it otherwise. And, as for leaving Sybil, that was of the least consequence. She'd done it. Why not Charles? And, because Charles had been brought up without much conscience, he'd probably escape the niggly little guilts that crept into Jessica's thoughts now and then.

Uncle John was also the family lawyer. She'd write to him immediately, hoping to get a letter to Charles before he headed off ... wherever.

Christmas morning dawned clear and bright, and, despite the fact that Jessica had no kin to celebrate with, she rose in very good humour. This had always been a time for merriment in the Windsor household and that was where Jessica had spent most of her Christmas holidays. She dressed in her second prettiest frock, a soft brown wool dress with touches of cream lace at the neck and wrists, showing off her dark hair and almost black eyes. She took particular care with her hair, rolling it high on her head as was the fashion of the day, instead of the neat, tight chignon that she usually wore at the nape of her neck. The shorter strands of Jessica's hair that refused to be contained with hair pins curled slightly, softening her rather severe countenance.

She descended the stairs right at nine, the appointed hour for breakfast.

Mrs. Carson was in the big diningroom, fussing about. Only Mr. Mason was at the table, gumming away at his festive meal. Jessica nodded to him and wished Mrs. Carson a Merry Christmas. The woman looked extremely nice today. Gone was the stark white look. She had on a very attractive gown of ruby red. Her hair was quite attractively arranged, and there was just enough gray in it that it contrasted nicely with her dress.

The empty chairs about the big table bore witness to the partying of the night before. No one worked on Christmas Day, so many took the Eve before as a special time for drinking and dancing. Jessica had known about this, as the girls at the hospital had gone to these dances, but Jessica had chosen to stay in her room, wrapping her few parcels and having a leisurely bath. She'd had to carry the water for herself, as Hazel too had gone off with a fellow. But still the young nurse had enjoyed her quiet solitary evening.

"This is a particularly fine breakfast, Mrs. Carson," she complimented her landlady, and the older woman flushed with the praise. There was fruit, which was normally scarce in the North at any time, but worse in the winter months. There was porridge, eggs, bacon, buns, both sweet and salty, pots of jam and honey and, as always, maple syrup, which Jessica was developing quite a taste for. Tea and coffee were kept hot on the stove in the corner. "I don't know when I've been so hungry," she added. She was truly enjoying her feast and was rather sorry for Mrs. Carson that the others were not down to appreciate her efforts. Mr. Mason continued to eat his share without comment, but apparently savouring every morsel.

"They were all out last night," Mrs. Carson said, gesturing towards the seats of the missing men. It was impossible to tell if she was censuring their actions or simply showing her disappointment in their absence.

"Yes, I heard them come in," commented Jessica, and she could not help the smile from stealing across her mouth. Several of the men had returned at about one in the morning, making quite a bit of noise as they came upstairs. Mrs. Carson had followed them, whispering to them to be quiet as there were others in the building who deserved their sleep. The more the men tried to be quiet, the more noise they seemed to make, bumping into things, and giggling like children. Rather than being annoyed, Jessica had been quite amused by it and wished that she'd been able to watch their ascent, but she'd had to content herself with simply listening, and it had not been an unpleasant sound. She'd fallen right back to sleep and she had dreamed very happy dreams of holidays gone by, spent at Fairview with Abigail. There had been no sadness in her thoughts, only warm memories.

When Mr. Mason had had his fill, he begged to be excused and shuffled off into the parlour. Jessica took the opportunity to give her gift to Mrs. Carson. She had slipped the little parcel into her pocket as she'd left her room and now she took it out and placed it beside Mrs. Carson's hand. "A very Merry Christmas to you, Mrs. Carson." The older lady looked truly surprised.

"I didn't 'spect this," she began, obviously flustered. "I thought I told you that nothing was expected of you. Now you've gone and done this." She was scolding the girl, but

Jessica was not to be embarrassed that easily.

"I just wanted to say a special thank you for making me so comfortable here, Mrs. Carson. There's no need to fret over it. It's a small thing, but I do appreciate your kindnesses towards me." She smiled her sincerest smile and that seemed to relax her companion. "Here, let me help you, " she reached over to assist Mrs. Carson in putting on her new broach. It was a small filigreed silver rose and it looked extremely nice against the woman's deep red Christmas dress.

"You are awfully kind, dear," the lady spoke to Jessica, her voice quivering. "I shall enjoy having such a pretty bit of jewellery. Mr. Carson didn't set much store in things like this, so I don't have any - but my wedding ring." She looked down over her chin and admired the little ornament. "I have nothing for you, Miss Baxter, but this letter that I was to deliver to you at this meal." She reached into her pocket and pulled out an envelope with 'Miss Jessica' written on it. "He gave it to me last night," she explained.

The handwriting was unfamiliar to the girl and she was reluctant to open it in front of Mrs. Carson. She put it down beside her plate and continued with her meal.

"Are you not going to open it, child?" asked the inquisitive Mrs. Carson.

Jessica felt obliged and carefully opened the letter. It was a very pretty Christmas Card, the kind that one might see on the shelves in the stores, the kind one might give to someone 'special'. It was signed George Dickerson and there was a message under his signature. She chose to read the message later.

"How very nice. It's from Mr. Dickerson, but I guess you already knew that," she smiled at her companion who was simply bursting at the seams to see Jessica's reaction to the card. She was disappointed when the girl said no more. They finished their meal in comparative silence and then Jessica stole up the stairs to her room, where she might read Mr. Dickerson's note in private.

"If you are not doing anything special today, Miss Baxter, I'd be pleased to have you join me in a walk.

Doctor Evans has assured me that you'll not be needed
at the hospital. I'll be by at one in the afternoon, if
that's all right with you. If not, I'll simply have a very
large piece of Mrs. Carson's delicious mincemeat pie and
be on my lonesome way."

Jessica thought that the last few words were a bit
unfair, but she was amused nonetheless. She'd been hoping
to get out to the Peters' place to give them their gifts, and
now she would have an escort. That pleased her, as she was
more than a slight bit worried about wandering too far from
the town by herself. She'd heard stories of wolves and bears
lurking about the outskirts of town when the food was scarce
in the bush. She was not aware that bears hibernated, so she
feared them equally as much as the timber wolves, that she
could hear howling in the dead of night.

In the several hours that she had to put in before her
caller would come, she decided to walk to the hospital and
give her gifts to what staff was there. Pamela was scheduled
to be on duty, and, of course, Doctor Evans was almost
always there.

The sunshine was deceptive. It was extremely cold out
of doors. The smoke from the chimneys rose straight into the
air, white-gray columns of heat escaping the little wooden
homes. Frost formed quickly in her nostrils and she pulled
her scarf up under her eyes but even her eyelashes were
tinged with white and she was thankful that her journey was
short. She realized that she'd have to be better prepared for
the walk in the afternoon.

Some effort had been made by the patients and staff at
the hospital, to make things as gay as possible for Christmas
Day. There was a small tree in the back of the tent, decorated with colourful little bits of paper and the odd real glass
ornament — the kind that Jessica remembered from her days
in England. Pamela wore a bright red ribbon in her hair,
which, on a normal day, would have been unforgivable, but
today was a nice gesture. There was a sort of punch available to anyone who wished it, and some nuts and fruit, the
fruit being very special in the winter in the north.

"Merry Christmas, Pamela," she greeted the younger nurse enthusiastically.

"Why ever are you here today Miss Baxter?" asked the girl, genuinely surprised at her appearing on the holiday, when she needn't have.

"To bring you this," replied Jessica, as she handed the astonished nurse a gift. "And to wish everyone well on this special day."

Pamela tore open her parcel and was pleased at the sight of an especially pretty handkerchief. It was edged in lace, and was far too attractive to be used for any ordinary purposes. She would wave it about when she was out with a fellow, and maybe even put some scent on it. "You are very kind, Miss Baxter. But I've nothing for you," she pouted. It seemed to be Jessica's day for making people feel uncomfortable.

"That isn't necessary, Pamela, it's just a gesture of thanks for helping me through these first few months." The girl relaxed with this and looked back to her gift. She was pleased.

Doctor Evans had been witness to this, standing by, silently smoking his pipe. When Jessica turned to him, he motioned for her to come with him. He did not go far, simply out of earshot of the others. "And I suppose you've something for me, young lady?" he asked. He seemed very sure of himself, but this did not spoil it for Jessica.

"Yes, sir," and she produced an awkward looking small bundle from her pocket. "I was hoping to improve the air about here with this gift." She teased him, as he opened the wrapping to find a new pipe. "Now, could we dispense with that old thing?" She nodded towards his now unlit old pipe, hanging from the corner of his mouth.

He grinned and shook his head. "Why, this here pipe's but a dozen years old." She held her nose in a rather rude way, and he added, "Well, I guess it's about lived out its span. I'll try this new one, but it won't be the same." They both laughed.

"And I've something special for you," now it was Jessica's turn to be surprised. He took her by the arm and led her to the very back corner of the hospital, where he had a makeshift office set up. From a desk, he picked up a rather large parcel and handed it to her. Her astonishment showed on her face and that seemed to please him. Slowly she unwrapped it and in it was a beautiful black cape, lined with a bright red satin. She was too stunned to speak.

The doctor just stood there, his eyes gleaming as Jessica ran her hands over the cloth. Finally, he thought he must say something. "It's not new, you know. But it's not old either, in the real sense of the word. Only been worn once, actually. By someone very special to me. Now I'd like you to have it." With that, he took the garment from her hands and placed it about her shoulders. It was a full length cape, obviously designed for a slightly shorter woman. He noticed this and added, "Good, it won't drag in the mud come spring." He evidently expected Jessica to wear this lovely thing. It was not intended to sit in a closet to be brought out on occasion, but was to be worn, often.

"Are you going to tell me to whom it belonged?" the girl inquired, her voice soft and quite full of emotion.

"Some day, Miss Baxter. Some day." She noticed that his eyes were quite moist as he looked her up and down in her (nearly) new finery. She would very much have liked to hear the story right now, but it seemed an invasion of his privacy to press the issue.

At precisely quarter to one, the doorbell at Mrs. Carson's rang, and in walked Mr. Dickerson. Jessica was in her room, but she heard it and somehow knew who it was. She refused to go down before the time, so she busied herself with rearranging her closet to accommodate the new cape. She ran her fingers over the smooth lining and caressed the woolen outer shell. It was a nurse's cape. Of that much she was certain. But whose? And how old was it? She had no way of knowing the answers to these questions, so she'd just have to invent them. Doctor Evans had been in love with, or even married to, a nurse who died? Ran off? The second solution was infinitely more interesting. The wounded man kept this cape all these years hoping that the girl who'd left it behind would return to him.

But now so very many years had gone by, and it was too

late. So he thought that Jessica might like it. But why her? Why not Pamela or Gloria? He'd known them longer. Did Jessica remind the doctor of someone? She surely would like to know the answers to all of these questions. Perhaps Mr. Dickerson knew, they seemed to be good friends. She hurried down the stairs, anxious to inquire, but then slowed, as she did not want her haste to be misunderstood.

She found Mr. Dickerson in the kitchen, at the table, eating his large piece of mincemeat pie. He was going to 'have his cake and eat it too', claiming the consolation prize when Jessica had already made her mind up to go with him.

"Please do not interpret this to mean that I don't want to go walking," he exclaimed when Jessica entered the warm kitchen. He rose and she motioned for him to sit back down.

"No sir. I can quite imagine that Mrs. Carson's pie would be irresistible." The landlady chuckled at this. She was always pleased when someone bothered to compliment her on her cooking efforts.

"I would very much like company on a walk to Pete Peters' place. I've a gift for young Jesse, and a small thing for Mrs. Peters." He continued to eat his pie, but now there was a hurry in his motions, as though he could hardly wait to be off. "Is that alright, Mr. Dickerson?"

"Excellent, Miss Baxter. It's a good day, a bit cold, but nice and clear and no sign of a storm. We should be there and back before dusk, if we go quickly." He thanked Mrs. Carson profusely for the treat and she thanked him for his enjoyment. They exchanged special, knowing glances, and then he led Jessica to the front hall where he suggested that she don her warmest against the cold day.

"I've been out this morning, Mr. Dickerson, and I quite agree. There's a nip in the air and I've chosen a very warm hat and muffler." He helped her on with her things, even buttoning her boots for her and they were off.

"You've been to the Peters' house before, sir?" she asked as he headed out in the right direction.

"Pete's an old friend. He's done work for me in the past. I know his wife Jeannie, too. And young Bert. He must be seven or eight by now?" When she did not answer, he contin-

ued, "I've not met your namesake, though," he glanced at her
and saw her eyes grin. He could not see her mouth, as it was
covered by a big woolen scarf. She was happy that he knew
about young Jesse and probably about her role in his delivery.

"He's a delightful boy," she murmured, her heart warming to the thought of seeing him again. "Looks like his mother," she added.

It became necessary to walk single file, so conversation
was limited until they reached the clearing around the
Peters' home. The dogs set up quite a howl, announcing their
arrival, and before they could knock, the door was thrown
open by Mr. Peters.

"I can hardly believe these eyes of mine. George
Dickerson and Nurse Baxter. Jeannie, come quickly." He
added a few words in Cree and his wife was soon at his side,
smiling the biggest, whitest smile that Jessica had ever seen.
She did not remember feeling more welcomed at anyone's
home before.

Their outer wraps were taken from them and hung on
nails in the log wall. They were advised to keep their boots
on, as the dirt floor was cool. They soon found themselves
sitting around the barrel stove, soaking up the wood-fire heat
and inhaling strange odours from the pots boiling there.

"Jeannie, tea," ordered Mr. Peters and Jeannie immediately set to making a pot of tea. "I'm sorry that I don't have
anything stronger, George," he apologized, "but we don't get
much chance to buy whisky nowadays." Almost before he
had finished his sentence, Mr. Dickerson jumped up, went to
his great coat and withdrew a bottle of liquor from one of the
pockets. Mr. Peters grinned and wet his lips. "Might of
known," he muttered.

"I thought we might just need a little for frostbite," Mr.
Dickerson said, and both he and Mr. Peters slapped their
knees and laughed. Jessica was to discover that, in the sum-
mertime, it was snakebite that they claimed to carry liquor for.

"May I see the baby?" asked Jessica of the young Indian
woman, signing her speech with motions that indicated that
she had a baby in her arms.

"Uhuh," nodded Jeannie and she rose to fetch Jesse from

his resting place. She handed the sleeping child to Jessica and the girl would like to have explained that she did not want to disturb the youngster, but it would have been too much of an effort. She sat with Jesse in her arms, as he wriggled, stretched, yawned and then opened his big dark brown eyes. Upon seeing the stranger, his mood quickly changed and he looked as though he was going to cry, but Jeannie reached over, touched him, cooed a few words in his ears and he settled down to study his new attendant.

When Jessica looked over towards where the men were sipping on cups of spirits, she noticed that Mr. Dickerson stole glances at her, and there was a mellow look in his eye. Before Jessica could tire of her charge, the mother took him to the corner where she changed him and then nursed him. She made no effort to hide her bosom, and no one in the room seemed to notice or care. Only Jessica, who, despite her efforts not to, blushed.

"The fire's getting to you, Miss Baxter?" inquired Mr. Dickerson.

"No, I'm quite all right, thank you," she accepted a cup of tea offered her by Mr. Peters and was surprised to find that it tasted nothing like any tea that she'd had before. It was very sweet, and she learned that it was sweetened with maple sugar. The tea itself was made from a bark of some kind, and was, not only warming, but medicinal as well, claimed her host.

"I've known of men sick weeks with fever, get well with just one cup of this brew," he boasted. Jessica's medical background made it impossible for her to believe this, but she was not about to argue, especially when she was enjoying it so much. It was not until she said yes to the second cup that she realized that there was a generous dollop of spirits from Mr. Dickerson's bottle in it. She chided the men for deceiving her, but continued to drink slowly from the cup.

"I've brought a little something for Jesse," Jessica explained to the father, when Jeannie and the baby rejoined the group. He quickly translated this to his wife, who beamed at the news. Jessica handed her a parcel, which she tore open like a child. Wrapped in a bit of lace that Jessica had purchased for Jeannie was a small wooden locomotive. Jessica had discovered it on the shelf at the local store and had fallen in love with it because it reminded her of the mode of transport that had brought her here, to this place. Jeannie spoke to her husband, but looked at Jessica all the while.

"Jeannie thanks you, Miss Baxter. She says that she will teach the boy to remember you when he plays with it." That made the girl feel very good.

"Please tell her that the bit of lace is for her," she asked and her wishes were quickly translated into Cree.

"My wife thanks you again, Miss Baxter. You are very kind, she says."

It was only then that Jessica realized that she should have brought something for young Bert. The boy had been sleeping in the corner and had been awakened by his mother's excited voice. Jessica looked helplessly at Mr. Dickerson who seemed to read her mind. He withdrew a pocket knife from his trousers and slipped it to her. There was not time to wrap it of course, but she handed it to the young boy and wished him a Merry Christmas.

He was overwhelmed by the gift. The stoical Indian side of him would not let him express his gratitude, but the English part of him made his eyes shine and his lips curl in a half-smile. "My son is pleased," explained Mr. Peters.

And so the next hour went, four adults, a child and a baby sitting on blankets on the floor, around a barrel stove, talking a mixture of English and Cree. It would certainly go down in Jessica's memory as her most unusual Christmas Day ever!

Food was offered, but Jessica declined, explaining that they must be off, as she was expected at the boarding house for the holiday meal. She was genuinely sorry when they got up to leave, but she realized that time was important, as it became dark so early in mid-winter.

When they were once again on the path, she thanked Mr. Dickerson for the gesture with the pocket knife. He explained that he understood her dilemma and that he liked the boy and so there was really nothing more to say.

They arrived at Mrs. Carson's just as darkness set in.

The boarding house looked warm and inviting to Jessica, whose nose was almost white with the cold. She had her hand on the doorknob when she suddenly remembered that she wanted to ask Mr. Dickerson about Doctor Evans' past, so she forgot the cold and turned and looked up at him. He was smiling down at her, the whisky leaving a glow in his eyes, and his moustache was at a comical angle as he grinned. She almost forgot what it was that she wanted to say, her desire to laugh was so strong.

"Doctor Evans gave me a beautiful Christmas gift," she began. His expression did not change, so she continued. "It's a very extravagant cape . . . a nurse's cape." Now one of Mr. Dickerson's eyebrows arched and she knew that she was on to something. "I was wondering if you might know to whom it previously belonged." Her companion shifted his gaze, seeming to settle on some spot in the middle distance. His silence did not discourage her. "Did the doctor have a nurse in his family? Maybe a wife, or a sister, perhaps?"

Mr. Dickerson's eyes took on a different glow. No longer simply the aftermath of a few drinks of whisky and a cold walk, they seemed now to reflect some distant thought, at once both sad and beautiful. Jessica had to know! She stood there, waiting, and finally Mr. Dickerson spoke, still staring off into space.

"John Evans had a sister, Bertha. I saw her only . . . once." His eyes glistened even brighter now, accentuated by the light streaming out of the parlour windows.

"I didn't know them as youngsters of course, but apparently, they were inseparable. Bertha worked in a shop in Toronto and took care of John when he was in medical school. She dedicated her every moment to him, feeding him, clothing him, making a home for him. When John finished his schooling, and began to earn a living, he insisted on repaying his sister. He would have given Bertha anything . . . anything. She wanted only to go into nursing and work by his side when she graduated." He paused, obviously quite moved by the tale. Jessica was standing breathless, anticipating the end of the story and not quite sure that she was ready for it.

"It was Bertha's graduation day and John and she were

riding in a buggy, heading back to their flat from the festivities at the hospital when there was an accident. It was on a busy city street and the traffic was frantic. Horses were hot and fretful and suddenly a stage careened across an intersection and overturned John's buggy. Bertha was thrown from her seat and run over by the stage. Her back was broken. She died there, in her brother's arms." His voice broke and he looked away. Jessica put her hand out and touched his arm. She could feel that he was shaking. It was not a time to ask questions so she remained silent. But her dark eyes cried out for an answer. This trembling man knew this story so well. Why?

As though in answer to her unasked question, he said softly, "I was on that stage." He turned and walked slowly away.

Big, fluffy flakes of snow began to fall, softening the edges of Jessica's vision as she watched Mr. Dickerson, collar up, hands in pockets, walk slowly down the street. The contrast between the peaceful white view in front of her and the hot red turmoil that she felt in her heart played havoc with her senses. It was not the time to join the others inside, as their laughter seemed harsh and unfeeling.

A quietness had dropped over the town that was almost holy. Sleigh bells could be heard, muffled, in the distance and the neigh of a weary horse. Aside from that, the town was silent. The usual traffic, both pedestrian and horse-drawn, had slowed to a trickle and Cobalt became a picture postcard place. The wooden shacks seemed a little less shabby, and the deep ruts in the slushy roads filled with clean white snow, and the evergreen trees, with their heavy branches, leaned toward the ground in a humble pose. Jessica stood there, alone on the porch, ignoring the Christmas cheer from within as she remembered John Evans' story, and she wept. She cried tears for Bertha, the nurse who never had a chance, and for Doctor Evans, who had spent these past years trying to fill the void with hard work and sacrifice. And then she wept for Christmases gone by, for friends that she'd never see again and her tears made her feel empty.

She dried her eyes with her handkerchief and opened

Mrs. Carson's front door to another world.

"Here she is!" announced Hazel, rushing over to help Jessica off with her outerwear. "We were just beginning to worry, Miss Baxter," she added with a warm smile. The usually sullen girl had a glow about her that was most appealing. She had on her Sunday best and her pretty hair was piled high on her head in a fashionable manner. "They're waiting dinner on you," she said as she scurried off.

Jessica entered the parlour and was astonished by the festivities. Every available lamp was on, making the room so bright that she noticed corners that she'd never noticed before. There was a tree decorated with colourful glass balls and animal-shaped ornaments. There were bowls of fruit and candies and nuts about the room and everyone seemed to have a glass in his hand and a grin on his face.

"Merry Christmas, Merry Christmas . . . " it went on until Jessica was certain that she'd greeted everyone. As she headed for the kitchen she was met by Mrs. Carson, arms outstretched, carrying a platter with a turkey on it. The smells of spicy stuffing and cranberry sauce told Jessica that she was very, very hungry.

The combination of good food and good cheer helped the girl to shed the sadness and the loneliness that she felt, and she was finally able to contribute something to the celebration by way of light-hearted conversation.

There were two guests at the table, and it seemed that they'd be stopping at Mrs. Carson's for several weeks. Once was a Mr. Barrett, a dynamite salesman, up from the United States making his semi-annual round of the mining camps. He was a handsome man, extremely well dressed and polished looking. Jessica was genuinely interested in his unusual occupation and was looking forward to talking with him about it. When he said that he had samples of his wares with him, the girl felt uneasy and her manner showed it. Mr. Barrett enjoyed this, as did the rest of the table.

The second stranger was a geologist named Harper and he was up from Toronto doing some work for a mining company. He was quiet and studious looking and seemed just a bit nervous of his surroundings. Most of the men at the table were quite boisterous, the whisky punch having taken effect, and poor Mr. Harper just got more and more quiet. He appeared relieved when the meal ended and everyone retired to the parlour. He did not join the rest, but went directly to his room, which, apparently, he shared with Mr. Barrett.

"So, you're from Merry Old England?" Mr. Barrett asked of Jessica as they sat side by side on the settee. It was a strange expression and not the first time that the girl had heard it. This time it tickled her 'funny-bone' and she giggled. It was so uncharacteristic of her that both Mrs. Carson and Hazel stopped dead in their tracks and stared at her. Jessica blushed and put her hand over her mouth as though she had hiccoughed, but she could not erase the smile.

"Did I say something funny?" asked the salesman in a smooth, suggestive tone.

"No, sir, it's not that. Perhaps I've had too much fresh air today, or the punch . . ." She gestured towards the table with her glass, which was empty, and before she could say anything more, Mr. Barrett took it and refilled it.

"Maybe this'll get you laughing right out loud," he said mischievously as he handed her the glass.

She would like to have declined, but something inside her wanted her to relax, to give just a bit, to enjoy the company of these pleasant, harmless people, so she thanked him and sipped of the mellow, fruity liquid.

There were some scraping sounds and suddenly an organ appeared from a small room that opened off the parlour. Jessica had always imagined that it was an office of some sort, as the door was always tightly closed, but, when she glanced in, it appeared that it was more like a small library.

Mrs. Carson sat to play and soon the room filled with Christmas hymns. The woman had been an organist at her church many years ago, and that was all the music that she remembered. It was enough, though. The group joined in song and soon Jessica's strange English accent was lost in the tumult.

Dancing was suggested, and, despite the lack of space, they made a valiant effort to dance. Jessica found herself in

Mr. Barrett's arms, twirling about and it was not unpleasant.

Dear old Mr. Mason surprised everyone and relieved Mrs. Carson at the organ and played a jig. This music was new to Jessica and she retreated to the settee to watch the others. Hazel was having a great time, her big blue eyes sparkling as she flirted with the men she danced with.

A pang of envy waved through the Englishwoman as she watched this. It looked so very easy, a nod of the head, a lowering of the eyelashes, a pout, they were all so effective that Hazel could have her pick of any man in the room as she danced about. She chose the 'explosive man' as she seductively called Mr. Barrett and the two of them danced round and round to Mr. Mason's playing and the foot stomping of the others.

The room was made warm by all of the activity and Jessica had finished her punch before she knew it. Her cheeks were hot and the beat of the music made her want to move. When Mr. Barrett saw her mood, he passed Hazel off to Mr. Rogers and went to Jessica, pulling her up to her feet.

"Here, I'll show you how," he said as he began to move her about the floor, much to the pleasure of all but Hazel.

"I'm so . . . so . . . awkward," apologized Jessica, breathless as they whirled about.

It was dreadfully unfair of the American, as it was obvious that Jessica could barely keep up with him and that she was a bit tipsy with the punch. But the persistent man would not let her rest, practically carrying her around the room.

"I'll take over now," a strong, familiar voice said and Jessica found herself being handed from one man to another. She looked up into Mr. Dickerson's eyes, and there was anger there.

Totally confused, she wanted to ask what he was doing here at Mrs. Carson's and what it was that he was so serious about, but she had difficulty forming the words. She was, as the saying goes, 'under the influence'.

Mr. Barrett shrugged his shoulders and went back to Hazel who was more than pleased to have his attention.

Mr. Dickerson led the swooning Jessica to the stairs and then up them. "This is your room, isn't it?" he whispered

roughly in her ear. He was carrying her now and she was
almost lifeless in his arms. She nodded when she recognized
her surroundings. He carried her in and sat her on the edge
of the bed.

A weariness overcame her and she could not sit up. She
toppled over on her side, curled up in a ball and went to
sleep. It was a drugged, dreamless sleep and it was many
hours before she awoke.

When she did, she was astonished to see Mr. Dickerson
sitting in a chair staring at her.

"I might have known," were his first words, and they
made no sense whatsoever. The anger that Jessica had witnessed earlier was still there and she could not account for it.

"Whenever that scoundrel comes to town, there's trouble," he said, and once again she did not understand. She
wished that he would explain himself, but she was in no condition to ask questions as her head hurt and she wasn't too
sure about her stomach. She shifted about in bed and came
to the realization that she no longer had her frock on, but
only her underthings. She wondered how she got that way,
but was afraid to ask.

"Would you like a glass of water and some salts?" asked
her companion.

That sounded like a splendid idea and she edged her
way slowly to a sitting position. She watched as he poured
water from her pitcher into a glass and added an envelope of
powder. It fizzed up and he handed it to her. His demeanour
had softened and he looked almost sorry for her. She drank
the potion and it was quick to work.

Now, to the problem at hand - what was she doing in a
bedroom alone with Mr. Dickerson? Her eyes asked the
question and he answered.

"When I heard that Roger Barrett was in town and
staying here, I was worried. The man has a terrible reputation, Miss Baxter, for, er . . . seducing young maidens, as it
were. The mining camps are full of girls who have . . . succumbed to his charms, believed his lies, and regretted it." He
seemed embarrassed by this conversation and had to turn
away from Jessica's gaze to continue. "I just didn't want you

to be added to his list." This last part was spoken so softly that she barely heard.

"It's probably safe to leave," he added in a much firmer tone. "They've all gone to bed. No one will bother you now." He reached for his coat that was lying on the chair, leaned over and blew out the lamp and darkness enveloped the room. There was a very quiet, very tense moment and suddenly he was gone.

Jessica's brain was too fuddled for her to sort out her feelings. She'd wanted to tell him to mind his own darned business - that she could take care of herself. But could she? These men played by an obviously different set of rules than the gentle aristocracy back in England. Was she capable of spotting the ne'er-do-wells? It was all too much for her tonight.

She rolled over to go back to sleep and in doing so, her hand brushed against something other than her ordinary coverlets. She felt around in the darkness and her hands recognized the wool and satin combination of Bertha's cape, put there by Mr. Dickerson while she was sleeping, to ward off the night chill. She pulled it up next to her face and fell asleep, her black hair spilling out across the red satin lining.

8

The New Year

The hustle-bustle of Christmas-time faded quickly with the New Year. Jessica took her turn and worked the next three weeks straight through, giving the other girls opportunities for making merry and visiting friends and relatives. Gloria went to see her family in North Bay and was stranded there when a severe blizzard brought with it heavy winds and snow, and that was followed by very cold temperatures and clear skies. Frostbite seemed the most common complaint, seconded by a sort of despondency that Jessica was to learn was called 'cabin fever'.

People holed up in their homes, shacks or rooms, waiting out the killer cold spell, and the inactivity led to short tempers, which oft-times led to fisticuffs. Excessive drinking impaired the good judgment of more than one northern native, keeping the hospital staff on their toes.

Jessica's birthday was on January 6th and it came and went without fanfare. She did not mention the occasion to anyone and celebrated it alone in her room. She was surprised with herself that she felt no depression about her solitude. Actually, she often cherished quiet moments with a good book, after the noise and confusion at the hospital.

It was early February when Jessica received a rather pleasant shock. She came home from the hospital after a particularly gruelling day spent with a very sick child who seemed to be slipping away despite the doctor's efforts to save him. She was tired and a bit cross when she opened the door to Mrs. Carson's boarding house to be met by Rosina.

Jessica's natural reserve gave way to expressive joy as the girls fell into one another's arms. Greetings and explanations poured back and forth until, finally, they were able to collect themselves and go in to dinner with the other boarders.

When Jessica asked where Rosina was stopping and saw a cloud pass over her face, she turned to her landlady and asked, "Might Rosina board with me, Mrs. Carson? It's a big room and we could share a bed until we could arrange for a second to be brought in." She ignored Rosina's shaking head. "I'd pay for it," Jessica added and Mrs. Carson smiled and nodded.

Settled. Rosina would share lodgings with her. A warm glow spread through Jessica and she realized that she may have been a little lonely after all.

"Jessica, I've got to talk to you," Rosina began when they were upstairs in the privacy of Jessica's room. The nurse stopped fussing about in her wardrobe, where she was trying to make room for Rosina's few belongings. Once again Mr. Dickerson's tent had to be removed to make room, and once again Jessica made a mental note that she should return it.

There was something ominous in the sound of Rosina's voice that demanded her attention.

"Alright, young lady, out with it," she said in a forced light-hearted manner.

Rosina was so obviously embarrassed about something that Jessica took her hand and held it in much the same way she would a patient's. "What could be so terrible, Rosina, that you'd look like this? And you're trembling." She squeezed her hand in a reassuring gesture and Rosina withdrew it and wrapped her arms about herself.

"There's really no way to say this, but plain out. I'm going to have a baby." She turned away, so as not to see the shock on her friend's face. Rosina knew that Jessica's quick mind would tell her that there had been no time to consummate her marriage. Sam had died immediately after the reception, and here she was, carrying his child. The poor little Canadian girl could not imagine this happening in Jessica's aristocratic society, but of course, she was wrong. This sort of thing had been happening since Adam and Eve, and Jessica wanted to make sure that Rosina knew this.

"Rosina, you silly goose, look at me!" She waited as her friend turned slowly, shyly towards her. "Don't you see how wonderful this is. You'll have something of Sam's, forever. I'm so happy for you!"

The relief on Rosina's face was accompanied by a rush of happy tears.

"I thought you'd think little of me. I was so scared," she blurted. "I didn't know where to go. I was so alone. O, thank you Jessica, so much." She wiped her tears with her sleeve as her friend searched for a handkerchief. "Thanks again," smiled Rosina as she finished drying her eyes with her friend's lavender scented linen.

A deep sigh came from Rosina and it said more than any words could. She'd been under such a terrible strain, certainly the worst in her young life and suddenly a friend, with just a few kind words, had eased her burden and for that she would be eternally grateful.

The young women shared a bed that night, and for several more before a new bed was delivered and then they settled into a shared life.

"We could use someone like her, Doctor," Jessica was speaking with Doctor Evans about hiring Rosina on at the hospital. "There are so many occasions when it would be advantageous to have a non-medical, sympathetic person do the bedside comforting, freeing the rest of us for work of a more critical nature." She was not going to lose this conversation. She wanted it too badly. She knew that, with corsets and loose clothing, Rosina could disguise her condition for months to come and by that time, the woman would have made herself indispensable — hopefully.

"She's quick to learn, sir. And she's clean and honest." Jessica went on extolling Rosina's virtues until finally the doctor interrupted.

"Yes, Miss Baxter, you win. We'll give it a try. But you must understand, this is only a trial. Nothing more. And the money, there won't or can't be much. Our budget is so small ... but, we'll give it a try."

The very next day, Rosina Beauville Hobson began

work at the Cobalt Hospital under the watchful but kindly eye of Doctor Evans. Gloria and Pamela accepted her arrival without comment, and when it became obvious that Rosina was no threat to them, they became friends.

In mid-March a sudden warm spell turned the town to mush. Horses and wagons were bogged down in the streets and laneways and small local streams flooded with the melting snow. The frozen ground could not absorb the moisture so it stayed on the surface causing impossible and sometimes impassable situations.

And sickness.

An influenza hit the town and one in three was struck with it. Jessica told a white lie to Doctor Evans, claiming that Rosina was sick, when, in reality, Jessica insisted she stay home, away from the sickness, for the sake of her baby. No one questioned her absence, as, one by one, they succumbed to the virus. Jessica could not remember when she'd worked this hard; staying at the hospital twelve to sixteen hours at a stretch, occasionally not coming home at all.

The tent was crowded and more than once the orderlies, when not actually sick themselves, tripped over the extra cots placed in the narrow aisles. The town's people prayed for a cold snap, believing that the sickness would go with the unusually warm spell, but the warmth and the virus lingered. A hospital comfortably equipped for twenty-four patients bulged at the seams with forty to fifty people at one time.

"This is ridiculous, sir" Jessica spoke to the doctor when several more patients were brought in. "A town this size without a proper hospital!" She groaned as she looked about the crowded room. The air smelled badly of vomit and dirty bedpans. People had been hired and some had volunteered to help, but it was almost impossible to stay ahead of the problem. "We've got to build a proper hospital!" Jessica added, punctuating her statement by hitting her fist into her hand in a very aggressive gesture.

Doctor Evans was extremely over-worked and it showed on his face, but he managed to muster a smile and a nod. "When this is over, Miss Baxter, I'd like to talk with you about just that subject." He hurried on to his next task, with no more conversation, but something in his tired tone gave her hope and something to look forward to.

By mid-April, things were back to normal. A cold spell settled in, and, sure enough, there were no new cases to report and those who were stricken, bettered. Twelve people had died during the siege and eight of those were children. The frozen ground made burial impossible, so the dead were stored in wooden boxes in a well-locked shed at the edge of town. The painful memories faded with time and children took to calling it the 'dead house', using the windowless walls as a target for their snowballs. Life went on.

"I'm going to Toronto to see about that hospital you spoke of," Doctor Evans told Jessica. He was very generous in suggesting that it was her idea, for, in reality, he'd been lobbying for funds for some time. Armed with the hospital's ledgers, filled with statistics regarding their most recent epidemic, he looked forward to success this time. He had the town fathers behind him, and even a promise of some local monies if he could just manage to get provincial consent. "I guess I'm sort of leaving you in charge, Miss Baxter. I'll be gone six to eight days, I figure, and there shouldn't be too much happen in that time." They glanced about the tent and each one smiled at the contrast with several weeks earlier. The sense of order had been re-established and the comfortable, familiar smell of antiseptic had replaced the smells of sickness.

"What are your chances for success, Doctor?" queried the nurse.

"Probably a whole lot better if you were to come along," his eyes betrayed a fondness and respect for Jessica that was at once flattering and disturbing.

"Well, we know that can't be, or could it?" She suddenly envisioned the excitement of the big city, of meeting with officials and she knew that she would enjoy that.

He shook his head slowly, "I won't say I haven't thought of it, Miss Baxter, but not this time." He sounded disappointed, so Jessica disguised her own chagrin.

"Well, have a good time and, of course, good luck." She was very sincere on both counts. She wished him good luck on his venture, for everyone's sake, and she wished him a good time, because he deserved it more than anyone she could imagine. He'd worked for the entire month, not missing a single day, and his fatigue showed in his face. There was a grayness in his complexion and the whites of his eyes were tinged with red. Jessica had not noticed this before, they'd both been too busy, but upon studying him now, she saw that the epidemic had taken yet another toll.

"Don't hurry, sir. We'll be fine here." She spoke cheerfully, wanting him to go away with an easy heart.

"Yes, I'm sure you will be, Jessica," he said softly, speaking her name for the first time.

George Dickerson, who had been away for most of the winter, returned to Cobalt on the very train that was to take Doctor Evans south. Jessica could not help but wonder if it was by design, as Mr. Dickerson seemed always to appear when most needed.

"You're looking a bit peaked, Miss Baxter," was his greeting. She knew this to be true, but bristled under his scrutiny.

"It's been a rough few months, sir." It seemed incongruous to be talking bad weather and sickness under the bright blue winter sky. It was still cold, but sunny, and there was the slightest hint of an honest spring in the air.

"Yes, I'd heard," he spoke almost apologetically and Jessica had to smile at his manner. "I've been out west for some of the winter, and in Ottawa. But news of the North has a way of trickling through," he explained.

They were walking together, back to the hospital, Jessica holding her skirts up to protect them from the slush and the mud.

Suddenly a thought occurred to her, and, before she thought, she spoke, "What if I were to shorten my skirts, Mr. Dickerson?" It was a most unusual, unexpected question and it brought a laugh from the gentleman.

"I mean it, sir! This is really rather silly. Winters and springs in this country do not lend themselves to modesty. I seriously think I'll find a seamstress and have at least my winter dresses cut back to above the mud line." She was accustomed to hanging her dresses near the stovepipe at night, and then brushing the dried mud off before wearing them again. It was a nuisance and the hems of her gowns were beginning to fray with the constant and vigorous brushing.

Mr. Dickerson realized that this was a serious subject, so he changed his manner and agreed. "It makes good sense, Miss Baxter. Why, you might even start a trend. I never could understand how it was that you women had to traipse about in your long dresses, sweeping the dirty streets. Yes, it's a very good idea!"

And so, with Mr. Dickerson's endorsement, Jessica and Rosina, unable to find a seamstress willing to take on such a shocking task, lopped off five inches of skirt and spent the next few evenings hemming their revised frocks.

That was just the first of several changes that Jessica made in the next little while.

"Mr. Menzies, if you've a moment, I'd like to speak with you." Jessica asked of the gentleman when he was delivering meals one day. When he joined her, she said, "I understand that you, along with Mr. Chow, own the laundry on Lang Street?" When he nodded, she proposed, "I'd like to engage you to do the hospital linens." He looked surprised and then glanced around, no doubt for Doctor Evans. As if reading his thoughts, Jessica continued, "It's quite alright, Mr. Menzies, I have the authority to do this. Doctor Evans has put me in charge." He seemed to relax. He was a man in his mid-thirties, rather non-descript in appearance, but extremely polite and with more than just a hint of an education.

"I've always understood that Mrs. Pearce took care of the hospital whites. She's still in business, isn't she?" Mrs. Pearce ran a boarding house close to the hospital and Jessica assumed that her proximity to the hospital had secured her the laundry contract, but Jessica had been constantly disappointed in her handling of the job. By the same token, she'd always been impressed with Gus Menzies' manner and abilities.

"Mrs. Pearce understands," was all that Jessica could say. Actually, Mrs. Pearce did not understand, but Jessica was within her rights when she took the job away from her, faced with continuing poor service.

That was enough explanation for Mr. Menzies and he reached out and shook the nurse's hand by way of sealing the bargain.

"Mrs. Hobson will be working with you . . . for a while at least. She knows our needs and expectations." Jessica called Rosina over and introduced her to Mr. Menzies, then left them to work out the details.

Despite the fact that she may have made an enemy of Mrs. Pearce, she felt good about her venture into the business world. She enjoyed the handshake that made her feel 'in charge' and she enjoyed the knowledge that the hospital linens were in good hands.

"Well, I think it's disgraceful . . ." The statement was made quite loudly in Miss Ema's millinery shop while Jessica and Rosina were shopping a few days later. Rosina's guilt made her blush and try to hold in her rounding tummy, but she needn't have bothered, as the criticism was directed at her companion, not her. Jessica paid no mind but went on with her inspection of a particularly attractive bonnet. She had no intention of purchasing such a frivolous hat, but she was in need of something to focus on to keep her from turning at the sound of Mrs. Pearce's strident voice.

". . . and her a medical person, and all . . ."

Here it was, mused Jessica. Mrs. Pearce had been festering for days, ever since Jessica had informed her of her decision to give the hospital whites to Mr. Menzies and 'that Chinaman' as Mrs. Pearce referred to Mr. Chow. Jessica was clever enough in the ways of the world to know that she would not get off scott free and she had been expecting some sort of retaliation.

"Women have quite enough a time of it, what with all the foreigners wandering about, but now, tempting them with their short skirts. They deserve just what they get," Mrs. Pearce pronounced, sounding ever so much like a judge, meting out a sentence.

"Miss Ema, I'd like to try this one, if you please," Jessica indicated to the shop keeper who had been standing to the side, looking somewhat mortified. The woman rushed to the nurse's side and removed that bonnet from off its stand.

"Oh, it'll look ever so nice with your dark hair," proclaimed Miss Ema in a clear, loud tone, quite loud enough to be heard by the gray-haired Mrs. Pearce and Mrs. Brooks who were standing close together at the doorway. "You do have the loveliest hair, Miss Baxter."

Jessica smiled her thanks to the thoughtful woman. It was plainly clear that she was putting the older, gray-haired Mrs. Pearce in her place and even though Jessica felt that she could handle this on her own, she appreciated the lady's efforts on her behalf.

"What do you think, Rosina?" Jessica asked, after the soft beige bonnet was placed properly upon her dark tresses. Out of the corner of her eye she could see that the old biddies at the door were openly staring at her, and she was enjoying it so much that she thought she might just buy the bonnet, despite the fact that it was obviously extravagant.

"Oh, Jessica, you look just beautiful!" Rosina took the cue from Miss Ema's behaviour, and between the two of them, they made it seem that Jessica was both visiting Royalty and some sort of stage princess. Mrs. Pearce could stand it no longer and stormed out of the shop, slamming the door behind her. Jessica shook with laughter but sobered up when Miss Ema shook her head from side to side.

"Why, what is it, Miss Ema? Surely you're not afraid of those old gossips?" inquired Jessica as she carefully, and very slowly, removed the pretty hat from her head.

"Well, I've been here longer than you, Miss Baxter, and, well, I know about Mrs. Pearce's tongue. And Mrs. Brooks' too. They're really quite, well, vicious, dangerous."

Miss Ema was a spinster in her mid-fifties. She'd come to Cobalt with her brother, years before, and even though the odds had been in her favour, she never managed to find a husband. The town gossips thought her too particular, but the woman seemed quite content to go about her business and take care of her brother in her own quiet fashion. The shop had been purchased with some monies that William, her brother, had made in a strike up north, and that was enough to keep the proverbial wolf from the door.

"Mrs. Brooks was responsible for a woman being run out

of town about a year ago. The woman, a Miss Van . . . something or other, was staying at the hotel, and, well, the story goes that she was a business woman." She blushed and turned her head briefly away. "I knew the woman, and she was really very nice. Told me she was waiting for her fellow to come back from up north, way up north, and that she'd told him she'd be waiting here, in Cobalt, for his return. No one, at least, not Mrs. Pearce and Mrs. Brooks and their crowd, believed her, and they had her run out of town. The church and all, well, you know." It was obvious that Miss Ema enjoyed a bit of gossip herself, but she did not have a vicious bone in her body, so the girls were not in the least uncomfortable listening. "About a month after the lady left, her man came looking for her. He'd made some money up in the Klondike area and came back to claim his bride. When he found she wasn't here, he headed back for the Klondike. Guess he's still there. I find myself wondering where the young lady went." Her voice was rather sad and far away, and Jessica and Rosina felt sorry for both Miss Ema and the lady who was run out of town.

Miss Ema cleared her throat and spoke, "So, Miss Baxter, you see that Mrs. Pearce is not a person one would want as an enemy." She tilted her auburn head to one side and smiled a wistful smile. There was a trace of pain about her eyes and Jessica wondered if Mrs. Pearce had, in some way, hurt this delicate person too.

"Thank you so much, Miss Ema. I really appreciate your warning, and I will watch out for her, I promise. And, in the meantime, I think I'll just take this hat." Jessica didn't know if she bought the hat out of pity for Miss Ema's sad eyes, or if she just wanted to shock the town gossips. But, whatever her reasons, she exited the shop with her new hat perched at a jaunty angle atop her head.

It was just the next day that Doctor Evans echoed Miss Ema's warning. He came back from Toronto in a good mood. Whether that stemmed from any sort of success with the hospital board or from a social event, he wouldn't say, but he looked rested and smiled a lot, even when cautioning Jessica about her new foe. "She's a devil, that one, Miss Baxter.

You'd have been better off to put up with gray linens, than tackle that she-wolf."

"Is that why you've been 'putting up with' her inferior work all this time, sir? Has she got something on you?" A cloud passed over the doctor's face, but it passed quickly.

"She's got something on everyone, Jessica," he said, and laughed outright.

"Well, she's not going to best me, sir," announced Jessica and she trounced out of the hospital into the cold, forgetting in her haste to do up her coat and she was immediately sorry. The last storm of the season was at its peak and the wind, although not as cold as it had been all winter, was so damp that it seemed to pass right through her. She tugged at her scarf and hurriedly did up her buttons. She would not have admitted this to anyone in the world, but her ankles were cold.

"Rosina, I've got such a chill," exclaimed Jessica as she entered their room. She hastened over to the stove pipe and stood facing it, trying to get the dampness out of her being.

"Perhaps this will warm you up," Rosina said as she handed her friend a letter. "Came in today's post," she explained. "I think it's from your brother."

Jessica took the letter from Rosina's hand and stared at it. She'd heard nothing from Charles for so long. She tore it open and glanced quickly through it, her eyes resting on just one sentence. "Of course, you must come home", and she knew that her mother was dying.

Jessica lowered herself onto the settee, suddenly more exhausted than cold. She'd been anticipating this news, but, by keeping busy, she'd managed to store it in the very deepest recesses of her mind. Now, with a jolt, that dark place was open, exposed to the light and it was overwhelming.

"Jessica, is something wrong?" the gentle Rosina was quickly on her knees before the distraught woman, looking up at her face, ready and anxious to give her unhappy friend solace.

Jessica shook her head slowly from side to side, but her tortured eyes said yes.

When she did not speak, Rosina asked, "Is it Charles? Is there something the matter with Charles?" she spoke his name as though she knew him.

Her friend found her voice, "No, Rosina, not Charles."
She gestured towards the letter, "He seems fine. It's our
mother. He's found out that our mother is . . . well, very ill."
She sighed a deep sigh, her shoulders rising and dropping in
rhythm with her breath. "I'm not surprised, Rosina. This
isn't sudden. I've been expecting it, actually, though not from
Charles. It seems so peculiar that he'd know in Africa before
the news arrived here. But that matters not." She stood up
and began to pace. "What matters now is, do I go back . . .
home, or not?"

She knew it was expected of her. What family was left
would certainly have the right to presume that she'd come -
but she didn't want to. And the awful truth of that shook her
to her very core. She did not want to go back to England to
watch a stranger die; to bury a stranger — a woman who had
never bothered to disguise her indifference towards her only
daughter, and who now had no recollection of the past. She
would not even know if Jessica was there. And, conversely,
she would not even know if Jessica was not.

Rosina looked so pitiful that Jessica realized that she
must explain things to her. She sat down again and drew the
girl up beside her on the settee. "Rosina, remember when
you came to me with your 'secret'? You said that there was
no way to say it but straight out? Well, I guess that's what
I'll have to do." She sat back wearily in her seat and began,
"My mother and I were never close, Rosina. I don't know
why, we just never were. She had a lifestyle that simply did
not lend itself to the love and care of children." She lowered
her voice, "Especially girl children."

There, it was out! She'd actually said aloud the words
that meant she felt that her mother had favoured Charles, or
at least was less indifferent towards him. She'd always felt
this, even as a child, and she'd waited until now to say it. In a
strange way, it felt good.

She sighed another of her deep sighs and continued,
"After Father's death, Mother sort of went to pieces. They
were very close. They did everything together. You see,
Father didn't work, so they were able to play with one anoth-

er all the time." She drew a deep breath and hoped that she didn't sound too bitter.

"With no one to fill her time, Mother became, well, rather eccentric. She may have been destined to premature senility, or maybe his death hastened it, but, for whatever reason, Mother began to slip away, to lose her senses. It started simply . . . forgetting where she put her gloves, missing a luncheon appointment. Then it became critical, as she'd forget where she was, or where she belonged. She was hospitalized for a while and then released to me."

A great dark cloud passed over Jessica's face as a flood of resentful memories eased their way into her consciousness. "I have to be honest, Rosina," she looked at her friend, "and say that I hated being responsible for her." She flushed at the statement, embarrassed, but not guilty. "She could never bring herself to be responsible for me, and there we were, very low on monies for the first time in all our lives, and I had to care for her. It seemed rather unfair to me." She looked at Rosina's sweet face and wondered if she understood her resentment. The girl's face betrayed nothing so Jessica went on. "Finally, I could take it no longer. I was working at the hospital, and I would have to lock her in our flat while I was gone. It was difficult to get anyone to sit with her, as she was, well, so unpleasant — so demanding. One day, I came home to find she'd started a fire in the grate and practically burned the house down. It was then that I knew that I must have her . . . committed."

It was the very first time that Jessica had uttered that word. Doctor Fairley had spoken it once, when she went to him for help and advice, but she'd never spoken it herself. She couldn't even write it in her letter to Charles. But, that was precisely what she'd done — committed her mother to an institution for the insane. Sybil Windsor Baxter, of noble birth, was reduced to spending the end of her days with 'halfwits', 'morons', 'the demented'. It should have been a fitting end for one so bent on self-indulgence, but, even the slighted Jessica did not wish it on her. And Jessica's role in putting her mother there had left her with nightmares that seemed never to end.

Jessica had been staring into the middle distance during the minutes that followed her last sentence and was brought back to reality by Rosina's sobs.

Strange. It was Rosina who shed the tears for the sad story. Not Jessica. Jessica's emotions were varied, but anger was prevalent. Fatigue, mixed with an almost boredom prompted another heavy sigh. The story was tiresome. She'd lived with it for so many, many years. She should be relieved that it was ending, for surely with her mother's death, she could also bury her family-related frustrations. Surely she could expect this. Surely she deserved no less.

Rosina made no comment on her friend's confession but went about her business. There was something in her manner though, that suggested to Jessica that she might be critical of her friend's feelings towards her mother, as Jessica remembered that the girl had been close to her own before her untimely death. The poor Englishwoman was entirely too weary to care just now, so she undressed and crawled into her bed. She was still chilled, and somehow, her quilts offered more warmth than her friend or her stovepipe.

"You may tell Mrs. Carson that I'll not be down for dinner, Rosina," she said as she buried herself under her covers.

Sleep did not come easily, despite her efforts. Every time she closed her eyes, she could see her mother's face, so she would open them and stare at the ceiling. Eventually her mother's countenance was there too, and Jessica could not stop the memories . . .

"Miss Baxter! Pardon my saying it, but you look positively dreadful!" Doctor Fairley cornered Jessica in the hospital, concern written all over his face as he looked at the haggard nurse.

She turned her head aside, well aware that the deep, dark circles under her eyes were most unbecoming. "Perhaps we could have a cup of tea and a talk?" he asked. She really didn't want to and tried to beg off by mumbling something about her nursing duties. Doctor Fairley stepped over to the nurses' station and said, "I'll be needing Miss Baxter for a spell," with such authority that no one queried him.

"That's that, young lady. Now, to my office." Once inside his office he ordered tea and cakes and settled into a deep leather chair behind a busy-looking desk. He motioned for Jessica to sit across from him and she did.

"Now, what is it that is so terrible as to ravage such a lovely face?" His words were light, but the tone was one of caring. He was kind. And it was obvious to Jessica that he was not going to let her go without some explanation, as he stared at her intently over his tea cup.

It should have been so easy to have blurted out the truth, to have said — My mother is going crazy, pass the biscuits please. But Jessica was not one for taking the easy or obvious route. She liked Doctor Fairley. She liked him a great deal. She'd even fantasized a romance between them, in one of her tired half-sleeps. It may have been this softness that she felt for him, or it may have been Windsor pride, but whichever, she could not bring herself to speak of the nature of her mother's illness.

So she lied. Not big lies, sort of half truths. She confessed that her once rather affluent family had fallen upon hard times. That truth somehow did not embarrass her. She said that she was living with her invalid parent and that she was working long hours because of their expenses.

He distracted her momentarily from her discourse as he wrote something on a piece of paper. She concluded the story by promising to take it easier.

He smiled his doctor smile. He didn't believe her, at least the part about taking it easier, and she knew it. But that was alright because he had something on his mind, of that she was certain. He was not ready yet to tell her of his plan, so the visit ended on that note.

She hurried back to her station and she felt better than she had for months. And she didn't know why. She'd been careful not to tell the good man what it was that was really bothering her most, yet she felt that he knew enough to help her . . . somehow.

Jessica did not have to wait long to find out how. Several days later, Mr. Johnston, the director in charge of the nursing staff called her into his office.

"It seems you've come to the attention of Doctor
Fairley, Miss Baxter?" he queried, smiling at her over
glasses that were perched on the end of his nose. He
glanced down, "I have a request here, from the good
doctor, that you be transferred to his office, to replace
Mrs. Potts who's had to give notice." Jessica knew that
Mrs. Potts was going to have a baby, and, of course, was
expected to leave before she began to 'show'.

The young girl was flabbergasted. She knew little of
such matters, as she'd never aspired to the position of
'Doctor's Nurse', but she immediately realized that she
might expect less ward work and probably a bit more
money. Of course she was interested and told Mr.
Johnston so, very quietly, of course. But her heart
soared. For the first time in a very long time, she felt
like singing.

As a matter of fact, she did sing as she made the dinner that evening, and she did not allow herself to be upset
by her mother's constant complaints and ramblings.

They spent a very quiet evening, an almost normal
one, as Sybil sat thumbing through a magazine and
Jessica wrote to Charles, telling him of the positive
changes in their lives.

Working for Doctor Fairley proved to be a very good
change for her. She had less heavy work, and the slight
increase in pay allowed for a few extras that pleased the
greedy Sybil, so that she grumbled less.

One day the doctor announced, "I'm going to visit a
sick friend of mine in the country, Miss Baxter." Her
mind raced to the things that she might do to help him
prepare for the trip. She liked her job. She liked her
doctor, and she tried to anticipate his needs. But she
had no way of anticipating his next questions.

"I was wondering if you and your mother might come
along? You would be of some assistance to me, Miss
Baxter." He stood with his back to her, lighting a pipe,
but she could sense his expectancy in the slope of his
shoulder, in the way he was breathing. It was a most

extraordinary request, and she knew not how to answer. Of course she wanted to say yes. Her mother had been quite well lately. The additional money had seemed like a salve to her troubled mind and life had been reasonably pleasant. Jessica thought that maybe, just maybe, Sybil would behave.

"I should like that, Sir. I think perhaps Mother might like it as well. It has been quite some time since we've been to the country." She tried to keep the excitement that she felt in her heart from surfacing in her voice. He turned and smiled a wide smile at her and she knew that she had to try.

"Yes, Sir. I think that we may be able to go. When would that be, Sir?" she asked.

"A week Friday. We'd take the train to Croydon and then we'd have James' carriage at our disposal. James is the father of a dear friend of mine, Dr. James Cousins. He's gone abroad, to the United States, to a large clinic there, where he teaches. I try to look in upon his father several times a year. The old fellow has a bad heart that bears watching." The doctor seemed quite relaxed and pleased with his nurse's response.

Jessica had to be very careful just how she broached the subject to her mother. She rehearsed her conversation all the way home. She knew that she must make it seem that the trip was planned for Sybil's pleasure and not hers, or the doctor's. If her mother was in one of her 'moods', it would be best not to mention it at all. And Sybil was in one of her moods! The flat was in shambles when Jessica arrived home. Absolutely everything had been removed from the drawers and cupboards and a feeble attempt had been made to stuff the belongings into travelling bags.

"It's time that we moved back home, Jessica," was Sybil's announcement. And, to anyone not familiar with their circumstances, the statement sounded very sane.

"Mother!" exclaimed Jessica. "Whatever are you doing? Stop it! Instantly!" There was anger and exasperation in her voice and as removed as Sybil was from reality, she recognized the tone and it triggered off one of her fits.

It was very late that night before Jessica finally stumbled into bed. Sybil's tantrum had gone on for hours, ending only when Jessica had been able to get a sleeping potion into her.

The fatigued nurse lay on her bed, wanting to cry, but unable to. Frustration and resentment welled up in her as she realized that it would be impossible to go . . . anywhere with her mother. Whatever could she have been thinking? Away from Sybil, it had all seemed quite plausible, but she knew now that Sybil Baxter would never leave this flat again, unless she were dead or hospitalized.

She told Doctor Fairley the next day, quite abruptly, turning her head aside in hopes that he would not see the pain in her eyes. But he heard the pain in her voice and asked gently, "Is there anything that I can do, Miss Baxter?" But she just shook her head and walked away.

About a month later, when Jessica arrived home from work, Sybil was in a coma. The flat smelled of smoke, but there was no fire, only remnants of one that had burned itself out in the grate. The flue was not open, so the small fire must have filled the flat with smoke and Sybil must have been terrified. Her breathing was weak and Jessica could not rouse her. She went back outside and hailed a carriage. The driver carried Sybil downstairs and placed her gently on the seat. She looked very young and beautiful, thought Jessica, and she felt sorry for her.

Sybil was not destined to make the return trip. Her stay at the hospital was lengthy and ended with her trip to the asylum.

No longer able to keep the truth from Doctor Fairley, Jessica told him of her mother's condition. He looked in upon her periodically, although it was not his area of expertise, and finally advised the girl to commit her to Flesherton House, a home for the insane.

Despite her resentment towards her mother, it was not an easy decision for the girl and she delayed it as long as possible. In the end, the decision was more financial than anything else. The asylum would not cost her a penny, as Sybil Baxter would become a ward of the state, whereas the hospital stay was draining what little capital the girl had left.

Finally, she said yes, and quickly signed the papers when the Doctors Graham and Fairley presented them to her.

She wrote to Charles, informing him of her act and received a very vague letter in return. He'd not been to visit once in the last year, claiming that it was too hard on him to see his mother that way. He continued to live a somewhat carefree life, staying first with one friend and then another. He was such an amiable chap that no one seemed to mind. He promised he'd drop in on his mother when next in that area, but Jessica knew full well that he had no intention of doing so as long as he thought that she'd do the family duty, and, of course, she did.

Twice a week, she'd take the train out to Flesherton, and visit Sybil. Sometimes they would actually have a conversation, but mostly they just sat there and stared into the gulf that had always been between them.

Doctor Fairley announced his engagement to Margaret Cousins, his friend Jamie's sister, and shortly after that, they were married. Jessica could not help but wonder if things would have been different had she gone to Croydon with him that time. She'd never know.

But this much she did know. She had to get out from under the pall of her existence. Her visits to her mother became more and more meaningless and her relationship with Doctor Fairley deteriorated into simply a doctor and his nurse situation. There was nothing for her here. Nothing.

Then came the advertisement about the desperate need for nurses in Canada, and Jessica saw a way out.

It seemed to Jessica that she had just finally drifted off to sleep, after her weary reminiscences when she was awakened by Rosina's return. The girl seemed to be trying to make as little noise as possible, but she was getting rather

awkward in her movements, and she bumped into the washstand near the door, sending the soap dish rolling across the
carpet. She glanced over towards Jessica, whose eyes were
open but a slit, and she caught the gleam from the light in the
doorway reflected in those deep brown eyes and she smiled,
"Sorry, Jesse, but I did try," she apologized as she retrieved
the china dish and put it back on the stand.

Jessica thought that she detected a purposefully warm
note in her friend's voice and she sat up. "It's alright, Rosina,
I wasn't quite to sleep," she fibbed. "How was dinner?" she
asked, trying to establish a conversation.

"Pork," was Rosina's answer. Jessica knew that the
girl's stomach wasn't quite up to par and that certain foods,
most particularly fatty ones, left Rosina a bit queasy.

"Sorry about that, Rosina," she smiled at her friend.

"Oh, I filled up on potatoes and bread. No matter."
There was still a bit of tension in the air and neither girl
seemed able to direct the conversation to what it was that lay
between them. Rosina began to prepare for bed, despite the
early hour. As she moved about the room, Jessica tried to
rehearse just the right thing to say. It was only when Rosina
came upon Charles' letter still lying on the settee that she
broached the subject.

"I'm sorry about your mother, Jessica." Her back was to
Jessica as she unbuttoned her dress. When she turned
around, there were big silvery tears sitting on her lashes.
She walked over to Jessica's bed and sat down, taking the
hem of her nightdress to dab the corner of her eyes. "I'm trying real hard to understand what you said, about your family
and all, Jessica. But it's so different to my feelings. My
mother went and died on me, when I really needed her, and I
miss her, so you can see it's so different from you?" She
seemed to want some response so Jessica nodded her understanding. "I wanted her to go on living, but, now that it is all
over, I guess I really wanted her to go on living for me. She
wasn't happy, Jesse, and she was in terrible pain. It was
kinda selfish of me to want her to go on. So, you see, when
you say that you don't seem to care about your mother, well
it's just kinda hard for me to understand. But, in a little bit

of a way, I think I do. And I'll know why if you don't go back there, Jesse. I'll understand." In her simple way she was giving Jessica her blessing and it was a gift that Jessica would not soon forget. The two embraced and nothing else was said of the matter. Nothing else was needed.

9

Another Wedding

"How long is your friend going to work, in her condition?" asked Doctor Evans of Jessica the next morning. It took the nurse quite by surprise, as she'd been thinking of her mother, and of how she should handle her family.

"I, well . . . I don't know, sir," was her honest answer.

"You know that it's just fine with me, Miss Baxter. As long as the girl does her chores, she's welcome. But you know how the town gossips. Most unusual for a woman to venture out so late in her term. Do you know when she's due?" Jessica knew the doctor well enough to know that he was not just on a fishing expedition. He was likely concerned, and of course, he had a right to know.

"I'll talk to her, Sir," she promised. But right now she really wanted to talk to him about another matter. She cleared her throat and began, "I received a letter . . ." her statement was to be left unfinished, for at that moment two men tore into the tent, not stopping until they were at the doctor's feet.

"Doc, there's been a cave-in!" the first man managed to blurt out.

While he was catching his breath, the second continued, "Over at the Trueway Mine. 'Bout two hours ago. Must be ten men trapped. They sent us for you." The urgency in their voices was matched by the doctor's quick movements. He reached for his bag and his coat and turned to Jessica. "I'll send a runner back for you, if I need you, otherwise, please take care of things here."

He was gone before she could ask where the property was or how long he might be gone.

"Gloria, where is the Trueway Mine located?" she asked of the nurse who'd come to the station when the men had entered.

"Not far. I'd say about ten, fifteen miles north and west of here. Is that where the doctor's gone?"

"Yes," replied Jessica. "There's been a cave-in and those men were sent to fetch him. Does this happen often? What exactly is a 'cave-in'?"

The younger nurse seemed pleased with the opportunity to enlighten her superior and she gave a pretty good account of what a cave-in was all about. "Sometimes men get trapped down there, and, well, often they die because of no air, or at least no good air." She looked sad, and Jessica wondered if perhaps she'd lost someone in one of the mining disasters. "Sometimes they bring the men up, and they can tell, at least the doctor can, that they just died slowly of the bad air. I guess it'd be better to be hit on the head with one of the big timbers than to suffocate." She shivered and Jessica felt a chill rush through her too. If she was going to make her future here in the mining country, she'd best get used to these disasters, for they weren't about to end.

"Mr. Menzies and I just heard the news," said Rosina as she returned from the laundry. "Has the doctor gone already?" Jessica nodded. "The whole town's buzzing. I've never been here when there was so much excitement, well, except for the fire," her voice trailed off temporarily as she referred to the fire that had taken her husband's life. "Everyone who can has gone to the mine, including Mr. Menzies, and it's several miles away. Wonder what they're going to do out there?" It was a very good question. There wasn't a lot to be done, except for the skilled miners who'd be working against the clock to free any men still alive, and, of course, the few women about who had men working in that mine on that shaft. Jessica could well imagine what it would be like at the mine shaft and shuddered.

"It's time to go home, Jessica," Rosina told her friend several hours later, but Jessica shook her head.

"Doctor Evans left me in charge, Rosina, I think I'd better stay. You go ahead and please explain to Mrs. Carson for me." The young woman promised to and soon Jessica was left alone in charge of the quiet hospital. A young man who worked for Gus Menzies brought the meals for the patients and there was a plate for the doctor, which Jessica picked at. She administered medication to those in need of it, helped a few to settle in their beds and then she went to sit at the desk to wait.

It was as though Providence had supplied her with such a wonderful excuse not to go to England. Not that she really needed one, as she had pretty well made up her mind to stay, and let John, their uncle/lawyer, do what was necessary when Sybil died. But now, she had such a wonderful feeling of being needed that it overshadowed the few small guilts that hung about in the back of her consciousness like tiny clouds threatening rain but passing by without fulfilling their promises. It would be impossible for her to leave this mining camp when there was such a need for medical help. She was feeling almost kindly towards the catastrophe when one of the men who had come with the news of the cave-in returned to ask her to come with him.

"Doc says he needs these things," the man passed her a list of medical needs scribbled out on a scrap of paper in the doctor's hand. "And he says he needs you too."

There was an urgency about the man that made Jessica hurry. First it was necessary to get Gloria or Pamela back for the night along with one of the orderlies, more for protection than anything else. She dispatched Mr. Bellows, the messenger, to fetch them, and she quickly gathered the necessary equipment for the doctor. Mr. Bellows returned with Gloria and young Jack Rumble in tow. It was quite dark now, and she was not so comfortable in the cold night as she had been when thinking about this disaster back in the confines of the warm tent.

They went first to Mrs. Carson's where Jessica ran in to tell them where she was going and to fetch a few warmer pieces of clothing in a bag. She said a nervous goodbye to Rosina and was gone into the black night.

Jessica could not remember such a terrible ride in her entire life. The cold was a very minor part of her discomfort. The wagon bumped along dirt roads and there was nothing to protect her from the hard boards of the seat. She tried folding her skirts up under her backside to ease the pain, but the motion of the wagon made that impossible. She tied her scarf tightly about her face and neck, but it too seemed to defy her, working loose and trailing out behind as they sped as quickly as the horse could pull them. She felt that her companion was driving dangerously, but she was afraid to mention that fact, as she did not know what awaited them at the other end. He might have a friend lying there, in need of assistance, so she bit her tongue and did a great deal of praying.

Occasionally there would be a glimmer of light in the bush, and her heart would brighten, thinking that they'd arrived, but they would scurry past a small prospector's cabin, the warm light shining out the window, quickly disappearing into the night. The sound of a wolf could be heard above the noise of the horse's hooves hitting the hard earth, and she shuddered. The light from the wagon displayed only a few feet forward, there could be any number of awesome creatures, just standing at the side of the road, and she would not have seen them. Perhaps it was best that it was so dark.

Once the horse shied, rearing up on his back legs and Mr. Bellows had quite a time calming him. "Must be a wolf," mumbled the man by way of explaining his horse's behaviour. "It's about the only thing that'll spook old Dan." That was comforting.

It was only forty minutes from town to their destination, but Jessica was certain that they'd been travelling most of the night. Her entire body ached from the tension of just trying to stay on her seat and her head ached from the wind and the fear. Then, suddenly, up ahead, there were many lights and she knew that they were almost there.

There was nothing in Jessica's training to prepare her for what she was to see in the next few hours. A makeshift hospital had been set up in the mess tent and in it were at least two dozen men, some dying, some dead, some hurt, but alive. Doctor Evans was working feverishly on a young

miner who was screaming out in pain and Jessica was glad
that she'd brought more morphine with her.

"Oh, there you are, Baxter. Here, come and hold this
tourniquet while I give this man another dose." Jessica flew
to his side and grabbed the stick that kept the pressure on a
bloody bandage that was wrapped around a man's upper arm.
The lower part of his arm was missing, just a gaping, oozing
mess below his elbow to indicate that he'd been whole just
that morning. She held fast, knowing how crucial it was in
these conditions to lose as little blood as possible, and she'd
turn even harder whenever she saw so much as a trickle of
blood appear at the wound. Doctor Evans jabbed the bleeding man with a needle, and shortly his head rolled to one side
in sleep.

"I'll try fixing him now, Baxter, you go over there, see
that fellow in the corner, he's been hit on the head — a timber, I think, and I'm afraid he's bleeding into his brain." He
looked at Jessica, who had involuntarily gulped for breath.
"You going to be alright?" he asked, and before she could
answer, "Of course you are, girl," and she sped off to hold a
young man's head on her lap while he bled to death.

It was so unusual, she was so distant from what was
going on. She managed to stay detached from the horror of it
all and function very professionally. She went from one casu-
alty to another, administering first aid, giving solace, and in
some cases saying the last rights of the church, in answer to
the requests of some of the miners.

"This'n here, he's always praying, Ma'am, goes to church
every time we're in town," and Jessica, remembering her cat-
echism, spoke the soothing words to the dying.

"I'm going to need you over here," called Doctor Evans
and she picked her way through the crowd on the floor to
where the doctor was sedating a miner in preparation for
amputation. "I'm going to need help." Suddenly the memory
of Danny from Burks Falls came rushing back to Jessica and
she had to fight the sorrow in her heart.

"Yes sir," she replied as she swallowed hard and thought
of other things. One thought that came to her mind was self-
centered, but she could not dismiss it: this seemed a very

high price to pay for not going to England to watch her mother die.

"Ever done a transfusion?" the doctor asked of Jessica, not looking at her, as he way busy with the unconscious miner. When she didn't answer immediately, he growled, "Well, have you?"

She gulped. Transfusions were very chancy procedures, even in sterile hospital conditions. She'd witnessed several, and was reluctant to tell the doctor that, in each case, the patient had died, from . . . complications. "Yes, Sir, I've been at a few."

He glanced at her, looking hard into her eyes — she wasn't sure for what. Fear, perhaps? Or maybe knowledge? He might very well be looking to Jessica for guidance. She wished with all her heart that she could take charge, and give the exhausted man courage to take a chance. But, she too was afraid. The stench of blood and vomit made it difficult for her to stay above the horror about her and to think along the clean, clear medical lines that would be necessary if they were to attempt anything so incredible as to take blood from one of the unhurt men and give it to the dying amputee.

She closed her eyes tightly for a moment, remembering as best she could, exactly what she'd seen in the operating room at the Old Vic. Jessica was a good nurse. She did not forget much of what she learned along the way. Slowly, the procedure came back to her, and just as slowly, she opened her eyes to stare into the doctor's. "You remember, don't you, Baxter?" There was a triumphant tone to his voice. Once again, his faith in this English-woman was well founded.

"We must find a donor," she said quietly to him, as she looked about the circle of men who were standing about the tent. They obviously knew nothing of the doctor's intentions, probably none of them had even heard of a transfusion.

"Yes," the doctor murmured back. "Anyone in mind?" he was practically smiling now. A sense of adventure had taken over the two of them. They had nothing to lose, as it was abundantly clear that the young miner, lying unconscious between them, was going to die, and soon, without a replacement for the great amount of blood that he'd lost.

"There's a healthy looking young man standing over there, talking to that chap with the broken arm," Jessica remarked, remembering the stresses placed on the good health of the donor. "He seems of a pleasant nature," she noted, as she watched him helping his buddy to light a cigarette with his one good arm.

The doctor looked over towards the duo and nodded his head in agreement. "He's as good as we're going to get, I expect," was his reply, and he headed over towards the tall, healthy looking stranger.

When he returned, he had Bob Aston in tow, a very young, very genial fellow who also looked upon the whole thing as an adventure. The doctor had assured him that there was absolutely no danger to him, and that there was at least a fifty-fifty chance that, with his assistance, the nurse and he might save Eff Langley, the dying man. Bob knew Eff and was rolling his sleeve up in preparation for the transfusion. What a delightful fellow he is, thought Jessica, as she helped Doctor Evans to prepare for the ordeal.

Jessica was responsible for the donor, Doctor Evans was responsible for the recipient. Jessica preferred it that way. Bob was extremely easy to work with. She applied a tourniquet to his upper arm and very soon, the veins in his lower arm bulged, making it easy for her to select the one she wanted to 'tap'. She attached the needle to his arm with bandages, once the needle had found its mark, and slowly released the pressure on his upper arm. The tubes were made of rubber and it was not possible to tell if it was working properly until a tiny, steady stream of bright red blood appeared at the end of the tube where it met the bottle that was lying below the table on the floor. A sense of relief flooded Jessica as she watched the bottle fill slowly. This was certainly the easy part. Getting this life-giving fluid into Eff was to be the hard part, and that was Doctor Evans' part.

"Alright now, seal it off. Don't take the needle out of his arm. We may need more, it's hard to say. Here, up here, gently now." He ordered Jessica about in a tone mixed with command and endearment. They were sharing something here that would be a bond between them forever.

"You're going to have to hold it up there. We've nothing to hang it on. There, I've found the vein. Now, slowly now, slowly, release the pressure." Jessica was pinching the tube closed, and now she released her grip and she could feel the liquid move between her fingers. Gravity was doing its job once again, and the blood was finding its way into Eff's veins. It all seemed too easy. You took blood from one person, gave it to another. Why was the success rate so slim? And was there anything that they could do to increase Eff's chances for survival? These were questions that Doctor Evans and Nurse Baxter could not answer as they stood there, tense and tired, watching the bottle empty into the man's prone body. They repeated the process with another bottle of blood before they withdrew the needles and began their watch.

Jessica remembered back to the hospital in England, and how the patients had just slowly passed into the next world. In the beginning, their colour had brightened with the new blood, but then they'd paled again. Their breathing became shallower, their pulse rate slowed until it just stopped. It was not a violent death, but it bothered everyone connected with the transfusion because in theory, the procedure should have worked. Yet time after time, the patient died. There had been the ones who had lived. Jessica and Doctor Evans both knew that, and with a little bit of luck, Eff would be one of them. Only time would tell.

Jessica took the first watch. Doctor Evans was so obviously exhausted that the girl insisted, and he was quick to curl up on the floor and drift off. Jessica sat next to the patient and held his hand. She often took his pulse, which was weak, and wrote it down on a paper that she had. She saw in the dim light that his colour had improved, but she did not allow herself to be excited by that. Bob, sitting on the other side of the cot, noticed the colour, but she shook her head to indicate to him that it was not necessarily a good sign. And the two of them sat out their vigil.

Jessica would doze off occasionally, waking when her chin reached her chest, embarrassed with herself, but quite unable to stop. It was hours later, when she was in this semiconscious state that Eff's hand moved in hers. Just a twitch, and it was warm. It had been quite cool earlier in the evening. She did not want to alarm anyone with false hope, so she very quietly leaned forward and placed her head on his chest. His heartbeat was firm and regular and she could feel his breath against her hair. She reached for his wrist to take his pulse and was amazed at how strong it was. It was only then that she found the nerve to look at his face. An involuntary gasp escaped her lips as her look was returned by the patient's, his big brown eyes shiny and alert. She bent her head to hide the tears of relief and said a silent "Thank you".

News of the incident at the Trueway Mine spread quickly throughout the North. Prospectors, trappers, miners, and salesmen carried it with them like their tobacco, to be pulled out when time allowed and enjoyed slowly. In the telling, the tale became larger than life and both Jessica and Doctor Evans were embarrassed with the large doses of esteem that came their way. They knew that Eff's transfusion had been an incredible stroke of luck, most particularly for Eff, but also for them. It could have gone either way and so often it went the other way, the sadder way, when the recipient of fresh, wholesome blood simply slipped into a coma and passed away. But when trying to explain this to their admirers, they simply seemed modest, so, finally, they stopped explaining and tried to ignore the praise.

"Miss Baxter," Jessica heard her name called and turned to see a messenger at the doorway of the hospital tent. He delivered telegrams from the local office, and usually his appearance set people's hearts to pounding, as it seemed always to be bad news that came via the telegraph wires.

"Yes, what is it?" she snapped, immediately sorry that she had, as Craig Hunter's face instantly fell. Craig did not write the cables, and it seemed so unfair that he should be the one people growled at whenever they received unpleasant news. "Sorry about that, Craig, but, I'm — well, I'm rather busy." It was a poor excuse for bad manners, but it was all that she could think of to say. She'd long been expecting the news that Sybil had died and been buried, and she knew that she should anticipate some criticism from abroad because she'd chosen not to attend. She felt no guilt about it, no guilt at all, and she was rather pleased to have it over. "How's your wife?" she asked kindly of the messenger as she signed a receipt for the yellow envelope.

"Fair to middling, I 'spect," he smiled a grateful smile at the nurse. "Baby's due soon, so she's kinda slow, but not poorly."

"Tell her to take it easy, Craig, and she should send for one of us as soon as she's in labour." Mr. Hunter was shuffling his feet and looking at the ground. It was obvious that the conversation was embarrassing him, so Jessica took pity on him and ended the conversation with a pat on the shoulder and a thank you.

She looked for a quiet place to read her news. The hospital was almost empty. Spring had arrived and the town had emptied itself of most able-bodied men. The trappers were out on their lines, the prospectors were out at their claims and the rest of the townsfolk were slowly recovering from a long, cold, bitter winter.

"I must say, Jessie, I'm rather disappointed in you. Everyone expected you here and when you didn't arrive, I had to come. Poor show. Mind you, I was able to get a fortnight off, 'compassionate leave', they call it, and that was rather jolly. I'm a bit overdue going back, but Uncle John is sure he can straighten it out with my commanding officer.

Well, the old girl's gone, Jessie, and I don't mind saying I'm not too upset. She didn't look anything like herself, you know. They made me identify her, and I almost couldn't. Actually, there were two old dolls who died at the same time, and it was not easy to tell which one was Sybil. Sad.

But, I've decided to forgive you, sister dear — for not coming, I mean. One would have to assume that the medical business in Cobalt is not just the easiest. Mind you, life isn't all that great in Africa. Oh, we're not in any danger — at least Freddie and I aren't. You remember him? Played cricket with me at Canterbury?

Anyway, he and I are mates now, and it sort of makes things more bearable, having one of your own kind to live with. We do have some jolly times, I'll tell you.

Uncle John will be sending an account of Mother's affairs to you. I asked him to, as I've little privacy where I am lodging. The blacks will rob you blind if you're not careful. So, let me know what old John says, and all the best to you, sister dear.

Your loving brother
Charles"

There were no sad tears for Sybil's passing. But an incredible sense of relief poured over the young woman and she heaved an audible sigh.

"What's this?" asked Doctor Evans. "Sitting here just staring into space? That's not like you, Miss Baxter." He then noticed the yellow paper in her hand, recognized it for what it was and changed his approach, "Is there anything wrong?"

"No, sir, nothing. Everything's just fine." She was reluctant to add that she'd just received news of her mother's death, because she knew that she did not represent the normal grieving daughter, so she shoved the message into her pocket and grinned at the doctor.

"Well, that's much better. I've come with news and I wanted a good reception." He sat down beside her on the bench that patients often sat upon when waiting their turn to see the doctor. "I've had a telegram of my own, Miss Baxter, and it just might mean good news for us." He let his glance sweep the entire room. "Doctor Humpherson, from Toronto, is going to pay us a visit this summer." He let his audience digest this piece of news before continuing. Jessica had heard of Doctor Humpherson, as he was one of the important men that Doctor Evans had gone to see when he last approached the government about a proper hospital for Cobalt.

"That is good news, Sir. Do you feel that your visit had some effect on the powers that be?"

"Not really, girl. I've a feeling that that episode with

Eff Langley probably did us about as much good as anything
else. Word has a way of getting around, and George
Dickerson was telling me that they were talking about it on
the train last time he went south. Seems that between North
Bay and Toronto there were several medical people who
showed a great deal of interest in the story. Of course,
George, being a good friend and all, well, he just made us out
to sound like Florence Nightingale and Louis Pasteur.
Doesn't ever hurt to have a man like George Dickerson in
your corner, I'll tell you." He was looking at Jessica and smiling as he spoke and she flushed under his scrutiny. There
was something about the mention of Mr. Dickerson's name
that always brought some reaction or other from her.

"Perhaps," she murmured, and changed the subject to
hospital business.

Rosina was waiting for Jessica at the door of Mrs.
Carson's when she arrived home that evening. She'd stopped
going to the hospital just the week before, as the muddy
spring roads were difficult to traverse, and her condition had
become quite obvious now. "Jesse, oh, how I've been waiting." She had the appearance of a girl with a secret to share
and she was simply bursting to tell it. She helped her friend
with her boots and wrap and then steered her into a quiet
corner of the parlour. "I've got to ask your opinion on something, Jesse, and, well, I guess it's got to be soon." Jessica
had absolutely no idea what it was that had her friend in such
a dither. She tried to guess, but she was not of a romantic
nature, so the signs escaped her.

"Well?" she asked, her head cocked to one side like an
inquisitive pup.

"Well, I've had a marriage proposal!" Jessica almost fell
off her chair. How very busy she must have been not to have
noticed her friend's involvement with a gentleman.

"Oh, Rosina, who?" she'd have given the world to have
been able to guess.

"I knew you'd be surprised, me in my condition and all.
But, of course, the gentleman knows," she looked shyly down
at her protruding abdomen. "And he's quite pleased. Said
he's always wanted children. Isn't that something?"

It was Jessica's turn to near burst. "Who?" she asked again.

"I thought you might have guessed, Jesse. It's Mr. Menzies. He's, well, he's been so specially nice to me and all. And I am fond of him. And I think he'd make a good husband and father. And, what I wanted to ask of you, should I marry him when I don't feel the same way as I did with Sam?" Her lovely eyes shone with excitement, but, in the very deepest part of them, there was a sadness that would probably haunt her forever. She was right to question marrying Mr. Menzies, thought Jessica. If Sam would always be between them, it would not be fair to this kind and generous man. She did not know what advice to give the girl. She had so little experience to call upon when it came to affairs of the heart.

She knew that she had to say something, as Rosina obviously set such store by her opinion.

"I'd say yes, Rosina." She was immediately glad that she'd said that, as Rosina exploded into happy tears and put her arms about Jesse and gave her a big squeeze.

"Oh, thank you, thank you," she murmured over and over. Jessica sat there with Rosina in her arms, praying that she'd said the right thing.

It was a warm spring morning when Rosina and Jessica, bride and bridesmaid, headed for the little church on the hill, where, once again, Rosina would say her marriage vows. The young women were in exceptionally high spirits, as they tucked their skirts about them in the carriage driven by Doctor Evans, who had agreed to 'give the bride away'. There were suggestive comments made about Rosina's un-bride-like condition and the girls giggled as Rosina patted her round tummy.

So often marriages were precipitated by impending births, but, generally, the brides still wore an air of innocence. Not so Rosina! She was long past being able to hide the fact that she was expecting a baby, and soon! And there'd been no attempt to disguise the fact as she'd dressed for the occasion, her soft yellow-beige outfit hanging loosely below her bulging abdomen. The colour of her dress was remarkably like her hair and, as the soft spring sun danced off her, Jessica could not help but admire her loveliness. Rosina was everything that the Englishwoman was not — small, dainty, despite her protruding tummy, soft and very feminine. Jessica, on the other hand, was tall, big boned, dark and rather austere looking. She had no illusions about her appearance and had always been content with the adjective 'handsome'. Abigail Windsor had been 'handsome' in her youth, and that was quite good enough for her granddaughter.

"How very unsporting of you, Doctor Evans, to have the two most attractive young ladies in Cobalt all to yourself," teased George Dickerson as he helped the women down from the carriage at the front of the church. He offered his arm to Jessica, the doctor took Rosina's and they entered the church. Mr. Dickerson helped the ladies with their wraps and then hurried away as he was to be Gus Menzies' best man.

There were only a handful of people sitting in the front pews as Jessica, followed by Doctor Evans and Rosina, strode quietly down the aisle. Mr. Dickerson and Mr. Menzies were waiting at the altar and, for a fleeting moment, Jessica fantasized that it was her wedding to George Dickerson and she flushed to the roots of her hair at the thought. When she looked into Mr. Dickerson's eyes, she was sure that he'd read her thoughts and she quickly turned away, her heart beating heavily in her chest. She could feel him standing close to her, hear his breathing and had difficulty with her own. Very little of the marriage vows filtered through the dreamlike daze that Mr. Dickerson's disconcerting presence created and Jessica was quite relieved when she realized that it was over.

She turned abruptly to follow the bride and groom down the aisle. George Dickerson took her arm and pulled her closer to him. "We're supposed to leave together," he whispered, and, of course, he was right. So they walked, arm in arm, down the aisle, Mr. Dickerson enjoying himself far more than Jessica thought he should and Jessica herself far less than Mr. Dickerson had hoped that she would.

The party that followed was at the Prospect Hotel. A portion of the dining room had been cordoned off — reserved for the 'Menzies group'. It's often imagined that certain thoughts are best left unsaid, and sometimes it's true, and often times it's not. The similarities between this wedding reception and the one less than a year ago, floated about the table like too-full balloons, ready to burst when someone spoke too loudly, or laughed too shrilly. So they didn't. The party took a quiet, nervous tone, so the men did what Northern men do so well: they got very drunk.

"You ought to be ashamed of yourself, George Dickerson," chastised Jessica in her most English voice, speaking to the inebriated gentlemen as a whole, really. "And you, Mr. Menzies!" she glared across the table at the groom, but her withering look was wasted on Rosina's new husband, who's eyes were becoming slits through which he stared adoringly at his bride. Rosina, much to her friend's chagrin, did not seem in the least put out by the men's behaviour. Jessica was disappointed and wished that the doctor had stayed, but he'd been called away on a case.

Remembering the awkward incident at Christmas, Jessica was determined not to drink and her abstinence seemed to irritate Mr. Dickerson. With a thick tongue, he tried to explain to her that she was safe with him and his convoluted logic escaped her. She was relieved when the doctor returned, but her pleasure at seeing the sober gent quickly soured as he seemed determined to make up for lost drinking time by indulging in two drinks to everybody's one.

When the party broke up, Jessica found herself being escorted back to Mrs. Carson's by Doctor Evans and Mr. Dickerson, one on either side of her and more than once she teetered under their lopsided weights.

As luck would have it, Mrs. Pearce and several of her old cronies were walking towards them as they went past the Post Office. Doctor Evans, in an extremely extravagant gesture, doffed his hat and bowed to the ladies. The sudden release of his weight caused Jessica to stumble and Mr. Dickerson's weight shifted at that precise moment, causing the two of them to topple.

"Well, I never!" exclaimed Mrs. Pearce as she picked her way around the couple, who were intertwined about one another in the mud.

Dr. Evans, unable to resist, smiled a lecherous smile at her and said, "Obviously!" and then burst into raucous laughter as the ladies beat a hasty retreat. He then sat down on the ground beside Mr. Dickerson, pulled a flask from his coat pocket, took a long draught and passed it to Mr. Dickerson.

"Ladies first," Mr. Dickerson said, and was quick to pull the flask back when Jessica took a swing at it. "Tut, tut, Mish Baxter," he cautioned with a boyish grin and he took a long swig of the liquor.

A soft rain had begun to fall, adding to Jessica's misery. Her lovely new hat had gone flying in the melee and her hair had come out of its chignon. It hung damp and stringy about her shoulders, giving her an almost child-like appearance.

Mr. Dickerson was not too drunk to notice the change and he stared, the way only a child or a tipsy person might - mouth ajar, eyes opened wide, head cocked, admiration written all over his face. She gave him her very blackest look, but he was not to be put aside.

Quite the contrary! Without taking his eyes off her, he said, more to Jessica than his friend, "You know, Doc, I'm going to marry this black-eyed woman some day!"

"Not very damned likely," was her sharp retort and she was quickly sorry that she'd resorted to such profanity, as it brought even wider smiles from her companions.

"Me thinks the lady disagrees, most profanely," giggled the doctor and with that, Jessica managed to free herself of her muddy trap, stagger to her feet and head home. Never had she been so totally mortified in her entire life. She'd be a long time forgiving those two, she vowed as she wavered up the stairs at Mrs. Carson's, the mud on her skirts making the way difficult.

"Damn, damn, damn," she muttered.

10

Doctor Fairley's Visit

Rosina settled into married life and Jessica, once again, learned to appreciate her own company.

She soon forgave Doctor Evans his disgraceful behaviour the afternoon of the wedding, but remained cool towards Mr. Dickerson. She told herself that the good doctor had been led astray by his less than perfect friend, but, in her deepest heart, she knew that one was as bad as the other — or as good.

"I think my time is very close," Rosina said to Jessica one day. She'd come over on the nurse's day off for a visit, and for advice. "I'm not scared, really, but I guess I'd just sort of like you to tell me that everything's going to be all right," she looked shyly at her friend.

"Everything is going to be all right," echoed Jessica, and they both laughed.

"I really mean it, Rosina. The doctor's here and he's not going anywhere for several weeks, so . . . " she put her arm about her friend's narrow shoulders and squeezed. "We'll both be here."

"I was hoping you'd say that. You see, ever since you birthed that half-breed, Mr. Menzies has had so much respect for your birthing knowledge. I think he'd be pleased if you were there with Doctor Evans." They both knew that she meant, 'you were with me'.

"I promise, Rosina. I promise."

It was only eight days later that Jessica was called upon to fulfill that promise. Rosina Hobson Menzies gave birth to

a seven and one half pound baby girl whom she named Mary,
after her mother.

"Much obliged," murmured Mr. Menzies, as he shook
first the doctor's hand and then Jessica's, after the delivery.
It was most uncommon for women to come to the hospital,
usually they chose to deliver in the privacy of their own
home, but Gus Menzies had insisted and tiny Mary Menzies
was born in Cobalt Hospital, making her a very special little
girl indeed!

Gus Menzies, upon receiving a "yes" to his proposal, had
begun building a house for his new family, and, until it was
finished, they were living in rooms behind the laundry. The
odour of soap, bleach and blueing was ever-present and they
looked forward to the day when their house would be finished.

"You know, Jesse, he's really quite a comfortable man,"
Rosina was speaking of her husband's finances, not his disposition, although she admitted that the word did describe his
disposition as well. "I'm really very lucky, Jesse, when you
think of it."

"So is he," replied the loyal Jessica.

"Oh, of course you'd say that. But I'm not much of a
bargain. And, Mary, well, he treats her like his own, and, you
know, I just can't do anything wrong. It would be right easy
to get spoiled, it would."

Jessica could only assume that Rosina was so accustomed to being ill-treated, first by her family and then by
fate, that she imagined herself to be better off now than she
really was. Mr. Menzies was pleasant enough, but no great
prize in Jessica's estimation. But, as long as Rosina and
Mary were happy, that was all that mattered.

"You know, Jesse, we have a silver mine," whispered
Rosina.

Jessica was truly surprised. She knew that Gus
Menzies was involved in several businesses in town, but,
somehow, she'd never imagined him in the mining business.
And his wife had said 'mine', not just stake.

"Where, Rosina?" she inquired of her friend, who was
caressing the infant Mary in an effort to lull her back to sleep
after nursing.

"Oh, I don't rightly know. But it's sort of north and east of here, I think," she answered vaguely, her brow furrowed in thought. "Yes! I think he said it's over near Quebec. Fancy that, Miss Baxter. A silver mine. Why, we all might be rich some day." She tried to adopt a regal air and was so comical that both girls dissolved into laughter, waking the baby from her near-sleep. "Oops," giggled the young mother and they lapsed into silence while Rosina once again rocked the baby back to sleep.

Late one evening when Jessica was sitting at the hospital with an elderly gentleman who was dying of pneumonia, Doctor Evans approached her and asked, "How's old Fred doing, anyway?" Jessica simply shook her head. Her patient was ghostly white, thin and almost without respiration. When he did breath, his rasping could be heard throughout the tent and everyone moved about on quiet feet and spoke in hushed, church-like tones.

"It won't be long now, girl," the doctor observed as he felt for a pulse and opened one of the old man's eyes. "Not long." He then pulled a chair up beside Jessica, not offering to relieve her of her unhappy vigil, but willing to share it with her. She smiled her appreciation and then looked back, watching for the almost imperceptible rise and fall of the patient's bony chest.

"It's probably not the best time to talk of this, Jessica," he said. She always felt warm when Doctor Evans slipped and used the familiar when addressing her, "But it's not always easy to get a good gossip in during a busy day," he continued.

She glanced at him in the semi-darkness, and she could perceive an excited glint in his eye that was absent in his respectful tone of voice. She arched her eyebrows in question, still remaining silent in deference to the old man who was dying only inches away.

"I told you that I knew Doctor Fairley?" He waited for some response, and, not finding it, went on, "He's coming to Canada. Actually, he's probably here now. He's written and asked if he might come up here for a visit - wants to see what an outpost hospital looks like, and how we operate, and all that." He fell silent for a moment and Jessica was afraid that, in the quiet, he might hear her heart which had begun to thump quite loudly in her chest.

Fred Lane breathed another of his hoarse breaths and the rattle of death could be heard quite plainly now.

"No," remarked the doctor, very softly, "It won't be long now." He patted Jessica's hand and went to get the necessary papers to fill out upon the man's death.

There was a touch of unreality about the next hour. Jessica went through all of the motions necessary under the circumstances, but it was as though she had hired someone else to do the ghoulish chores as she, Jessica Baxter, moved gracefully aside, her mind filled with memories and an unnatural titillation at the thought of seeing Doctor Fairley once again. She watched herself as she bathed the corpse and put clean linens about him, but the sorrow was not there.

Her mind was back in England, standing in the cool, clean halls of the hospital, flirting with Doctor Fairley, and, despite the fact that she stopped in her reverie to remind herself that the doctor was married, she was unable to stem the blood-rush that she felt when she remembered.

"Well done, Miss Baxter, it's always such an unpleasant task," spoke Doctor Evans kindly. And then, "Are you all right?" He had just noticed her flushed cheeks.

"I'm just tired, sir," she answered, with total honesty, as she was suddenly emotionally exhausted.

"Well, off home now," he ordered and she was quick to obey.

"Pardon me, but it's Nurse Baxter, isn't it?" a voice from Jessica's past asked, just a few weeks later. She was sitting at a make-shift desk doing some paper work and she'd not noticed the approach of two men.

"Be calm!" she commanded her heart.

"Doctor Fairley, how very nice to see you again, Sir," she stood up and extended her hand. His warm and comfortable touch opened the floodgates of her memory. She smiled such a spectacular smile that even Doctor Evans was astonished.

"And what a pleasure to see you, Miss Baxter," Doctor Fairley responded enthusiastically.

They both turned to look at Doctor Evans who had coughed to gain attention. "I just knew that you two would be glad to see one another," he commented slyly.

Jessica felt some embarrassment, but, if Doctor Fairley did, it was not obvious in his manner.

"I'm certain you're quite busy here, Miss Baxter. I was wondering if you might do me the favour of having dinner with me this evening? Assuming, of course, that there's some decent place to dine in this town."

She smiled her agreement, but something in his manner had her on the defensive. She'd become quite proud of Cobalt in the short time she'd been there and she was in no mood for snide comments about its lack of social amenities.

It was agreed that Doctor Fairley would pick her up at Mrs. Carson's at 8:00 p.m., and they'd dine at the Prospect Hotel. Doctor Evans whisked his visitor away on a quick round of the hospital and they disappeared out of the front door.

Jessica approached her lodgings with mixed feelings. She was excited at the prospect of dining with Doctor Fairley. She could not understand or deny that. She was a bit uneasy because she was nervous that he might make disparaging remarks about her new home town, and there was a very slight element of guilt hovering over the other two emotions.

"Oh, bother," she thought. A nice hot meal, followed by a hot bath and a good book, would do her a great deal more good than that dinner engagement with Doctor Fairley.

She was seriously considering sending a note to the hotel with her regrets, when the front door to Mrs. Carson's flew open and George Dickerson stepped out.

"Good evening, Miss Baxter," he said, dripping with good humour. "I fancied that it was time for me to plead for your forgiveness." In a very theatrical gesture, he dropped to one knee and placed his hands in front of him in a prayer-like fashion.

Despite herself, she laughed, "Get up, Sir," she demanded, "You look ridiculous." Her words were stern, but her face bore traces of humour. He was a most engaging man, this George Dickerson.

"And, in order to win back whatever modicum of respect

and admiration that you might once have had for me, I'd like to take you to dinner and dazzle you with my knowledge of literature and stamp collecting." He had such utter confidence in himself that Jessica felt truly badly about having to refuse the invitation.

He was, after all, just a man, and his ego was a fragile thing. "I'd be pleased, sir, but I'm unable to this evening." The look of surprise on his face was embarrassing, and she had to remind herself that this very same man was responsible for the most embarrassing moment in her entire life.

"But, dear lady, I've already instructed Mrs. Carson not to set a place for you at dinner," he explained awkwardly.

"That was rather presumptuous of you, Mr. Dickerson. But, in actuality, you've done me a service, sir, as I am dining out this evening and was about to announce the same to Mrs. Carson." She sounded so formal that she was amused even herself.

She moved away, a bit angry with him for assuming she'd be so willing to share his company. He was both enchanting and aggravating at the same time and his presence always left her in a state of agitation.

"Are you supping with the Menzies?" he inquired.

"No," was her simple reply as she edged towards the doorway.

"Doctor Evans, I would expect?" he asked.

"No," she said and some perversity in her nature enjoyed his dilemma. "Just an old friend," she explained and left him standing there, with a silly look on his otherwise handsome face.

The nurse was not truly committed to her dinner date, so, forgetting her fatigue, she ascended the stairs to her room with renewed anticipation.

Only her best frock would do, and she hurriedly fetched it from the wardrobe and placed it near the lamp so that she might examine it for mud or other stains. There had been staff for this sort of thing in Jessica's former existence, and she was always a bit irked when she had to do it for herself. Mrs. Carson did her laundry for her, for a slight charge, but Jessica was responsible for the heavier garments and her boots, shoes and slippers. Raising the hemline of her dresses had certainly improved the mud situation, but splatters often reached well above her skirtline.

After some rigorous brushing, she was satisfied that the outfit was as neat as she was able to get it, and she turned her attention to washing herself and selecting clean underthings, as she usually felt quite grimy after a day spent at the hospital.

It was spring and certainly a great deal warmer than it had been in the previous months, but it was not warm enough for summer underthings. She selected woolen stockings which she fastened to garters that hung from a woolen vest. She wore soft woolen bloomers and a pretty cotton petticoat. Nothing that she owned seemed quite as white as she was accustomed to, but she was reluctant to complain to Mrs. Carson, so she put up with the untrue whiteness of her personal belongings. Someday she would have the nerve to send her things to Mr. Chow's, but just now, it simply wasn't worth irritating her landlady.

She took a brush out of her travelling bag and applied it to her boots, adding a small bit of polish until they shone.

Jessica's hair was long, thick and lustrous, and on special occasions, she chose to wear it high on her head in a fashionable roll. Carefully, she brushed it out of the chignon and placed the forms upon her head, like a crown, around which she would roll her hair, achieving the effect that she wished. The shorter, finer hairs about her temples and ears had a natural curl to them and by letting them remain short, Jessica was able to create a softness about her face that she needed to offset her customary black-eyed, austere look. Once again, standing in front of the oval mirror above her washstand, in the subdued lighting of her oil lamp, she reminded herself that she would never be 'pretty', but must settle for striking, attractive or handsome.

Just before exiting the room to await Doctor Fairley in the parlour, she applied a bit of scent to her wrists and her handkerchief. It was lavender, and helped to re-enforce the softness that she was trying to create.

George Dickerson had managed to finagle a dinner invitation from Mrs. Carson, probably the portion originally intended for Jessica, and he was sitting with the other boarders, having a pipe and a gossip in the parlour. It would be impossible to avoid him, so she entered the room and sat on the settee, waiting for the door bell.

"Looking splendid, Ma'am," murmured Mr. Simmons as he sat on a chair next to the settee. He was a shy man, but he obviously couldn't help but sneak glances at Jessica, glances that registered admiration.

"Thank you, Sir," she replied, politely, and she stole a glance at Mr. Dickerson, who appeared to be concentrating on his pipe. When he did look up, Jessica caught his eye, and there was anger there, or perhaps jealousy.

She was not enjoying his discomfort any more and hoped that the door bell would ring immediately. And, when it didn't, on the pretext that she'd forgotten her gloves, she left the parlour and went back to her own room, where she stood, just inside the door, until she heard the door bell. As she stood there in the darkness, she could feel her own pulse throbbing in her neck. Her face was warm and each heartbeat made her more uncomfortable. Was it Mr. Dickerson? Or was it the prospect of dinner in the company of a man with whom she had once fantasized that she was in love? Her heart was like a stranger to her, she knew so little of it.

"How marvelous you look, Miss Baxter," exclaimed the good doctor when Jessica re-entered the parlour. Mr. Dickerson was gone, much to her relief.

"Thank you, Sir," she acknowledged, and they left the room to enter the small foyer together. The doctor helped Jessica on with her coat, and in doing so, seemed to let his hands rest upon her shoulders a bit longer than she thought necessary. It was not unpleasant, but it bothered her, and she instinctively pulled away. The gesture did not go unnoticed.

"Oh. You have a carriage, Sir," she remarked when she saw Mr. Menzies poised at the end of the walkway. Gus Menzies, among his many other ventures, operated a carriage rental, and could often be seen driving one of his vehicles himself, when there was not sufficient staff to accommodate his sometimes busy trade. He tipped his hat to Jessica, but did not speak.

"I simply could not imagine walking about this muddy town, Miss Baxter. I really don't know how you put up with it." Jessica could not remember this trait of Doctor Fairley's but then she'd never seen him out of his own comfortable hospital circle. He seemed a bit of a pompous fellow, but, Jessica reasoned, so would her brother Charles in a similar situation. And, quite honestly, they could not be blamed, for she recalled her own horror at conditions when she first arrived.

"It's not really so dreadful, Sir, once you get used to it. And, of course, this is the muddy season. We've only just gotten rid of our snow. It's sure to dry up . . . come summer." She said this with some trepidation.

It took only minutes to get to the Prospect Hotel, and soon they were sitting comfortably in the diningroom. Obviously, the doctor had arranged things in advance, as the manager was there to greet them, and a table was set with some extra care and style. The menu wasn't extensive, so they placed their orders quickly. Wine was delivered in an ice-filled bucket, and a sense of celebration encircled their table.

"I must confess, outright, Miss Baxter, that my reasons for asking you to dinner are twofold," began the doctor, in an extremely secretive tone. Jessica instinctively looked about to see whose ears he might be trying to keep this conversation from. It was then that she spotted Mr. Dickerson, sitting in a corner. His back was to her, but the bearing was unmistakably his. She was both flattered and angry that he should be there, assuming he was there to spy on her. Doctor Fairley must have noticed something in her eyes, as he looked over his shoulder, and seeing nothing untoward, asked, "Is there something the matter? You look as though you'd seen a ghost."

"No, no sir, everything is fine. I just thought that I knew someone who just left, but I think I must have been wrong," she lied. She turned her attention fully to him, determined to not let anything interfere with this visit. "I'm fine, sir, you were saying . . .?"

"I was saying that my reasons for asking you to dinner

were twofold," he repeated. "Firstly, I should like to tell you of your mother, and her last days." He looked softly at the girl, who'd given an involuntary shudder at the mention of her mother. "It's important that you understand, Miss Baxter, that I'm in complete agreement with you in your decision not to go back to England for her final days. It would have been quite pointless, as she knew no one. From what I gather from Doctor Evans, your time was much better spent here, in the, ahem, wilderness, of Canada than it would have been standing beside the sickbed of one whose mind was, well, so far gone." He was trying to set her mind at ease, that was apparent, but he was not being totally successful. She wondered if it was his manner, or if she was destined to feel this way whenever she thought about her decision. She was still convinced that she did the right thing, but, would she ever be free of the niggling little guilts?

"I instructed the hospital not to notify you, but to get in touch with your brother, but, somehow, messages got crossed and you were sent for. Perhaps it was your brother, I don't know, but we were told to expect you, and when you didn't arrive, I was concerned. I wrote to Doctor Evans and he assured me that you were well, and, that was quite enough for me." He had placed a warm soft hand over hers, and she felt a rush of kindness towards him. So often the messenger was guilty of the message — she must remember not to fall into that sort of judgment again.

"Thank you for understanding, Sir," and, anxious to get off the topic, she asked, "You said twofold, Sir?"

"Yes, I did. Well, Miss Baxter, I've been offered an excellent position with the General Hospital in Toronto. I very nearly didn't consider it, what with my wife's ill health and all. But, it was such a great opportunity and, well, I must confess, I thought of you when I made my decision. I'd like to take you away from all of this." He swung his arms about him as if taking in all of the town. "I would be needing a good nurse, no, an excellent nurse, by my side, and it's been reported to me that the nurses trained in England are the best in the world." He beamed at her, probably expecting some show of embarrassment at his compliments. But it was not there. Jessica knew that she was a good nurse. She was not overtly proud, but in her heart, she knew that her schooling was superior to that of the other nurses. What did bother her though, was that the doctor seemed to think that she required a 'saviour' — that she was simply whiling away her time here in this primitive town, waiting for someone, some man, to come and save her. She was extremely independent. She could, and did, take care of herself, and, although the prospect of working in a big city hospital once again had its appeal, she would only go if she felt good about it. She was not going to feed this man's ego by allowing him to think that he was doing her some great favour by offering her a position next to him. Quite the contrary, she'd be doing him a favour! That is, if she went. And she had absolutely no idea if she would go or not.

Doctor Evans hovered about Jessica in much the manner of a child who doesn't let the cookie jar out of sight if there's the slightest chance that someone might come along and open it. He fussed about over his book work, checked the drug cabinet, several times in fact, and just manufactured one chore after another, anything to keep him close to the nurse, lest she might want to tell him of her dinner date of the previous evening.

If she did notice his rather peculiar behaviour, she paid no heed as she went about her daily routine. It finally became too much for the doctor and he descended upon the 'cookie jar' like a hungry boy. "You're most annoying, Miss Baxter," he began abruptly. She was startled into looking up quickly at him, quickly enough to catch the trace of humour about the corners of his mouth, which instantly turned into a frown.

"What's that, Sir?" she asked innocently.

"You bloody well know what I mean," and, of course, she did. It was apparent during the conversation of the night before that Doctor Fairley had spoken to Doctor Evans about the possibility of Jessica moving to Toronto to take up the most attractive position at his side. It was most unkind of her to keep Doctor Evans on tenterhooks.

"Oh, yes ... Doctor Fairley ... right?" she knew that she

was right.

"Of course, Doctor Fairley," he bellowed, and there was a very slight tinge of bad humour in his tone now.

"You'd like to know if I'm going to Toronto with him?" she asked.

"'You'd like to know if I'm going to Toronto with him?'" he mimicked and now it was her turn for a bout of bad humour.

"You needn't be so sarcastic, Sir!" she retorted and was embarrassed when Nurse Gloria turned to look at her. She hadn't realized that their conversation had become so loud.

He appeared contrite. "I'm sorry, Miss Baxter, it's not fair of me —" he was going to go on, but Jessica interrupted.

"No, Sir, I'm the one who should be saying I'm sorry. It was rather childish of me not to talk this all out with you immediately"

"But I had no right to yell at you, or to be so rude . . ."

"No, Sir, it is not your fault," she tried again to apologize.

"No, Miss Baxter, I insist . . ."

Suddenly they realized what a ridiculous conversation this had become with each party insisting on being more guilty than the other.

"I'm certain that I'm more sorry than you," Doctor Evans said most officiously.

"Yes, of course, Sir," she mock-bowed her acquiescence, and they reached out and touched one another in an unusual display of affection.

"We'll order tea and have this out," Doctor Evans announced and turned to instruct one of the orderlies to fetch tea.

"I'm glad, Sir, because I'm in serious need of someone to talk with," Jessica began as they sat side by side on a nearby bench. "I was thinking of going to Rosina, but heaven knows she has her hands full with young Mary, and she doesn't need my problems just now." She sighed a deep sigh and he reached out and took her hand in a comforting gesture.

"My, my, to be so young," now he sighed a weary sigh, "And to have so many opportunities stretching out before you." He had a lot of concern in his voice and a very slight touch of envy.

Jessica detected the envy and inquired, "You'd go,

wouldn't you, Sir?"

"Perhaps," he said slowly, "Perhaps I might have, years ago, but now, well, now you couldn't pry me out of this north country with a stick of dynamite. I like it here. I like the people, the seasons, the fresh air." He paused and added quietly, "And, to be perfectly honest, Jessica, I like being a big fish in a little pond." He glanced at her, and she nodded her head in understanding.

"Now, Doctor Fairley, while he's young and clever, he may just become an important man in that big city hospital, but he may also just become another staff member - just one more doctor amongst all of those others. Now, I'm not saying that there's anything wrong with that - not at all, but, well, up here, I'm The Doctor, The Only One. I must say, I rather enjoy that." His voice became even softer. "It helps to make up for some of the other things in life that I may have missed."

They were silent for the next few moments. The orderly brought the tea and set it on a small bedside table that he wheeled over for them.

Abigail Windsor's elaborate tea trolley came to Jessica's mind as clearly as though she were sitting at Fairview. The hospital's thick, sturdy white cups and saucers became fine bone china, and, in place of the few biscuits, she envisioned trays laden with the fruits and cakes that Martha so enjoyed tempting her with. She smiled a winsome smile, her black eyes all shiny and soft.

"Now, it's your turn," remarked her companion, his voice a bit hoarse with emotion.

She was startled back to reality and thick porcelain and dried biscuits. She looked at him blankly for a second before she was able to speak. "Excuse me, sir, I was just remembering . . ." She poured the tea and, setting a napkin on her lap, took one of the sweet, hard cookies. She wanted to ask him about his last statement, wanted to know just what he thought he might have missed, but something in his demeanour suggested that she'd be best to leave things as they were. Someday, he'd confide in her, she was certain of that, but now, he was right, it was her turn.

"I must admit, Sir, that I'm considering Doctor Fairley's offer. Why, what nurse wouldn't? The city is quite lovely, I enjoyed what I saw of it before I came up here. And, even in England, I'd heard of the Toronto General Hospital, so it would be quite a thrill to be a part of it. Especially to be a 'special' nurse to a 'special' doctor." She stopped to see if he had reacted to any of this. He sat silent, not looking at her but staring at some point in the middle distance, his expression betraying nothing of what was going on inside.

She brushed crumbs from her skirt, slowly, deliberately, stalling, hoping for some comment from the doctor, but none was forthcoming.

"Doctor Fairley has given me two weeks to decide. He is coming back then, and, I assume, expects me to return to Toronto with him." It had all sounded so much more exciting in the diningroom of the Prospect Hotel. Perhaps it had been the wine, or perhaps Doctor Fairley's attractive presence, but here, in the dingy little tent hospital, perched on a narrow pine bench with a man she respected above all others, it sounded less like an opportunity and more and more like a sentence.

How can she possibly prefer to stay here, here in this dismal frontier town, where her petticoats are never quite white, where she has to tote water every time that she wants to bathe, where the cold weather sets in in October and stays until May, where the snow drifts rise halfway up the sides of the houses and the hospital is a mere tent? It is ridiculous. There is no choice. She must go to Toronto, to a well ordered, civilized existence to which she has been accustomed, where she may draw a bath whenever she chooses, where the weather is much warmer and where hospitals have solid walls and roofs.

Indeed, there really was no choice, and yet, every time that she tried to conjure up a picture of how it would be, the long sparkling white corridors of the Toronto General Hospital, her focus came back to the dimly lit room in which she was currently sitting and a warmth emanated from the stained brown walls that drew her like a magnet to the place. The smoky odour that once had offended her nostrils was like an opiate now, dulling her senses to the squalid conditions, lulling her into the security that came with the familiar.

Damnation! It was such an awesome decision, one she simply did not feel capable of making without advice.

"Sir," she looked directly at Doctor Evans, who seemed still to be in the distance somewhere. "Help me, Sir," she spoke with a desperate tone.

He finally turned. "Jessica, I'm not able to be fair in this concern. I've too much to lose and I'm not man enough to hand a treasure such as yourself over to another doctor. You'll have to seek other counsel. You must forgive me, my dear, but I'll not betray myself and send you happily on your way. Not so big a fool am I. No sir." He smiled a tight lipped smile and patted her hand, got up and left.

She never felt so alone in her entire life!

When Jessica left the hospital that evening, she was amazed at how warm the weather had become. There was a subtle breeze blowing that tickled the tiny hairs about her face. The air smelled clean, and there was a touch of newness about it. The girl realized that if she left now, she'd never get to see the summer of the north. Summer was spoken about in reverend tones by one and all during the long, cold winter. Token mention was given to the vicious insects that were a constant threat, but that was all. Everything else said about summer was good. She'd miss that. So deep in her imagining was she that she nearly fell into George Dickerson's arms as she turned the corner. Much like the proverbial bad penny, he seemed to turn up everywhere.

"Whoa," he exclaimed. "Such a hurry!"

"Sorry, Sir, I guess I wasn't paying much attention," she apologized.

"No matter, no damage done," he smiled, "But perhaps you need an escort the rest of the way home?" He extended his arm in a gentleman-like fashion and the tired girl took it.

"Thank you, Sir," she murmured, and they walked a few minutes in silence.

"You seem totally preoccupied, Miss Baxter. Problems?" he inquired.

"Not really problems, Mr. Dickerson, just . . . well, decisions."

"Anything that I might help you with?" her companion

asked of her.

Her dilemma was so great that she managed to forget some of the previous encounters with this unusual man, and she began to confide in him.

She told him of Doctor Fairley's visit, of the invitation to be a big city hospital nurse, and also of her reluctance to leave the Cobalt Hospital and of her own perplexity over her indecision.

"It should be so very easy. The obvious choice is surely the right one, but I'm having difficulty taking that course." They were sitting on the steps of Mrs. Carson's boarding house now, Mr. Dickerson having taken his jacket off and placed it on the dusty stair for Jessica to sit upon. He'd remained silent throughout her soliloquy, but his expression indicated that he was weighing her every word.

She went on to tell him of Doctor Evans' conversation, and she wondered out loud if she liked being the Best Nurse in Cobalt and that was why she was hesitating to go to Toronto where she'd be one of so many others. She confessed that she had enjoyed the respect and admiration that had followed the mining mishap at Trueway, and it bothered her that it might be just false pride that kept her there.

Finally, exhausted, she turned to her audience of one and was astonished at the look in his eyes. There was a softness that she'd seen parents bestow upon their children, a sort of kind protection there that made her feel instantly more comfortable. And yet, she reasoned, why should she place such an importance on a mere look. After all, he'd proven himself to be quite an actor.

Suddenly she rose, intending to go indoors, to the security of her room where she'd call upon her own resources to settle this matter.

"Please don't go," Mr. Dickerson asked, taking her by the hand and pulling her gently back to her seat on the stairs.

When she was once again seated, he continued, "You're going to think these words strange coming from me and you've every right to, considering my past performance," he grinned at her and she couldn't help but smile back.

"There's a specialness about this north country, Miss

Baxter, that I've not seen anywhere else. The California Gold Rush has been much ballyhooed and romanticized, as has the Klondike business, but here, in our area, there are untold riches begging to be wrested from the ground. Only special people can do that. Only very special people can carve out an existence from this hard Canadian Shield, and I, for one, want to be a part of that group." He spoke with a touch of pride. "Toronto's nice. It's safe. It's clean and it's well ordered. One could live a very, well, decent life there, I'm sure — but that's not for me. I want to be part of the growth of this area. And, somehow, I had imagined that you wanted the same thing." He was looking deep into her black eyes now and she was unable to turn away.

"I watched you with Jeannie Peters and her baby and was impressed. I saw you shorten your skirts even when the townswomen judged you badly. I've seen that specialness in you in the way you handle your job and the people around you. You are the kind of woman the North Country needs, to bring brave sons into the world. Please don't throw that opportunity away for a comfortable position in the city. There are many more opportunities for greatness here." She smiled, remembering the crowd that had greeted her after the successful blood transfusion at the Trueway Mine.

"You know it's true, don't you?" he asked, and she nodded.

"Well, then you'll stay?" his tone was not an assured tone — there was a fair bit of pleading to it.

"I still must think of this some more, Mr. Dickerson, but I truly do appreciate your sharing this with me. It's always good to get an unbiased opinion." She smiled her gratitude.

"But mine is not really an unbiased opinion, my dear lady, not by a long shot." They were standing now, and he bent forward as though he was about to kiss her. But instead, he moved a strand of hair that had fallen across her cheek and let his fingers touch her face for a brief moment.

"Not by a long shot," he repeated, tipped his hat, and strolled away.

11

The River

The next few weeks dragged ever so slowly for Jessica and the townspeople. Very warm weather had settled suddenly upon the North and no one was quite prepared for it. There'd been something enervating about the coldness of winter that floated away on the warm spring breeze and one and all suffered a kind of spring fever.

Jessica's fever was complicated by her decision to stay in Cobalt, and her doubts about that decision. She'd wired Doctor Fairley, but there had been no reply, and she wasn't certain as to how to interpret his silence.

"Beaver castors," Mrs. Carson said one day at breakfast after looking about the table at her group of lethargic boarders. "That's what the lot of you need — beaver castors. Works every time, I guarantee it!" And if her cheerful and energetic presence was any indication as to the effectiveness of her prescription, it was certainly something worth looking into.

"Doctor Evans, whatever are beaver castors?" asked Jessica of the man.

He chuckled and asked her, "You in need of a spring tonic, Miss Baxter?"

She nodded, "I guess so. I"m having the devil's own time getting things done recently, and I really can't imagine why."

"Well, my dear, there's nothing unusual about that. It's a common Northern ailment called spring fever, and I would imagine that you've never experienced it before. People raised in more temperate climates, such as the south of England, don't have to contend with the drastic season changes that we have here. The further north you go, the worse it is. But," he patted her back as he added, "Doctor Evans has a magic elixir that is guaranteed to lift your spirits and your energies." He led her to his desk from which he produced a bottle reminiscent of a whisky bottle. When she frowned, he explained, "No, it's not liquor, or at least, not in the usual sense of the word, but there is alcohol in it, I suppose just to make it palatable."

He took the cork off and passed it beneath her nose. She shuddered, and he laughed. "You really ought to try it, Miss Baxter. Best tonic I've been able to find," and he massaged the bottle in a loving manner.

Very timidly she took a sip and almost spat it out. "That's dreadful," she complained.

"No more dreadful than walking about in a tired stupor, I might venture to guess," he defended his medication.

He was right of course, so she took a larger swallow and felt it burn its way down her throat.

"I'll get a small bottle made up for you to take home," he offered, and she thanked him.

That evening, she dragged herself though the warm, dusty streets and up the stairs of Mrs. Carson's. She'd lost her appetite, so made her apologies about dinner and went off to her room. It was bath night, and she'd already made arrangements with Hazel to help fetch water, so she pulled the tub out of its corner and began to get everything ready. When she was certain that the evening meal was over, she began her trips up and down the stairs with the hot water, each step becoming more and more tiresome. She reasoned that a good taste of tonic might help, so she took a swig and imagined that she felt a bit better. Several trips later, she took another draught and she did feel better. By the time she had her tub full, she was feeling quite well indeed.

She locked her door, disrobed and stepped into the tub of water which she'd scented with lavender.

The hot water and the heady odour worked together to cause her senses to tingle. And, coupled together with several ounces of the tonic, which, as it turned out, was about 70 percent alcohol, Miss Baxter was in a very good mood indeed.

Forgetting that she was in a house that she shared with many others, she began to sing. Jessica Baxter did not have a good singing voice. Quite the contrary, her voice was too low for a female singer and too high for a male. But she made up for her lack of talent with her enthusiasm. She sang little girl songs that she'd learned in boarding school, and she sang hymns, and she sang silly risque songs that she'd heard her brother Charles sing, all the while sipping on the tonic.

Jessica Baxter was tipsy.

And it was a most becoming condition on her. Her olive skin took on a rosy tone that glowed. Her jet black eyes widened and shone as never before. The little hairs about her face and ears curled in a most engaging fashion.

Her singing voice improved as she lost her inhibitions, and she was in the middle of a ditty when there was a loud knocking at her door. At first, she did not hear it and went on with her singing.

"Miss Baxter, are you all right?" a voice penetrated the steam that rose about her like a London fog.

She sat up and instinctively covered herself, even though she knew that the door was locked.

"Yes," she managed, as she stood up, a towel draped about her form. "Yes, I'm fine."

"You have a visitor, Miss Baxter," Mrs. Carson said. "Doctor Fairley is here, and he'd like to see you," the woman was shouting so Jessica unlatched the door and opened it a crack. Mrs. Carson's eyes flew open at the sight of her boarder clothed only in a towel. "He's ... he's ..." she stuttered and finally found her tongue. "He's waiting in the parlour. Should I ask him to come back another time?"

"That won't be necessary, Mrs. Carson, I'll see him shortly." She hiccoughed and put her hand to her mouth. "Please tell him I'll be down in ten minutes, thank you," she spoke deliberately, elaborately.

"Very well, Miss Baxter," but her face indicated that it was, in truth, not very well at all.

Jessica closed the door in her face before anything else was said. "Doctor Fairley," she murmured to herself. "Good old Doctor Fairley," and she went about dressing herself.

It was about fifteen minutes later that Jessica descended the stairs. She floated into the parlour and Doctor Fairley rose to greet her. She had no way of knowing what effect her appearance had on the poor man. He'd come to beg her to go back to Toronto with him, as his nurse, but suddenly the vision of Jessica made his head spin. She was no longer Nurse Baxter, all clad in white and cold looking. She stood in front of him radiating warmth and beauty. And she was totally unaware of it, which seemed to add to her mystique. Her rosy cheeks had not been put there by the cold wind, but came from somewhere deep inside her. Her very dark eyes were now not just quite as wide as usual, but her lids moved slowly, sensually over them as she waited, smiling with a friendly smile. Her hair was disheveled and had the look of one who'd just risen from bed and it excited him. And the scent of her was most intoxicating.

Doctor Fairley was totally incapable of handling his feelings, so lost was he in her aura. "Miss Baxter," he spoke hoarsely. "Could we talk?" and he led her into the parlour which was occupied by several of the male boarders.

Jessica did not notice, but her appearance created quite a stir. Doctor Fairley noticed and, spying the door of Mrs. Carson's little office ajar, he led Jessica into it and closed the door behind.

"That's not necessary, sir," Jessica said, but not in an unpleasant tone, so the door stayed shut.

"Miss Baxter," began the smitten man. He was trying very hard to regain his composure, "I'm here because I chose to ignore your telegram," his voice drifted off as his eyes rested upon the top button of her bodice. It was not fastened, nor was the second and his eyes were rivetted there. Jessica looked down to see what he was staring at, but did not reason that it was simply an unfastened button or two.

"Are you all right, sir?" she asked innocently.

"No," he answered abruptly. "I'm not all right," and before she knew what was happening, he pulled her into his arms and kissed her. She struggled half-heartedly, as she was enjoying the embrace, her good sense having been dulled by the tonic and the lack of dinner.

"Jessica, you have to come to Toronto with me," he murmured into her ear in a lusty tone which frightened her.

She pulled away, the reality of it all descending upon her with a thud.

"Jessica, Jessica," Doctor Fairley's voice had a begging tone, and he refused to let her go, trying to kiss her again.

"Doctor Fairley, stop it!" she shouted, and just then the door flew open.

Before she could say anything, a strong male arm came between her and Doctor Fairley, freeing her of his embrace. She backed up and saw that it was Mr. Simmons who'd come to her rescue. She went to scream as he raised his arm, but before she could utter a sound, Mr. Simmons' burly fist connected with the doctor's chin, and he went flying.

"Oh, my Lord!" exclaimed Jessica.

"You all right, Miss Baxter?" asked her saviour.

"Yes, yes, thank you, Mr. Simmons," was her reply. She stood staring at the unconscious form of Doctor Fairley on the floor, not certain what to do.

"I'll take care of him, Miss Baxter," Mr. Simmons offered. "You'd best go back to your room," his voice was tender.

"But perhaps I should look after him, he's hurt," she said feebly.

"I'll do that!" announced Mrs. Carson in an authoritative voice. "You go to your room." It was an order.

With one last look at the poor doctor who was just beginning to stir, Jessica went back to her room and slumped onto the bed. Her head was spinning, and she wasn't sure that she wouldn't be sick, so she lay very, very still, until sleep finally overcame her.

It was well before breakfast that Mrs. Carson was back at her door. Jessica's memory of the previous night was hazy so she was puzzled by her landlady's opening remark.

"I can't have that sort of behaviour going on here, Miss Baxter." And as though in answer to Jessica's inquisitive stare, she added, "Coming downstairs in that condition. Why, I run a respectable house here. I've never had a bit of trouble, and now, fisticuffs, and in my office. It's not decent."

"I'm sure you're right, Mrs. Carson," apologized Jessica.

She did not reason that she'd done anything wrong, but she sensed that an apology was expected.

"Well, as long as we understand one another, Miss Baxter," snorted Mrs. Carson. She was about to head back downstairs when she added, "I might tell you, that if it happens again, you'll have to go."

How incredibly embarrassing for Jessica Baxter. To be threatened with eviction from one such as Mrs. Carson. Abigail Windsor must be rolling over in her grave, thought the girl.

Her pride would not let her miss the breakfast table, and, of course, she was starving from the night before. It was quite a meal, with everyone sneaking glances at her and then quickly attending to their porridge. She would like to have thanked Mr. Simmons, but his face and neck were beet red, and he seemed to be avoiding her altogether. She hurried through the meal and was glad to be off to the hospital.

"Good morning, Miss Baxter," greeted Doctor Evans and his tone suggested that he knew all about the night before.

Jessica, tired of the treatment she was getting, said, "Out with it, Sir. Just what have you heard?"

His eyes twinkled. "Well, actually, I haven't heard . . . everything, but I have seen Doctor Fairley. He came to me because he thought that his jaw was broken." He was thoroughly enjoying himself.

"And?" she asked.

"And, there may be a slight fracture, but he's chosen to wait until he gets back to Toronto to have it looked at." He paused, waiting for an explanation, waiting for her side of the story. When she offered nothing, he asked, "Must have been some fight?" and still, she said nothing.

"Come on, Miss Baxter. You've got to tell me," he pleaded.

"I have to do nothing of the sort, Doctor Evans!" she retorted hotly and walked away. She turned after a few steps and added, "And you can keep your damned tonic to yourself, Sir!"

And so it was that Jessica Baxter was freed of the wonder of Toronto. No longer did she doubt that she'd made the right decision. She was to learn much later that Doctor

Fairley's wife was bedridden, and that he had taken a young nurse as his mistress.

And so it was, also, that she began to search for more suitable lodgings.

"I hear the Robinson's are moving back to North Bay and their house is going to be sold, or rented," Rosina mentioned to Jessica during a visit one afternoon a few weeks later.

Jessica had told Rosina of her decision to move from Mrs. Carson's Boarding House, but she had not told her friend her reasons, so she was quite surprised when the young woman added, "It's a shame to be leaving there though, after just one silly little incident." Her tone was not judgmental. She was simply stating an obvious fact.

Jessica turned to stare at Rosina, her black eyes flashing, "What silly little incident?" she asked in a tight voice.

Rosina flushed, and her hand flew to her mouth in an involuntary gesture. "Well, you know . . . that 'thing' with Doctor Fairley . . . and Mr. Simmons." Her voice trailed off and her embarrassment was so obvious that Jessica almost abandoned her questioning.

"Just what have you heard, Rosina?" she demanded in slow, measured tones.

Poor Rosina. Her hands fluttered. Her eyes shone. Her lips trembled. "I, well, just that Mr. Simmons had to defend you, and that, well, that he hit Doctor Fairley square on the jaw." As awkward as she felt in her position in this conversation, she could not help but giggle at the image of big, burly Mr. Simmons hitting the dapper, much smaller Doctor Fairley smack on his neatly trimmed beard. Her humour was contagious, and Jessica's mood turned quickly to one of mirth as she plunked herself down beside her friend.

"Oh, it was just too funny, Rosina," she exclaimed, when she found her voice. "You should have been there." She then sobered up. "But, of course, you weren't there, so how is it you know all of this?" Her tone betrayed no anger now, just simple curiosity.

"Well, Mrs. Carson is thick as thieves with Mr. Dickerson, but I guess you know that." When Jessica nodded, she continued, "Well, Mrs. Carson told him, and he told

Mr. Menzies and Mr. Menzies told me."

"I wonder how many other people Mr. Dickerson has told? And Mrs. Carson?" she pondered out loud. Mrs. Carson's part in all of this made it even clearer to the young woman that she must find other lodgings.

"I doubt anyone else, Jessica," Rosina said sincerely. "Mrs. Carson's not such a bad sort, really. And Mr. Menzies and Mr. Dickerson are very good friends, and Mr. Dickerson knows that we care about you, so it didn't seem too awful that he should tell us. I really doubt that he'll tell anyone else."

The young nurse wasn't sure that she was ready to accept her friend's opinion of just what George Dickerson might or might not say or do, so she shelved that topic and got back to the Robinson's place. "Is it just for sale or did I hear you say rent?"

"I overheard Mr. Menzies and Mr. Chalmers talking. He's from the bank," she said, by way of explaining Mr. Chalmers. "And it seems that the bank owns the house and that they would like to sell it, of course, but if they can't quickly, they'd be willing to rent it. Are you interested?"

"Well, I certainly can't afford to buy a house. I'm not even certain that I can afford to rent one on my own, but I guess I'd like to know," Jessica answered.

"I'll ask Mr. Menzies to look into it for you," promised Rosina, and her tone suggested that they were through with this conversation and she was anxious to move on to another.

"We're having Mary christened Sunday next, and Mr. Menzies and I wondered if you would be her Godmother?" Her pretty young face shone with excitement.

"Oh, Rosina, of course I would," spoke her friend with enthusiasm. "I'd be delighted. Proud!"

"Mr. Dickerson has consented to be Mary's Godfather," the young mother quickly explained, and Jessica was both surprised and pleased. She was surprised because she'd not thought of George Dickerson in that light before. And she was pleased because she'd not seen the gentleman lately, and she'd like to be given the opportunity to ask him about his recent venture into the gossip market.

The Robinson place proved to be too expensive for

Jessica to rent by herself, so she continued to keep her ears open for news of accommodation.

"You might want to take our lodgings when our new house is ready, Jesse," suggested Rosina a few days later. "Mr. Menzies thought of it. It's really not too bad, honestly, and he'd make the most agreeable landlord." She smiled with pride. Her affection and admiration for her husband grew daily. "We'd get along just fine, Jesse. I know it. As long as you didn't mind the smell of soap and bleach."

"It would be a most welcome change, Rosina," Jessica replied honestly. "The stench of mud, dog dirt, and horse manure after a rain is hard to get out of my nostrils sometimes. To say nothing of that open sewage ditch to the south of town." Both women grimaced and instinctively their hands went to their noses. "Soap and bleach would be a most welcome odour to come home to, I should think." The nurse began to see all sorts of positive aspects in her friend's offer.

"Might I come about and have a look?" she asked. "I've not paid that much attention to your flat as I've never considered living there."

"Oh yes, soon — now, anytime," exploded her friend.

Jessica decided that she should wait until Mary's christening, which was only days away.

The warmth of the early spring had given way to a rainy period the likes of which the Englishwoman had never before experienced. There were rivers rushing down alongside the roadways where there'd been not much more than a thin, moist trickle the day before. The roads became impassable mud holes, and bridges washed away. The hospital had a dampness to it that would not go away, no matter how many stoves were lit.

One particularly steamy day inside the tent, Doctor Evans rushed over to her and said in a breathless tone, "Miss Baxter, grab your bag, we have an emergency." She knew better than to ask questions so she hastened back to where her bag and wrap were and prepared to go.

"There's a wash-out over at Eddy Creek and some people have been hurt. One or two drowned, I believe," Doctor Evans explained as they hurried, on foot, out of the town to the north. A really good horse with an experienced rider just might have been able to navigate the mire that was the roadway, but a buggy or a wagon had no chance.

There was a small encampment on the edge of what was usually a pleasant, meandering creek, but now a raging river. Unfortunately, the encampment was on the other side and it was now apparent that they'd have to cross by boat. Jessica was a fairly strong swimmer and not generally afraid of water, but this muddy, brown, swirling mass looked so dangerous that her heart gave a little shudder. Boxes and other bits of debris sailed past, and it was easy to determine the speed of the flow by their motion.

"Ah, ha, here comes someone with a boat," exclaimed the doctor as he stood on a solid rock searching the far bank.

Sure enough, two men were headed towards them in a flimsy looking wooden row boat. They were rowing frantically in an effort not to be swept down stream. They threw a rope to the doctor, and he caught it with expertise.

"Jump in, Miss Baxter," he ordered as he steadied the boat as best he could under the circumstances.

She could feel her petticoats rip as she leapt over the rough side of the old boat and landed on her seat with such a thud that it shook her through and through. Doctor Evans was soon beside her, and the men, not speaking, worked feverishly to guide the boat back from whence it came. They missed their spot by several hundred feet, having drifted downstream when they had to turn their attentions from rowing to fighting off a big tree that threatened to steer them down the angry river.

They walked back through the thick underbrush to the encampment in silence as soon all their energies would be needed for the emergency that lay ahead.

Despite her raised hemline, Jessica's dresses became sodden as they walked through the long wet grass. The rest of her was constantly being sprayed by the soggy branches that sprang back at her as she followed her guide through the bush. She could hear the moist earth squish under her feet as she picked her way, carefully, occasionally slipping on a wet stone and giving her ankle a wrench.

She approached the encampment with mixed feelings. Incidents such as this brought memories of the more pleasant, more ordered existence to which she had been accustomed for so long, and she could not stop the wonder that crept into her brain, the wonder of what she was doing here, now, on this cold, wet, dangerous shore so far away from England. But as swiftly as these thoughts entered her consciousness, they were swept away to be supplanted by an incredible sense of purpose that had been lacking in that other life. The discomfort gave way to excitement - what would they encounter this time? What would they be able to do about it? Her heart raced and her personal comfort and safety became unimportant as they rounded a bend to be met by a bedraggled group of very frightened people.

"Over here, Doc," one man called, pointing to a lifeless form on the ground. Another grabbed Jessica's arm, pulling her over to the broken body of a young Indian woman. A quiet murmur rose from those present, each one trying to explain what had happened, but speaking in hushed tones in the presence of death.

"This fellow's dead," pronounced the doctor in a toneless voice and in the absence of a shroud, he covered the man's face with the canvas flap of a knapsack. He moved on to the next.

Jessica bent over the slowly breathing woman, who was conscious, but unbearably silent, as though she was afraid to open her mouth, lest she scream out in pain. Jessica had heard of the stoical Indian and reasoned that perhaps it would be some sign of weakness if the woman cried out, so she respected her muteness and asked of a man standing nearby, "What happened to her?"

"Pulled out into the water," he gestured hopelessly towards the water and then pointed to some rocks, "Banged up on those rocks pretty bad. We pulled her in, but she's broke, I guess."

She was 'broke'. Jessica could tell by the angle at which the woman lay that she had sustained broken bones, perhaps even a broken back. Dragging her out of the river certainly spared her from drowning, but there was a good chance that the movement had aggravated the situation and, in all likelihood, if the spinal column was broken, the spinal cord may also have been severed.

She leaned over, closer to the woman's face, to stare into eyes almost as dark as her own. There was pain and fear there, and a control that Jessica had not seen before in man nor beast. The woman was dying. It was in her eyes, but she was not going to cry out. Even as Jessica stared, the light began to fade and soon it was gone. The big black-brown eyes stared unblinking back at her and the spark that had once made this young woman unique in the universe, slipped slowly away as Jessica watched.

It was several minutes before the nurse could bring herself to close the lids and cover the brown face. She would remember that woman's strength for the rest of her life.

As if in a trance, Jessica moved about the camp, ably assisting wherever she was needed, but none of the sorrow of it all touched her. She had seen the worst in the death of the young Indian woman and the rest was anti-climactic.

In a matter of hours all that could be done was done. And it was dusk.

"We'll have to stay," remarked the doctor in a matter-of-fact tone. This was the English woman's first camping experience, and she knew not what to expect. The flimsy tents that had housed the small group of men, women, children and dogs had been washed away by the angry, swollen creek, and as she looked about, she could not imagine where they were expected to sleep.

She needn't have worried. Doctor Evans, working with the men, built a lean-to out of cedar and pine boughs under which they made a very long bed, also out of boughs. While the men laboured at this, the one remaining woman, with the help of a very young girl, made a fire and by the time darkness fell, the crackling fire was large and comforting.

"You'd best dry your clothes, Miss Baxter. You'll get a devil of a chill if you sleep in them," Doctor Evans suggested, and he began to take off his outer clothing. Soon, much to Jessica's surprise, he stood beside her at the fire in just his underwear. The rest of his clothing was placed up on sticks so that it was close to the fire. Steam rose up from his heavy trousers in mute testimony that he would go to bed dry. He rotated himself in front of the fire, like an animal on a spit, only slower, and Jessica, wet to the bone, envied him his position.

She looked about and realized that no one was watching the doctor, so she began to disrobe. Her dress was heavy as she stepped out of it as was her petticoat which she would keep on and dry, like the doctor with his long johns, before the fire.

"I'll help," murmured the Indian woman as Jessica reached for her dress in preparation to taking it to the fire. Soon it too was hanging next to the doctor's trousers and jacket, steaming away at the fireside.

The cold drove her to the doctor's side, and he very kindly made no mention of her appearance. She felt naked and shy, but her good sense told her that she'd best follow the doctor's lead as modesty had no place in a situation such as this one.

One of the camp dogs sniffed at one of the bodies and was quickly beaten. He yelped and headed off into the bush to lick his wounds. "We'll bury them in the morning," stated the doctor when Jessica frowned. "They'll be safe 'til then."

Not only was she to spend the night in a communal bed with a group of total strangers, but she realized she was also to share this bank with a dead man and a dead woman. Such is the life of a frontier nurse, she thought, shaking her head.

"Something the matter?" asked Doctor Evans and the question was so ludicrous in light of the situation that she laughed involuntarily.

"Aha, a woman with a sense of humour," remarked her companion, a look of admiration taking over his face, which was now glowing from the heat of the fire. "It helps. Don't you think?" he asked, and she nodded, afraid to speak lest she laugh again.

It was about an hour later that the Indian woman determined that their clothing was dry, and they slipped it on. It was hot and felt good against her weary body.

"You'd best get right into bed," suggested the doctor, "Before you lose all the heat," and they trundled off to bed, where a spot had been left for the two of them.

"Take a swig of this," suggested the doctor as she settled into the boughs. "It'll keep you warm inside until sleep comes." She did not argue, but took a long draught from the bottle that he produced, shuddered and lay back.

"This is probably the most incredible thing that's ever happened to me," she whispered, not wanting the others to know of her inexperience. She could not resist verbalizing her predicament, and her companion was a compassionate listener.

"Jessica Sybil Baxter, of noble birth," she seldom mentioned her aristocratic background, but now it was necessary for the ultimate contrast, "Sleeping with strangers, men and women, on a soggy bank on a nameless river, with nothing to protect me but a few evergreen boughs. And," she added, "Not to forget the dead and the dogs and," she added faintly, "The hunger. You know, we had no dinner?"

"I know, Miss Baxter. We had no dinner, but, I think that these people lost all or most of their supplies, otherwise I'm certain that they would have offered. And, my dear, it's not a nameless river. It's Eddy Creek. And you do have more protection than a few cedar boughs, as you put it. The men are armed and watchful. The dogs are tied, the fire's well banked so no wolves or bears will come too close. Why, you're as safe as in your mother's arms." It was perhaps an unfortunate comparison, but Jessica understood and relaxed. She was warm, and the boughs were soft and no one had so much as spoken an unkind word to her, so she dismissed all of the unpleasantness from her mind and slipped off into a restless sleep. She dreamed of dogs and wolves, of the dead and the dying and suddenly she awoke, certain that it was still the dead of night.

Bright sunshine burned her eyes, and she was astonished to see that she was alone in the bough-bed. All of the others were working to ready themselves for the trip back across the turbulent waters.

She staggered to her feet, her joints aching with the dampness. "How embarrassing," she muttered as she straightened herself out.

"Hello, sleepyhead," spoke the doctor cheerfully. "Thought you'd died on us there."

"I wish you had awakened me. I feel just dreadful." She looked about, feeling awkward.

"There's nothing really for you to do, Miss Baxter. We're preparing to cross in three groups. We've decided to take the dead as they were Christians and deserve a church burial. I think you'd best go first with the woman and the children, and of course, two rowers."

"I'd sooner go with you, Sir," she didn't know why she said that.

"No, it makes no sense," he stated in an authoritative voice. "Your boat leaves in about ten minutes, I should guess," he said, as he looked about. "So get to it." He walked away leaving her confused and disorganized in the middle of the compound.

"Missy, come," instructed the Indian woman, leading Jessica to where the boat was waiting. She had the young girl with her from the previous evening and also a young boy who'd stayed in the background with the men up until now. He had a sullen look about him and viewed Jessica with suspicion.

The dogs came with them and a few of the belongings that had been saved. It was a dismal lot and Jessica wished for the energy to talk with the woman and the children, but she was tired and aching and the brilliant sun was giving her a headache. She contented herself with comforting one of the dogs that came to her after a blow from the young boy. She fondled the dog's ears and remembered the hounds at Fairview.

So many, many miles away.

The little craft rocked from side to side, sometimes lurching forward in a sudden rush, sometimes settling back with a thud, water spilling over the sides. It was a short trip, the far bank was clearly visible at all times, but quite long enough to soak Jessica once again and to cause her stomach to sicken. The combination of hunger and motion sickness turned her an ashen colour and the bright sunshine caused her to frown to protect her eyes. When she did let go of the sides of the boat to shade her eyes, the thrashing motion would dash her against the wood, her arms and sides bruising.

As they approached the shore, the Indian woman

pitched in to help direct the boat. Even the children knew what to do, as Jessica sat there, helpless. The young boy threw critical glances at the strange, quiet, white woman and she was embarrassed by her ineptitude.

Mr. Dickerson stood at the end of the shabby wooden dock as they finally nosed to safety. The look of relief on his face was profound. "Miss Baxter, you do show up in the strangest places," he teased, but she was so pleased for the attention that she mustered up her very best smile. Encouraged by this, he reached down and helped her out of the shaky craft, not letting go of her even after she was safely on shore. "You do look dreadful," he teased again, and she knew that this must be true. "We'll get you home right away and see if Mrs. Carson will allow you a bath, under the circumstances."

There was nothing in the world that would have pleased her more than a hot bath but she wondered if she shouldn't wait until the doctor crossed safely with the wounded and the dead. She expressed her concern, and Mr. Dickerson assured her that there were more than enough hands available to assist the doctor. She shielded her eyes and searched about and realized that the man was quite right, and she allowed herself to be led home.

12

The Train Wreck

Mrs. Carson was always ready to please Mr. Dickerson, and arranged to get Hazel to tote water for Jessica. After thanking Mr. Dickerson for guiding her home through the muddy paths and streets, the girl headed directly for her quarters, forgetting even her hunger.

When she stepped into her room, she closed the door and leaned against it. A fatigue settled over her that was so total that she suddenly realized that, as grimy as she might be, she was unable to fill the tub and bathe. When Hazel brought up the first two pails of water, she thanked her and told her that it was sufficient. She closed the door once again and caught sight of herself in the little mirror over the washstand. She was startled by her image. Her dark hair, which was usually so shiny and healthy looking, was dull and lifeless. It hung about her shoulders in a most unattractive fashion. Her face was flushed and dirty and her eyes shone in a feverish manner.

She put warm water into the china basin on the washstand and set to undressing herself. Her dress was heavy with the dampness and mud, and her underthings were ripped and a dirty gray. She washed as best she could under the circumstances, feeling quite guilty about slipping into bed knowing that she was still not totally clean, but it took the last little bit of her strength to just pull the covers up about her face. Her eyes burned as she closed them, and she knew that she was ill.

The high fever brought with it a series of dreams that

were often more memory than dream.

She remembered being sick with the measles and Grandmother Baxter ignoring the quarantine sign to smuggle treats into her room.

She remembered sailing with Charles and his friends, the clean blue of the ocean boiling alongside the sailboat until it became Eddy Creek with its debris floating by — here an old trunk, there the remnants of a tent, and there the body of a young Indian woman. Even in her feverish sleep, Jessica forced her attentions away from the lifeless form, and the dream moved on to the chastising stare of the young Indian boy who knew so well what to do when she, a grown woman, sat there helpless, and then, as dreams will have it, she was the child and once again back at Fairview. Charles was there, doing daring stunts on horseback, showing off for his sister who screamed for him to stop lest he hurt himself. He only laughed. Then he became the Indian woman with her broken body all hunched over the saddle, and her laugh was silent, her open mouth uttering no sound.

Jessica tossed and turned in bed, forcing herself to wake from the nightmares. When the room stopped spinning, she sat up, slowly, waiting for her hot eyes to become accustomed to the darkness, for it was now late afternoon, and the early evening shadows had filled the room. She made out where she'd dropped her bag at the doorway, and she struggled to it, opening it with thick, tired fingers. She reached for medication, and her hands found the little packets that they dispensed for colds and fevers. She mixed one with a cup of water, drank it and stumbled back to bed. It was then that she noticed that there was a tray with food and a tea pot which was quite cold to the touch, so she passed it by and snuggled back to bed, waiting for the drug to take effect. As she waited, she promised herself that she'd dream only pleasant dreams, think only pleasant thoughts, but, such was not to be the case. The swollen Eddy Creek splashed back into her memory and in order to avoid the disgust in the Indian boy's eyes, she stared out over the water, examining, once again, the pieces of people's lives floating by. There was a doll that she'd had as a child and when she reached for it, the boat tipped, and she was saved from plunging overboard by the boy, whose expression never changed. She tried to thank him, but it was no use. He looked right through her. She looked away.

On the bank sat Abigail Windsor in her rickety old wheelchair. Jessica tried to call out to her to be careful, so close to the eroded edge, but her voice made no sound. Abigail sank slowly into the water, to be joined by Martha, Sybil and Edward, and finally Charles, who wore an expression of disbelief on his handsome face. Bad things just weren't supposed to happen to Charles. He was too innocent. Jessica reached to pull him into the boat, but it was the Indian woman whose body came to the side, her big brown eyes staring up at Jessica in quiet suffering.

Again the girl rolled over in bed. Again she forced herself to wake and clear her thoughts, but as soon as she began to drift off, the faces all came back to her. In her semi-conscious state, she realized that they were all faces of the dead in the water, except for Charles, and in one incredible burst of horror, she woke up screaming.

It would be several weeks before she received word that Charles had been killed. He was drowned in the Mediterranean while on leave.

Mary Menzies' christening was postponed to accommodate Jessica, whose illness kept her in her room for six days. Mrs. Carson, grumbling good-naturedly, delivered meals to her or had Hazel do it. Visitors were few, as a mild influenza seemed to sweep the town, and people stayed close to their homes.

In the beginning, for a few days, Jessica slept a great deal. They were deep sleeps — dreamless. As the week progressed, her sleep was fraught with memories, sometimes pleasant, often not. She tried to stay awake to avoid dreaming, and she became restless. She hungered for good books, but there were few.

Rosina sent her regards, but, for Mary's sake, wisely stayed away. George Dickerson left town, as Jessica was to learn from Doctor Evans, who paid a short, awkward visit, and time dragged on.

At the end of it all, the girl had lost considerable weight

and was bothered by a sort of melancholy that was impossible to shake. Charles was ever on her mind, and, even though she did not yet know that he was dead, she felt a foreboding whenever she thought of him.

"Well, look who's here," greeted Doctor Evans cheerfully when she returned to the hospital. She was astonished that the walk had left her rather breathless and in need of a cup of tea and a sit-down. The doctor seemed to sense this and arranged for a pot to be brought down to them as they went over the hospital's patient charts.

The hot tea coupled with the familiar surroundings mellowed Jessica. She sighed a weary sigh and asked, "The young Indian woman . . . the one who died, was she buried from the church?" For some obscure reason, it seemed important for her to know.

"Why, yes, she was. Why do you ask?" The doctor was sitting back in his chair, arms folded, pipe in his mouth.

"Oh, no reason, I guess," murmured the girl and she lapsed into silence, staring off into the middle distance, almost afraid to close her eyes lest she see the Indian woman's face once again.

Jessica was very thin and pale, and the doctor was obviously concerned by her appearance and mood. She sensed his eyes on her, and she felt the need to say something else. "She seemed . . . I just thought . . . oh, I don't know. I just wish that I'd known her." She was tracing the edge of her tea cup in an distracted gesture. "I find myself thinking of her a great deal. I don't know why. I don't think of everyone who's died the way I do of her. She . . . well, she sort of haunts me." It was a strange choice of words.

"Her name was Rising Moon," spoke the doctor. "She was married to a white man by the name of Smothers, and it was her son who sat in the boat with you. Dan Smothers was the man who was dead when we arrived." He paused to light his pipe, and, noticing the interest in Jessica's otherwise tired eyes, continued, "She was not pulled out into the water. She jumped in to save Dan. The water was too strong, and she really couldn't swim. She was dashed against the rocks. It's unlikely that she knew that Dan was dead before she, too, died. I'd like to think that she didn't."

"She seemed so very young," mumbled Jessica.

"She was but nineteen. She was married to Dan at four-teen and her son is five years old. She was pregnant when she died." A shudder passed over Jessica, accompanied by a terrible fatigue.

"Perhaps you've come back too soon?" suggested her companion.

"No, no, I'm all right, Sir. I'm quite looking forward to work. My mind, when idle, plays terrible tricks on me."

He nodded his understanding and allowed her to go about her business.

The first Sunday after her illness was Mary's christen-ing. The baby did a great deal for Jessica's disposition as she was a darling, good-natured child. The attention paid the baby girl by her step-father was enough to melt the coldest heart, and Jessica had a truly wonderful day in the presence of her friends.

"I wish I'd lost the weight instead of you," laughed Rosina. Jessica's slender body was the topic of conversation, and Rosina probably sensed her friend's embarrassment. "I don't know just how I'm ever going to get my figure back." She put her hands just above her hips in an effort to control her thickened waist.

"My goodness, Rosina, you look marvelous," Jessica remarked in all sincerity. Rosina had bloomed from a young girl into a woman, and it was most becoming. Mr. Menzies nodded his agreement to Jessica's statement, quite obviously pleased with his young wife's maturing body.

Jessica experienced a moment of discomfort when she noticed his eyes caressing Rosina's form. She felt like she had when she'd peeked into Charles' post card collection of voluptuous women in various stages of undress. It was odd that in her capacity as nurse, the nude body held no fascina-tion whatsoever, but, in a situation such as this, she could not help but be titillated by the implications of a husband's ador-ing look. She turned her attention to Mary. There was a safe innocence about babies.

"Your cheeks are flushed, Miss Baxter. I hope you're

not getting sick on us again," spoke George Dickerson.

Jessica knew that he'd been witness to her discomfort with Rosina and her husband, and she flushed even deeper red. Nothing about her ever escaped his attention. She always felt a sort of nudity of the mind when he was near, as though, in some occult fashion, he was able to strip away all of the pretense that we protect ourselves with in the company of others, and get right into her feelings. He was dangerous in that respect. She did not always understand her own feelings and to imagine that he might be able to, put her in a most vulnerable position.

"I'm quite all right, Sir," she snapped, not looking up from the child in her arms.

"Good," was his only reply, but there was a subtle mocking in his tone.

The soggy spring slipped into summer, and with the more predictable weather, Jessica's mood and health improved. The letter informing her of her brother's death was no surprise, and her sorrow was spent before the fact.

It had been definitely decided that she'd move into the Menzies' lodgings when their house was completed later in the summer, so that was no longer on her mind.

The hospital routine became just that, routine. Nothing unexpected occurred, no outbreak of diseases, everyone was too busy making a living to become ill.

"It would probably be an excellent time for you and me to go to Toronto, Miss Baxter," suggested the doctor one day.

Jessica's heart skipped a beat. The slow, lazy days of summer, while not exactly boring, had a sameness about them that invited change.

"You and I would be going?" she asked with surprise.

"Well, I did tell you before that I felt you'd be an asset in our negotiations with the provincial fathers." He was referring to his ongoing quest for a proper hospital. "Doctor Gallagher from North Bay is willing to spend a fortnight here. Says he'd like to get away from the 'big town' once in a while, and there not being too much going on here just now, we'd be safe to go."

"Yes Sir. I'd be more than pleased. When?" she asked.

"Next Monday's train, I should think, providing Neal is able to get up on Friday."

The last of the gloom that had settled over Jessica began to lift. Rising Moon and Charles became memories that she could control, as she'd slowly learned to control the others — bringing them out of their cubby holes for inspection only when it suited her. She was far too busy planning her trip to Toronto to concern herself with the past.

Neal Gallagher did arrive on the Friday afternoon train and was met at the station by Doctor Evans. Doctor Gallagher was a tall, rather pleasant looking man with sandy red hair and beard and a mischievous gleam in his eye. He took an instant liking to Jessica and ribbed his friend about running away to Toronto with her. This sort of good-natured bantering did not embarrass the nurse. Quite the contrary, she enjoyed it, and she liked Neal Gallagher in return. He asked if he might come calling on her the next evening and she said yes.

"Good evening, Sir," Jessica greeted him when he arrived at Mrs. Carson's. He wore a big smile that set his eyes to twinkling. "You had no difficulty finding the place?" she asked, simply making conversation.

"Why, I was led right to your door by Doctor Evans," he claimed, his expression becoming quite serious. "I fancy he was trying to dispel any rumours about you two by throwing me at you."

"Well, I . . ." began Jessica indignantly, but she soon realized that the man was teasing her. "Sir, you are most unfair!" but her smile gave her away.

"I'm not at all, dear lady. You see . . ." he took her arm and led her down the porch stairs, "I've begun the rumour myself."

"Oh, you are a beast!" she exclaimed and withdrew her arm from his.

"I've always fancied that what Cobalt really needed was a bloody great scandal to set it on its heels. Put some spice in the dusty old town." He gestured around at the sorry houses and dirty streets and Jessica had to laugh.

"That may be so, Sir, but please pick on someone other than me. Why, I've enough problems with some of the local ladies already." She flushed when she remembered the incident with George Dickerson and Doctor Evans when they all fell in a heap in the mud on Lang Street.

"Aha!" he exclaimed. "The pretty lady does have some secrets. Come, share them with me." He stopped walking and stood in front of her, looking down into her black eyes. His presence made her catch her breath. He was so very male and so very, very sure of himself.

"It doesn't bear telling, Sir," she murmured, lowering her eyes and walking around him.

"Now you're being unfair! Here I am, on an errand of mercy, taking over so that you and Evans may run off to Toronto together, and you're not going to give me a tidbit of gossip to keep me humoured whilst you're gone?" He was most persuasive and Jessica was in a very good mood.

The evening was comfortably cool, the heat of the day having disappeared with the sun. The blackflies and mosquitoes, so plentiful earlier, were not in evidence just now, and the western sky was softening to an orange-pink glow.

"You must promise not to tell — anyone," she whispered. And when he nodded earnestly, she related the story to him, getting caught up in the telling. She talked for the longest time, recounting for him her encounter with Mrs. Pearce in the store, describing with her hands the beauty of that fated hat. She even told him of Mr. Simmons defending her by socking Doctor Fairley square on the jaw and rendering him unconscious.

Her audience of one was most entertained. He laughed so heartily that she had to join in and soon the tears were running down their cheeks as they leaned against the bank to catch their breaths.

"I shall never," he exploded, "Ever assume that Cobalt is a boring town. No siree — not now that Miss Jessica Baxter is in residence." He doffed his hat and bowed.

She in turn curtsied and that brought about a new round of laughter. How very much she liked this man!

The train left Monday afternoon and was to take them as far as North Bay, where they would stay the night and board another train for Toronto on Tuesday morning.

Travelling with a well-known, well-respected person made this ride very unlike the lonely journey to Cobalt so many months before. The good doctor seemed to know everyone by name and often inquired after their spouses and their children.

"You must have treated absolutely everybody in the North Country at one time or another, Sir?" asked Jessica when they finally had a quiet moment.

"Guess so," he agreed, settling back against the white linen headrest. "Even treated old Sam once or twice." Sam was the porter who'd helped them aboard, refusing the piece of silver that the doctor had tried to force into his hand.

He appeared quite weary and had already confessed to Jessica that he and Neal had stayed up quite late. Going over the hospital charts and procedures and polishing off a bottle of scotch was the the way he had put it. Soon his eyes were closed and his breathing indicated that he was asleep. Jessica turned her attention to the passing scenery.

It was very much the same as last time, but the colours were various shades of green, the leaves not yet beginning to turn. The sky once again was bright with sunshine, and she caught herself frowning to shield her eyes. She remembered her first encounter with George Dickerson, and his explanation of the 'sunshields' fashioned by the Eskimos out of whale bone. She could use a pair just now. She reached for the blind, intending to pull it part way down, as she did not want to miss all of the scenery, just the brilliance of the sky.

"Allow me, Ma'am," spoke Sam, who was passing by. He flashed an amazing set of teeth when he smiled. "You travelling with Mister Doc?" he asked quietly, as Doctor Evans was stirring in his sleep.

"Why, yes, I am," she replied just as quietly.

The old coloured man's eyes rolled in their sockets and Jessica was annoyed by the implication. Perhaps Neal Gallagher was right. There just might be rumours about this trip. She thought that she should explain to Sam that she was a nurse and that this was a business trip, but then she thought better of it. If she began now, she'd be repeating herself for a long time to come, so she smiled demurely and sat back, closing her eyes to indicate that the conversation was over.

The brightness of the day filtered through her closed lids, lighting up her thoughts. It would be impossible to sleep, what with the clickety clack of the train and the daylight in her head, so she contented herself with some selective day dreaming.

Jessica's thoughts drifted back to Saturday evening past, and the marvellous time that she'd had with Neal Gallagher. He was such a comfortable man to be with, witty, knowledgeable and attractive. She could not help but compare him to George Dickerson who, while being equally good looking and clever, was not comfortable to be with. She wondered why. Was it that she was more attracted to one man than the other? If so, which? The corners of her mouth turned up as she remembered Neal Gallagher's clowning ways and a frown appeared when her thoughts turned back to George Dickerson. Yet, if the truth be known, it was George Dickerson who made her pulse beat faster. It was George Dickerson who caused a shiver of excitement to jar through her whenever he was near. Perhaps that was why she was so uncomfortable about him. He was able to arouse her and possibly at some point to make her lose control, whereas Dr. Gallagher seemed to take everything so lightly that she'd never be in danger of not being in command.

She modestly reasoned that she was silly to go on with this exercise as she'd not been offered a choice between these two men, but she continued to wonder which would be the better pick.

Her face betrayed her inner turmoil and Doctor Evans, who had just awakened, asked, "A penny for your thoughts?"

She started in her seat, feeling very foolish at being discovered in such a 'school girl' occupation as daydreaming about fellows.

"I was just recalling things . . ." she murmured, her warm cheeks acting as a beacon for her childish thoughts.

"He's married," was her companion's simple statement, and she closed her eyes to hide her shame. Married! It had never occurred to her that the dashing young doctor was wed. He certainly did not act as though he was, or at least as she thought that he should act under such circumstances. Why, he'd even tried to kiss her good night. She'd easily been able to side-step his gesture, although she'd really wanted to kiss him. But all that changed with this knowledge. She was hurt and a little angry and tried desperately not to let it show.

"Really?" she remarked casually.

"Yes, to Oscar Johnston's daughter Mabel, from North Bay. Nice girl." He spoke matter-of-factly, but he did not take his eyes off Jessica's face, and she felt trapped into saying something.

"Odd, he didn't mention it," she said, and before another embarrassing second could creep slowly by, there was a tremendous crash up ahead, and it steadily reverberated down through the train, car by car, throwing them out of their seats.

"Probably a moose," said Doctor Evans, calmly. He appeared unflappable. "They often come out to the clearings — like the roadways or the railway tracks, trying to escape the flies that torment them. Hope we didn't derail, that's always such a nuisance. You stay here," he suggested, helping her get re-settled in her seat. "I'll go up front and see what's going on."

She nodded, rubbing the back of her neck which had been badly jarred in the sudden stop. "I'll be here," she said weakly.

Doctor Evans was back in only a few moments. "Grab your bag, Miss Baxter." And she obeyed, not asking why. They hurried through several cars and then he led her off the train. She had to jump into his arms as the last step to the ground was several feet.

"Up front," he called to her as he sped ahead. It was difficult to assess just what had occurred and suddenly she was too busy to care.

The first three cars were off the track, one on its side. The people in those cars were crying and moaning, some badly hurt, some merely stunned. The doctor motioned for her to stay out as he and several unhurt men climbed into the overturned car to determine the damage within. A woman with a baby clutched to her bosom was the first to get Jessica's attention as they sat on the gravel at the side of the tracks. The woman's eyes were round with terror as she withdrew from Jessica, swinging her torso to and fro as though she were soothing her infant. The baby was dead, probably having died instantly as its neck snapped when it was thrown across the car. The woman was bruised and bleeding slightly, but the real injury was to her mind, as she refused to believe that the tiny child in her arms, lying with its head thrown back at an impossible angle, a thin river of blood beginning at its open mouth, leaving a strange mark against its snow white skin, was dead. There was nothing to be done for the woman, her intense grief had placed her temporarily where no one could touch her, so Jessica took off her shawl and placed it around the woman's shoulders, taking care to drape it over the baby, thus shielding it from the stares of others. She murmured a few words to the woman and moved on to where a man lay writhing on the ground.

As she approached him, an incredible stench assailed her nostrils. The man was one of the train's stokers and apparently he'd been shoveling coal into the hungry boiler when the accident happened. At the moment of impact, the smoldering white-hot coals from the fire had lurched out of the open hot-box, showering upon him where he lay thrown against the engine wall. He'd had the wind knocked out of him, as well as sustained a terrible knock on the head, and he'd been slow to move. In those few seconds his clothes had caught fire and one of his mates had had the sense to throw him out of the engine room and roll him on the ground to put out the flames. Jessica heard this story as she administered aid to the suffering man, his mate muttering over and over, "It could've been me, it just as easy could've been me."

She had to go for morphine as she did not carry the drug with her, and she asked the one mate to stay with his friend who was slowly making less and less noise as he began to slip into a coma.

"Doctor Evans. Doctor Evans. Please Sir, where are you?" shouted Jessica amid the confusion. There was considerable smoke now as some of the nearby bush had caught fire, and the men were beating it out before it became an even bigger catastrophe.

"Here, Miss Baxter, over here," he answered, and she rushed towards the sound of his voice. His head appeared out of one of the train windows that was now more like a skylight than a window. "Help me!" he ordered, not to his nurse, but to a man who was standing on the ground below. "Help me move this man," and the two carefully moved a bloody body out of the car, placing him on the ground several yards from the tracks.

"Miss Baxter, can you get in here?" he asked, and she shook her head.

"No, Sir, I need some morphine. I've a badly burned man," she gestured back through the smoke, "And I've got to get back to him." While she was talking, the doctor disappeared only to reappear with a packet that he threw down to her. She scurried away to find her patient unconscious and past the need for medication. He was now deeply in shock, and there was nothing more that she could do for him here, on this dirty, smoky little patch of land. She reached for his face which was unhurt, stroked it, said a prayer and turned to go back to the doctor. The man died before she got back to him with Doctor Evans.

It was not easy for Jessica to get into the upturned car, but when she identified herself as a nurse, some men made a human chain and passed her up and in through the horizontal window. Doctor Evans caught her and eased her down into the debris which had once been a very comfortable first class coach.

There were about twenty people left in the car, all having sustained some sort of injury. Most had broken bones and a great deal of bruising. There were several whom the doctor thought might have concussions, and he'd been reluctant to move them around.

Jessica followed the doctor about, helping him wherever the need indicated. They ran out of what bandages they had in their bags, and she tore up her petticoats to create more. The hours slipped by, and she did not even notice when the daylight faded, and the lanterns where lit.

Eventually the episode went full-circle and Jessica was back with the woman with the baby. Someone had removed the child, but the distraught mother sat in an attitude that suggested that she still had the child in her arms. Jessica's shawl was still about her shoulders, there was pathos about the woman that shocked Jessica into doing something very out of character. She sat in the dim lantern light, placed her arms about the woman, pulled her slowly to her bosom, and wept.

Jessica felt a warm hand caress her shoulders and a soft voice uttered, "Not now, Miss Baxter. We're not done yet," and she turned her head to look into Doctor Evans' sad eyes. The light from the lantern flickered as if to go out, but he turned up the wick and, in the brighter light, she could see the toll that the day had taken on this caring man.

There was a deep cleft between his eyebrows, carved there by sorrow and fatigue. The whites of his eyes were bloodshot from the dense smoke that had, at one time, threatened the rescuers. His face, arms and hands were dirty with blood and soot. His shirt, so brightly white earlier in the day, was stained and torn where he'd quickly ripped off pieces to make bandages.

He smiled a weak smile when he noticed Jessica staring at him. "Here, let me help you," he offered as he rose slowly from his squatting position behind her.

She allowed herself to be lifted gently to her feet. The woman she'd been holding seemed not to notice her leaving and that brought a lump to her throat. She reached down and adjusted the shawl about the woman's shoulders and was startled when a hand moved up and patted hers. The lady never looked at the nurse, or acknowledged in any other way that Jessica had been there, but for this gentle, feather-soft touch, and it was then that Jessica knew that she'd be alright.

"Yes, Sir," she whispered in a hoarse, emotion-filled voice.

"There are others, Jessica," he said very quietly. "We were hit by another train, and there are more injured just down the track a bit." It hadn't occurred to Jessica that things could possibly be any worse than they already were.

"Others?" was all that she could stammer.

"Yes, others," he answered as he took her arm and led

her around the people and bonfires that had been lit in preparation for the long night ahead.

It was dark that night, and the mosquitoes, having no regard for the situation, were out in full force and as soon as Doctor Evans and Jessica moved away from the fires, the buzzing of the insects heralded their attack. It seemed so very unfair.

It was only several hundred feet down the track that they came upon the other half of the incident. The scene was similar to the one that they'd just left, but, fortunately, there seemed to be no loss of life. There was, however, a great deal of moaning going on and Jessica took a deep breath and wandered into the melee.

She and Doctor Evans had been there about fifteen minutes when they were surprised by the sound of singing. Just beyond the circle of light cast by the main fire, was a group of men singing and laughing, and it was such a welcome sound!

"Why, George Dickerson, you old son of a gun!" she heard Doctor Evans greet his old friend, and her heart stopped. Surely George Dickerson wasn't hurt! But of course not, she reasoned, else he'd be up here, near the fire with the rest of the wounded. There was a strong desire to edge over to the circle of men who seemed to be taking this opportunity to party, but she fought it and stayed by the injured, giving whatever assistance and solace that she could.

"Miss Baxter," called the doctor, and she knew that she must go.

"Yes, Sir," she answered as she peered into the darkness beyond.

"We have more injured," he replied, but there was laughter in his voice, and she did not know whether or not to take him seriously.

She walked slowly and carefully towards his voice until she could make out his form and that of George Dickerson and his friends. They had a very small fire going that did not illuminate much more than several feet, so she had difficulty making out what the doctor was talking about.

"George, the old buzzard, seems to have broken his leg." She failed to see the humour in this situation, but Doctor

Evans and George Dickerson chortled like schoolboys. She was convinced that it was all a ruse to get her over to where they were, and she very nearly turned back. Then she saw Mr. Dickerson's leg extended at a most peculiar angle. He was hurt. She was more concerned than she wanted to be.

"Yes, Sir," she agreed. "You seem to have broken your leg, Mr. Dickerson," she spoke to the man as she knelt down to inspect his limb.

"No matter," he replied, his words slightly slurred. It was then that she noticed the bottle that he held tightly against his chest. No wonder he wasn't making more of a fuss. She smiled to herself. He had already begun the medical proceedings by consuming his liquid pain killer as quickly as possible.

She looked up into Doctor Evans' eyes, and he nodded. They would have to set the leg, and that meant considerable discomfort to George Dickerson. She was unsure what to do next. Then the doctor invited her to join them in a drink. It became obvious to her that it would take a bit more of the demon rum to sedate the man to the degree that was necessary, so she sat down on the ground beside him.

"This here's Dicky Martin," George Dickerson began the introduction of the group, stopping occasionally to take a heavy swig of the bottle. He offered it around, but his friends declined. He was the only one hurt, and they must have known that he was in need of the drug.

"Dicky's an ol' buddy from up Liskeard way. Matter of fact, he was headin' home to see his wee wifey when your train hit us." He laughed at this, and the rest joined in. "Dicky's in a hurry to get home, 'cause his wee wifey's having a baby." For some reason or other he thought this funny, and slapped his leg in a comic gesture. It was a grave mistake, as it was his broken leg, and the pain almost rendered him unconscious. He managed to stay up, though, clutching his whisky bottle to his bosom.

When he was able to breath normally once again, he said, "An' over there we've got good old what's-his-name Jackson. Good old what's-his-name. And then . . ." The pain, and the liquor, were now taking effect, and he began to slide into a horizontal position. He slowly let the bottle slip away, and it was rescued by Doctor Evans, who took a generous draught of it before passing it over to Mr. Dickerson's companions.

Doctor and nurse worked quickly. They cut the injured man's pant leg up to above the knee, gently removing his boot and sock. "He'll be all right," assured Doctor Evans as he examined the broken limb more closely with the aid of his lantern. "You hold him straight. Sit on him if you must, but hold his thigh tightly while I pull." Jessica followed instructions, but felt so very awkward when she realized that the others were all staring at the proceedings. She was embarrassed because she no longer wore any petticoats, and she felt rather naked as she lifted her skirts about her knees and sat across Mr. Dickerson, who was lying motionless on the ground.

"That's it, Miss Baxter, now hold firm." She leaned forward and grasped the man's upper leg tightly. "Hold on," ordered her colleague as he twisted and turned the lower leg until, satisfied that it was in the correct position, he pulled and a weird snap could be heard quite clearly as the bone clicked into place. "Righto!" he exclaimed and the men applauded. He gave a silly little bow and motioned for Jessica to move to his side where they proceeded to put a splint on Mr. Dickerson's leg. It was a very primitive and very temporary, but would certainly do until they could get him to the hospital and place a proper brace on the leg.

Jessica put the sock back on the foot as best she could and reached for a coat lying nearby to cover the sleeping man. He looked so peaceful there in the warmth of the firelight. His handsome face, even in repose, wore a smile.

"You'd best stay here, Miss Baxter, and I'll do a final check on the rest of the wounded. If George wakes up, he probably won't be in nearly the pain that he was, but, if he complains, give him some more whisky. It can't hurt him." He wandered off into the darkness, leaving Jessica sitting alone beside Mr. Dickerson, the others having drifted off.

There was really nothing that she could do but sit and think, or perhaps, to sleep. Sleeping suddenly seemed a very good idea, as she was utterly exhausted and her neck, which had hurt her so much earlier, began again to ache. She longed for a good massage with some liniment, but there was no one to help, so she settled for trying to find the most comfortable position that she could, lying on the ground next to her patient.

The mosquitoes were at bay, the smoke from the small fire probably discouraging them. It had turned cool, despite the heat of the day, and Jessica longed for the shawl that she'd left draped over the bereft woman's shoulders. She did the best she could. She cuddled up beside Mr. Dickerson and managed to get a bit of the coat that was covering him over her upper body. She settled her head back on a clump of grass and was soon sound asleep.

There were no dreams to mar her slumber. She slept a deep, untroubled sleep and was awakened at dawn by a strange noise in her ear. She'd forgotten where she was and she was startled when she opened her eyes to stare into George Dickerson's.

"Well, hello!" he exclaimed, obviously more surprised than she.

She tried to sit up, but her neck was now so sore that the slightest movement sent a mean pain throughout her body. George Dickerson must have misinterpreted her reluctance to move away from him, and smiled a pleasant smile.

"What in the devil's name are you doing here?" and as he spoke, he moved his arm, which had been by his side, up to his head so that he might prop himself up, the better to see Miss Baxter.

She tried very hard to sound officious. "You were hurt in the train crash and Doctor Evans and I came to help." She avoided looking him straight in the eye as he always made her so nervous.

"You just happened by?" he frowned.

"Well, we were on our train heading to Toronto, and you were on yours going . . . well, wherever it is that you always go . . . and we crashed," she explained.

He seemed only to have heard the beginning. "You and Doctor Evans were on your way where?" he asked, shifting his position, the better to see her face. He winced with the pain as he moved, but ignored it.

When she tried once again to rise, he put his free hand on her shoulder and held her down. "You were going to Toronto, together?" and suddenly she resented his questioning.

In spite of the awful pain, she shook loose of his hold, which was really quite feeble, and sat up, her head reeling. "Yes, we were on our way to Toronto. Together," was all she volunteered. As with Sam, she saw no reason to explain further.

She stood up, shaking her skirts out around her legs. She felt most peculiar with no petticoats, and she longed for a hot bath and a change of clothing. She glanced down at the injured Mr. Dickerson, and he was not looking at her now, but at some place in the middle distance, a frown on his face.

"I'll go find the doctor," she mumbled and off she went.

Doctor Evans, when she found him, was full of information. They had a choice. They could continue on their trip south when a new engine arrived from North Bay, or they could return to Cobalt when an engine could be sent down from Latchford.

The cleanup would commence when crews arrived from Latchford, so, if they went north, they'd have to wait until the tracks were cleared before they headed south once again. The doctor thought it best they head back north so they'd be available to follow up any of the injuries that were transported back to Cobalt. The ones that headed south would soon be in North Bay where there was plenty of medical assistance.

13

The Fire

So it was, once again, that Jessica Baxter headed north on the T&NO Railway, in the company of George Dickerson.

The trip back to Cobalt was spent trying to keep the injured comfortable and that included Mr. Dickerson. He proved to be a rather troublesome patient as he refused to be fussed about. There was no doubt that he enjoyed Miss Baxter's attentions, but not when they were directed at his broken leg.

Jessica was tired and aching all over. She had no time for Mr. Dickerson's flirtations and was quite rude to him. He complained loudly to Doctor Evans, who admonished him, "For heaven's sake,George, stop your moaning. If you'd simply sit there and be quiet, Nurse Baxter wouldn't have to be so short with you," he said in defense of the exasperated Jessica. "Be good now, that's a brave fellow," he teased and Mr. Dickerson eased off. He put his head back on the headrest and closed his eyes. Not totally, though. There were tiny little slits of light that darted about, watching Miss Baxter as she moved about the car. "She's quite a woman, what?" whispered Doctor Evans as he walked by and spotted George's furtive glances.

"I'm going to marry her," Mr. Dickerson whispered back, a smile tickling the corners of his moustache. He closed his eyes for real and drifted off to sleep, the smile not leaving his lips.

Doctor Gallagher was not surprised when they arrived at the hospital with the injured, as he'd been warned through the telegraph system out of Latchford. He did not disguise his pleasure at seeing Nurse Baxter so soon again, and she, remembering what Doctor Evans had told her, snubbed him, and the poor fellow had no idea why.

The two younger nurses were in attendance so Jessica took Doctor Evans' advice and headed home shortly after all of the patients were settled in. George Dickerson grabbed her arm as she walked by, on her way out the door. "You are a fine lady, Miss Baxter," he said sincerely. "Please don't let my carrying on upset you. It's just my way," he spoke in a very direct fashion. "I'd be very proud, if after this leg's healed, I might come calling?" It was the very first time that he'd approached her on such a formal level and it rather confused her. She was at a loss to understand why, at this point in time, he'd turn to such gentlemanly behaviour. She smiled at him, and murmured something about it being all right. She turned to leave and noticed Doctor Gallagher watching her. He'd obviously witnessed the conversation between her and Mr. Dickerson.

She could not help but wonder if in turn, Mr. Dickerson had witnessed the encounter that she'd had with Doctor Gallagher.

It was a weary nurse who crawled in between her sheets that evening. She'd arranged for a bath, and, although it made her neck feel better, it seemed to take the last bit of energy that she had left. She'd brought her dinner up on a tray, and it sat beside her bed, on a chair, barely touched. Poor Jessica! There seemed so few quiet times between the crises.

She drifted off into a fitful sleep. It seemed impossible to get comfortable as the whipping motion of the train crash on her neck had left her with a spine that acted like a corridor down which pain might travel. When one portion of her body was relatively pain free, that very position would cause another area to ache. And, in between the times when she'd wake to move her hurting body, she dreamed the remembering dreams that she'd forced to the back of her mind, where she was able to keep them, most of the time.

"Jessie, dear, do sit straight," Sybil nagged at her daughter. It was enough to be reprimanded about her posture, which was actually quite good, but to have it done in a public place was quite unforgivable. She glared at her mother who did not notice, as she was busily engaged in a flirtatious dialogue with a house guest. Sybil, although apparently madly in love with her husband, was not above trifling with any available man's attentions. And somehow, she seemed to gather a prestige by belittling those about her. It was easy enough to do, as Jessica did not care enough to answer back. She was not in competition with Sybil, however much Sybil might think she was. But it irritated the girl to watch her mother use her wiles on men other than her father. Later in that same memory dream, she saw Sybil and her house guest in an embrace. It seemed quite innocent at first. Sybil was always gushing over some silly bit of information or other. But, as Jessica went to leave, she saw them kiss, and saw Mr. Waddington caress her mother's buttocks. There was a whispered promise, and then they spotted the girl.

"Whatever are you doing there, child, lurking about in the shadows. Why, one might think you were spying on your poor mother." There was absolutely no guilt in her voice. "Come, deary, surely you have something better to do with your time," and Jessica was dismissed.

It had been a very long time since Jessica remembered this occasion. There were others, but this was the first and it proved to be the most difficult to erase. Her father was in London on business. Jessica wondered just what business as he was not employed anywhere. In his absence, Sybil often invited couples to stay with her. There was a semblance of purity in her plan. The lonely country chatelaine, her husband off to - wherever. It was only as Jessica grew older that she realized that there was no innocence in much of what Sybil did. On this particular occasion, the wife of the man left Sybil's estate in a huff, to be followed, only several days later, by her smirking husband.

Awake once again, Jessica reached for a match and lit

her lamp. She was hungry now, and thirsty, and, for some reason, full of resolve. As much as she hated to be reminded of Sybil and her infidelities, it had suited a purpose tonight. Doctor Gallagher, however charming and attractive, was one of Sybil's men, and she was able to dismiss him with no difficulty. And then her attention turned to George Dickerson, and his invitation. If nothing else, the man was honest. He never pretended to be anything more or less than he was, and that was becoming a most cherished characteristic.

It was several weeks later that Jessica decided to move into her new lodgings. She was, in a small measure, sorry to leave Mrs. Carson's Boarding House as she'd grown to like her fellow lodgers and Mrs. Carson too. Even Hazel, with her sometimes slatternly ways, had become somewhat of a friend, amusing Jessica occasionally with tidbits of gossip about the local gentry, such as it was.

But Jessica felt that she could afford and needed something more private than she now had. It was understandable that men became entirely dependent upon the boarding house system. It had been her experience that they were quite incapable of caring for themselves — that is, of course, unless they were out in a tent in the bush, cooking over an open fire, where cleanliness seemed unimportant, and unless they had not cultivated a palate that craved something other than beans, strong black coffee and stale bread.

She smiled to herself as she packed her belongings in preparation for the move. It was gratifying to know that she could take care of herself. Oh, she realized that, given the same primitive conditions that the men tolerated whilst out prospecting, in all likelihood, she'd find it quite a struggle, but she knew that she could handle it. She'd watched and listened, and she was extremely resourceful. Yes, it was nice to be independent!

One article that she carried from Mrs. Carson's to her own flat was George Dickerson's tent. It had been with her since that first day, and she noticed while moving it, that some of young Danny's blood had stained the canvas. She decided to ask Mr. Chow to launder it — if that was possible, and she'd return it to the gentleman.

An unexpected tug at her heart surprised her when she thought of this.

Rosina had left the flat scrupulously clean, so Jessica had only to place her own things about the rooms, and she was moved in. It was very easy. The Menzies had left her a few pieces of furniture, but she knew that she'd have to begin to plan on buying some articles of her own. She made a list of her needs and tucked it away in her pocket — to be referred to in the future — and perhaps as things occurred to her, she'd write them down.

The trip to Toronto had been postponed indefinitely, as Doctor Gallagher could not stay any longer, and he wasn't certain just when he'd be able to come back. Thus Jessica was quite free to spend her spare time planning her new home.

Mr. Chow, who lived upstairs from her and ran the laundry that was at the front of her building, was most helpful. He took an instant liking to the woman and called her something that sounded like — 'Please-Missie-Jesse' — and he generally bowed slightly whenever he addressed her thus.

"I'm in need of some furniture, Mr. Chow," Jessica explained to him one day, shortly after moving in.

"Please-Missie-Jesse, honourable cousin is vely good, he will make whatever," he gestured with his hand to indicate that his cousin could make absolutely anything that Jessica might be in need of. They discussed her wants and Mr. Chow gave Jessica directions to his cousin's home which was far to the south of town.

The next day, Jessica took off to find Mr. Chow's cousin, another Mr. Chow. It was incredibly hot for the eighth day in a row. This sustained heat was most unusual for this part of the country, Jessica had been told time and time again. Jessica, too, was not accustomed to it. England may not have had the very cold winters that Cobalt had, but England certainly did not have very hot summers either.

She walked along the dusty road, remembering the days when deep mud had been there, during the spring. There were bone-dry ditches along the roadway where once there'd been flowing water.

She was thankful for her bonnet, as her eyes had never been accustomed to the bright sunshine, and she'd squint when she'd raise her head to make sure that she was taking the correct trail.

Mr. Chow, when she found him, bore a remarkable resemblance to the other Mr. Chow, both in appearance and manner. He spent a good deal of time bowing and nodding as she strained her ears in an attempt to understand his peculiar accent.

When the business at hand was completed, he offered her tea, and she readily accepted, as she was quite parched. He was about to excuse himself to go and prepare the tea, which Jessica knew to be quite a ritual, when a young man burst into the room. He stopped short when he saw Jessica, bowed, and backed up. Mr. Chow frowned in his general direction, obviously displeased with the young man's entrance, but, despite this subtle admonishment, the man spoke. His voice was hurried and excited, and, of course, he spoke Chinese. Jessica recognized not one word that he uttered. But whatever it was, it was important. She looked from one man to the other as they exchanged curt sentences in their mysterious tongue, and finally Mr. Chow turned and spoke to Jessica, most formally.

"'Scuse please, Missie," he bowed his apology, "but honourable nephew has brought most distressing information." His eyes became large, and there was fear there.

"What, Sir? What is it?" Jessica exclaimed.

"The town, please Missie, the town is on fire!" and suddenly Jessica could smell smoke!

It was unbelievable that a town Jessica had strolled through just hours earlier could have become such an inferno. Looking north from the vantage point of Mr. Chow's front porch, Jessica could see an unusual orange glow in the sky. She was far enough south of town that she could not see individual homes, but the illusion was that the entire town was ablaze.

Normally a very quick-witted person, the nurse was stunned into silence and immobility. Her brain raced in so many different directions — the hospital, there would be wounded — her home — her possessions — Rosina and the baby — George Dickerson with his broken leg — where were they? Where to go? What to do?

It was really only seconds later that she headed out on the run. She'd go to the hospital. Doctor Evans was always in command. He would give her direction. She would be safe with him. The wind was from the southwest so she was able to get quite close to the edge of town before the smoke and heat became unbearable. She swung to the west, keeping as much space as was necessary between herself and the fire. She could no longer run as breathing was painful now and her eyes smarted, distorting her vision.

The fire must have started somewhere in the central part of Cobalt, as there were homes untouched that Jessica passed on her way north. The people from these homes were packing up their belongings in preparation for escape.

Jessica stopped to catch her breath and she spoke to a man who was hitching up a rather nervous horse to a wagon. She leaned against a post, holding her bosom, trying to still the pain and fear that were pounding against her rib cage.

"What . . . where are you going, Sir?" she managed.

The man did not even look up, but muttered, "Seen these fires turn. Just like that. She may come back this way. We're moving over the creek," he gestured to the west.

"The whole town — surely it won't all go?" she asked hopefully.

"Maybe, maybe not," was his reply. He finally looked up and recognized the nurse. "Why, it's Nurse Baxter, what're you doing way out here?" It was a logical question as Jessica would not usually be in this part of town.

"I was just . . ." she was going to explain about her visit to Mr. Chow's and her furniture and all, but it seemed so senseless here and now. "I've got to get to the hospital. Do you think I'll make it by circling this way?" She recovered her breath and composure and was anxious to be off.

"Me and my family'll give you a ride up to near the station, but then we're staying 'tuther side of the creek and the lake." It seemed a wise move, and she'd like to have been able to do the same, but her training as a nurse would not let her put her own safety above that of others.

"Thank you, Sir," she smiled. "I'll go as far as that with you and continue on foot." The man and his family climbed aboard the old wagon, clutching their few possessions to their breasts, and they headed north. The poor horse was so fretful that the man had to whip him to keep him from bolting with fear. It was a frightening ride and Jessica was glad to get off where she did.

The station sat low in town and it offered a good view of the fire that was raging up the side of the hills upon which so many wooden houses were ready to feed the flames. Jessica could taste and smell the burning wood and decided that she'd have to protect herself with a wet cloth. She stooped down to tear a ruffle off her petticoat, and she wet it at the pump that stood near the station. There was a lineup of people at the pump, some gulping down water to soothe parched throats, others splashing it over themselves to cool flesh that had been too close to disaster.

When she glanced about, she saw a confusion that far surpassed anything she'd ever experienced before. Those fortunate enough to have a horse, were escaping on horse-drawn carts. There were riderless horses that galloped dangerously through the streets. The air was filled with cries, screams, neighs and now the crackling of fire as it ate up the dry wooden buildings. The fire wagon could be heard in the distance, and its usual commanding bell was lost in a sea of strong, more powerful sounds, the sounds of fear.

She held the drenched bit of cloth to her nose and mouth and began to pick her way to the hospital. She was heading against the stream of traffic and was knocked over twice before she was in sight of the tent.

What she saw then startled her. The fire was to the west of the tent, but very close by. There were people forming a bucket brigade from a local pump to the western side of the hospital and they were dousing the canvas with water as quickly and completely as possible. Occasionally bits of burning debris would land on the roof and immediately the townspeople would rush to the spot, climbing a rickety ladder held aloft only by the strength of dedicated men, to splash water on the pieces of charcoal.

But they were fighting a losing battle.

The few patients who had been in the tent were long before removed and there was a steady stream of people rushing out of the tent door, their arms full of whatever they could salvage.

Jessica fought her way past them and entered the steamy tent. Doctor Evans stood near the entrance directing traffic, a solemn look upon his face. "Miss Baxter!" he seemed both surprised and pleased.

"Sir! I came as quickly as I could," she ran to his side.

"There is nothing left to do here, Miss Baxter. Everything has been removed to the station." Jessica recalled seeing people headed towards the train depot, but had not associated their bundles with the hospital. "You'd best go there. The fire department has declared it to be the safest place around because of the lake, I should imagine. We've sent the word out that any wounded are to be sent there. This place is nearly empty, and it's sure to go."

Even as he spoke, the roof that had been steaming with the heat and the water, burst into flames, and it spread so quickly that they were lucky to get out with their lives.

The crowd that had formed the hospital bucket-brigade now moved away in search of another building they might save. Jessica and Doctor Evans stood away from the burning tent, silently, feeling the steamy heat against their faces, tasting the acrid smoke in their throats.

"I guess we won't have any difficulty getting our new hospital now, Jessica," the doctor spoke quietly, and they turned and walked down the hill towards the train station.

They could not return by the route that Jessica had previously taken as that street was now far too treacherous. They took back lanes and edged around buildings that were still standing until they, along with a flood of others, reached the depot. The wind had not turned. The station remained the safest place to be.

There were surprisingly few injured. Jessica had expected much worse. It was the despair that would be hard to reckon with, she imagined. Women with crying children at their knees worried about food. Men, unable to fight the fire because of age or infirmity, voiced their worries, often admonishing themselves for not stopping to save more of their belongings.

The medical staff wandered about, offering what comfort they could.

"The wind's turned!" a voice screamed into the doorway. The voice held terror which spread quickly about the crowded room. People rushed to the west windows where they could see the proof of the statement. The fire had indeed changed course and seemed now to be moving in a southwesterly direction. The station did not seem to be directly in its path, but dangerously close, and, if the outbuildings that surrounded the station caught fire, it seemed inevitable that the depot would go.

Before anyone could take charge, the crowd thronged to the doorway which was far too small for the crush and people cried out in pain as they were pushed and shoved against the doorway.

Doctor Evans cried out for attention, but only Jessica heard. Soon the last of the people limped out of the stationhouse, over the wooden platform, across the tracks and into the shallow lake.

Doctor Evans looked at the medical supplies that were piled high in the corner and realized that the two of them were not capable of saving them, so they too headed out, to the lake, where they would wait the fire out, waist deep in the warm water, praying that the fickle wind would once again change.

The air was foul enough to make Jessica want to retch. She fought the urge by keeping the wet piece of her petticoat next to her face. She waded about in the water, helping where she could. There was a woman who had her hands full with three small children so Jessica took the smallest into her arms and carried her about for a spell.

With the wind change came reduced visibility, and it was quite impossible to tell just what was on fire. If it hadn't been for the intense heat generated by the fire, they would not have been able to tell in which direction the town lay, as even the flames could not be seen through the smoke. Thick,

black clouds of soot fell upon them, causing choking and seriously affecting their eyes. In the confusion, some wandered
deeper into the lake and had to be fetched back as, even
though the lake was considered shallow, it was over the
heads of most people when they reached the centre.

And then, suddenly, a strong west wind swept down
upon them, and they were once again able to breath and see.
Cobalt, to the east of them, was still burning out of control,
but the station had been spared. There were no houses afire
close by, the blaze having moved up the hill away from the
centre of town.

Ever so slightly, people began to edge towards the
shore, much like careful cattle. Finally, they moved up to the
bank, crossed the tracks, climbed up on the platform and re-
entered the depot. It was a little like coming home.

Again, Jessica was surprised that no one was injured.
She had a fear that when the count was taken, someone
might be missing, perhaps drowned, but such was not the
case. Everyone seemed to be accounted for.

But the rest of Cobalt, that was quite another matter.
Those in the eastern side of town had no way to get to the
lake, and the optimists at the train station suggested that
they'd probably fled north or south until they were free of
the threat. But there were others amongst the group of sur-
vivors who were just as sure that many had been trapped in
the inferno and that only time would reveal the missing.
Jessica was of mixed opinion. It was inconceivable to her
that this much had been damaged with no loss of life. She
just prayed that the numbers were few. She further prayed
that Rosina, her baby, and George Dickerson were not on
that list.

It was dusk before it was deemed safe to move away
from the train station. People were restless, children were
hungry. The fire still raged far to the east of town, but had
seemingly done all of the damage it intended to do to Cobalt.

Forest fires were a constant threat that the early settlers of the North had to deal with. Bands of men left what
safety the town had to offer and followed the blaze, fighting
every step of the way until it was out.

And then came the time of reckoning.

Doctor Evans, followed by Jessica and then a few of the townspeople, wandered out into the street. A horse lay dead in the blackened roadway, the smell of burnt flesh filled the air. Wagons that had once been crammed with belongings stood scattered about, only the metal wheels still intact, mute testimony to the vulnerability of wood. Buildings smoldered, some levelled to the ground, others with some walls still standing, the wallpaper scorched and peeling.

Surprisingly enough, there were some buildings that had escaped the fire altogether. Jessica couldn't understand this. She assumed that a fire would consume everything in its path, but it seemed to have skipped and scurried about town, razing here, avoiding another next door.

Several hotels remained standing and plans were set into motion to billet the townspeople there. The telegraph office was gone, but so were the posts and wires leading out of town. A horse was found and a rider was dispatched south to Latchford to spread the news of the disaster. The railway tracks were untouched, so help would come from the south and then the north. Northerners were not new to catastrophes and everyone knew that help would soon arrive.

A quick walk about, and Doctor Evans began giving orders.

"Miss Baxter, go back to the station and set up a hospital. I'll send what cots and mattresses we're able to salvage and you enlist the aid of anyone you find that looks able. I'll go with these men and sift through the rubble for dead or injured," his face saddened, but only for a second. "We'll send what food we find down, and that station pump should be safe." He was very much in command, and the people around him seemed pleased to do his bidding.

"There's a stove at the depot, find pots for water and sterilize whatever. You may also want to heat what food we're able to find." He turned quickly and walked away.

Jessica, followed by a few of the women, headed back down to the station house just as the sun set in the west with a golden-orange glow and the fire sputtered to the east, casting a similar glow in the otherwise dark blue sky.

There were about forty people who spent the night at the depot. It was crowded, damp and noisy, and Jessica slept badly on the hard wooden floor. Doctor Evans did not return, so she was pretty much in charge. The group consisted of mostly women and children, and the few men who were there were elderly. Morning brought with it new problems that weren't so apparent the evening before. Black soot and gray ash formed a thick blanket over everything. Washing in the lake brought little relief as it was dirty, muddy, and warm. The pump, which drew cold clean water from some hidden spring, was slow, and there was also the fear that, like many other pumps during the summer's drought, it might dry up.

Food was scarce, and what little was found was eagerly shared by all, the children coming first. There was no immediate need for medical help, beyond the removal of a few cinders from tired, red eyes. Jessica grew anxious to be out, where she could better assess the extent of the damage, but Doctor Evans had sent her there to man the station and she knew that she must stay until he sent word for her to leave.

It was midday before the doctor arrived, accompanied by none other than George Dickerson, who walked with the aid of crutches. They were a grubby looking pair, but Jessica had to fight to keep from throwing her arms about them. The two were escorted by several other men, who had small portions of food to distribute amongst the families at the station.

"Fire's out," explained George Dickerson to Jessica as they huddled about the stove, waiting for the kettle to boil for a cup of tea. Amid the parcels that the men brought were several tins of tea, and everyone looked upon them as precious gifts.

"And the damage, Sir?" Jessica asked.

"Extensive," was Mr. Dickerson's reply. He busied himself with the firebox and then sat down on a nearby bench, his splintered leg thrust out in front of him. "I'd say about two thirds of the town is gone. And it's quite impossible to figure out how many lives were lost just now." Jessica gasped audibly. He looked up at her, "That's to be expected, Ma'am. These fires, when they come at night, usually take a greater toll. This one, well, most of the people saw it coming

and got out of the way. But not all . . ." he added soberly.
There was something in his manner that suggested to Jessica
that he was keeping news from her. Her mind flashed first to
Rosina and the baby, and then to Mrs. Carson's Boarding House.

In a shaking voice she asked, "Rosina, have you seen
her?" She was almost afraid of his answer.

"Yes . . . yes, your friend is safe," Doctor Evans stepped
into the conversation at this point. Jessica turned to look at
him and saw there foreboding.

"What is it, Sir?" she asked softly.

"Mr. Menzies. He's — well, he's dead," and as he spoke,
he reached out for Jessica, who looked, for a brief second, as
though she was going to faint. Jessica let him hold her shoulders as she fought back the tears.

"Where is she?" Jessica managed to whisper.

"She's at the Fraser House, Jessica. You may go to her.
We'll handle things here," offered the doctor, and, once again,
Jessica took off on the run.

She was completely oblivious now to her surroundings.
The enormity of the disaster centred around Rosina, not the
fallen town. She reached the steps of the hotel and had to stop
before climbing them. Her heart pounded in her chest, and her
head ached. She tried to think of what to say, but her mind was
blank. It was just important that she get to her friend.

She climbed the stairs and entered the foyer. There
were people everywhere. Some standing, some leaning
against the walls, and a few of the younger ones sleeping on
the floor in protected corners. She searched for Rosina but
did not find her. The big french doors to the diningroom were
open, and the crowd spilled over into that area. She made
her way through the crowd and began to circle the room.

And then she saw her. Rosina sat at the same table that
she'd occupied the day that she'd married Sam. The very day
that another fire had robbed her of another husband. Rosina,
merely twenty-one years of age, twice widowed by fire.
Jessica flew to her side, wrapped her arms about her friend
and buried her head in her hair.

"Rosina . . ."

It was a quiet cry that made Jessica realize that baby

Mary was on Rosina's lap. She reached down and scooped her into her arms. Rosina seemed not to notice. Both the child and the mother were blackened with soot and Jessica found herself wondering if they'd been with Mr. Menzies when he was killed. She did not ask. "There, there, Mary. It's Aunty Jesse. Everything's going to be alright," she crooned to the girl as she rocked her to and fro. "Everything's going to be alright." It was just an expression that one used at a time like this, but somehow, this time, it seemed so meaningless. How could everything ever be alright again? Rosina, beautiful, young, happy Rosina, alone again, and with a child to care for. Jessica was quite alone in the world, but it was different. For some inexplicable reason, Jessica belonged alone, at least for now. But Rosina — not Rosina. She was a happy wife. She'd loved her husbands — both of her husbands. She enjoyed fussing about them. In the short time she'd been married to Mr. Menzies, she'd become so very dedicated to him, perhaps out of gratitude, but perhaps too, out of love. And now, this loving woman, with so much to give, was once again alone, with no man to take care of, or to take care of her, and she seemed so totally abandoned.

Finally, Jessica had enough nerve to look directly into her friend's face, and what she saw there frightened her. A dull film had closed over Rosina's usually bright eyes and there was a hopelessness there that chilled Jessica's heart. It was not a time for silence. Instinctively, the nurse knew that she had to bring her dear friend out of shock, or lose her forever.

"Here, take Mary," she said briskly as she shoved the child into Rosina's arms. "Rosina," she practically yelled in her friend's ear. "Rosina, take Mary!" The baby began to cry. There was still nothing in Rosina's eyes. Jessica, fighting tears, reached out and slapped the woman, hard, across the face, and those nearby murmured their disapproval. "Rosina!" she yelled again. "Mary, take Mary!" and just before the child slipped to the floor, Rosina's arms curled up to stop her. "That's better, Rosina," remarked Jessica, kindly, still fighting tears as she noticed the red swelling on Rosina's face where she had struck her.

"Now, come with me. I need you." She took Rosina by the arm and fairly dragged her out of the hotel. She kept her eyes averted. She did not want to see that look in Rosina's eyes, and she did not want Rosina to see the tears in hers.

It was a strange sight, the two bedraggled women, stumbling down the street. The nurse leading the way, careful not to look back, and Rosina following obediently, as one in a trance, hanging on to her child with blackened hands. They were met by George Dickerson at the entrance to the station. He reached out to Rosina with one arm, his other needed to balance himself on his one good leg. She allowed him to pull her to him where she buried her head in his shoulder and began to sob. There was a tenderness about the moment that would live forever in Jessica's memory. This man, who seemed such a rogue, showed such great tenderness when the occasion warranted it. She breathed a sigh as she turned away, eyes burning with hot tears.

My God, it was such a difficult life, here in the primitive North Country. She began to wonder again what she was doing there. It all seemed so futile . . . and then, just when things seemed to be the darkest, the train rolled in. The joy and excitement with which it was welcomed brought a new feeling to Jessica's heart.

Things were never entirely hopeless. Even here, in this God forsaken wilderness. Just when everything was going so wrong, people came and did the good things that people do in an emergency, and even the toughest, most cynical heart had to be gladdened by it.

There were cars full of clean linen, barrels of fresh water, mattresses, cots, and, most importantly, food. Boxes and boxes of food. A sort of hysteria hit the crowd at the depot as they helped the Latchford crew to unload. There were medical supplies to be taken care of, and Jessica busied herself with this chore.

The most incredible thing happened then. A party atmosphere arose from the blackened rubble that was Cobalt, and everyone who could, joined in. The wounded were made comfortable, and even supplied with liquor to help ease the pain. The food was cooked and shared by all. Small parties developed at the various buildings that were used to billet the townspeople. Some people slept on the train. As evening darkness fell, children were bedded down, bonfires lit, bottles passed around, and everyone exchanged stories about where they were when the fire hit, what they did, where they went, what they saw and felt. A camaraderie that knew no social borders was experienced by all. It was temporary, and everyone knew it, but it was here and now that mattered, and 'when the chips were down', as the saying went, you could depend on these tough Northerners to pull together and do the right thing. Jessica felt good!

It was a long night, and it showed no promise of ending. People were reluctant to go to bed, almost as though they were afraid to miss something. It was New Year's Eve once again, and the hearty wanted to stay awake to see the dawn - the dawn that would bring with it so much promise. The plans to rebuild Cobalt were formed that very night. Promises were made, time and supplies were donated. Some people wandered from group to group, keeping each informed about what was going on at the other bonfires. To make the affair even more festive, a short train came down from New Liskeard, bringing with it more provisions, and fresh party-goers. Liskeard had suffered through a fire, and people compared notes about major catastrophes, one topping another with stories of fear and heroics.

Gus Menzies' name came up several times during the night and, each time, Jessica was prompted to go over to where his widow lay, arms wrapped around her daughter. But Rosina did not hear her. She was off in her own memories. Doctor Evans had given her a sedative.

As near as Jessica could piece together the different accounts of Gus Menzies' death, it had happened like this — Mr. Menzies was driving north out of town, his wife, child and some belongings in his wagon. He stopped often to pick up townspeople who were fleeing on foot, the flames fairly licking at their heels. The poor frightened horse could not manage such a load, so Mr. Menzies handed the reins over to another man and got off the wagon to run alongside. He pulled at the horse's harness, encouraging it through the most dangerous part, and when on the other side, Rosina noticed that he was no longer there. She handed Mary to a woman in the back and jumped off herself, going back to the fire to find her husband. She never found him. The wall of fire engulfed the street behind them, and she was pulled bodily away from the scene, not allowed to rush into the flames to die with her man. She fought, clawed at the men who held her captive, until there was no fight left, and she was returned limp to the wagon that stood several hundred yards away, in safety.

Those on the wagon knew that they owed their lives to Mr. Menzies, but Rosina did not hear their praise and thanksgiving. Her mind closed over the events of the day, shutting out forever the horror of it all.

George Dickerson was sitting beside Jessica when she heard one of the accounts of Gus Menzies' heroism, and he slipped his hand into hers and gave it a squeeze. Poor George Dickerson. He too had suffered a loss. They'd been good friends, Gus and George. Jessica, in a most modest fashion, squeezed Mr. Dickerson's hand in return and was rewarded with a smile that melted her heart. His eyes were brimming with tears, and they shone in the light from the fire. She was drawn to him, much as Rosina had been earlier, and she leaned over to place her head on his shoulder. She fell asleep there, nestled next to him, a feeling of security wrapping itself around her like a blanket.

14

New Beginnings

What was left of the summer was spent rebuilding Cobalt. Things would never be quite the same. Of course not. But the townspeople were given an opportunity to make a fresh start and those who chose to stay did just that.

Mr. Chow's laundry had been partially burned and a lot of Jessica's belongings were gone, or ruined. As fate would have it, Mr. Dickerson's laundered tent was spared, but the magnificent cape that Doctor Evans had given her was spoiled by the smoke and the water. Even Mr. Chow's attention could not save it, and it was with a sad heart that she disposed of the garment.

Jessica moved back to Mrs. Carson's.

The hospital was one of the first buildings to be erected, and, despite its size, or lack of it, the Cobalt and District Hospital was like a castle to Doctor Evans and Jessica.

Houses sprang up everywhere. Businesses reopened and new businesses were begun. There was a hustle about the town that gave everyone hope.

Quite a few people had moved on, however. Some were sorely missed, and others, not so. Jessica knew somehow that she would never go. Too much had happened here to bond her to the country, and in spite of her youth, she became a solid citizen, almost an oldtimer of Cobalt.

Rosina . . . she stayed, more because she had nowhere else to go, than for any great love for the town that had widowed her twice. She changed a great deal after the fire. Oddly enough, the house that Gus Menzies had built for her withstood the blaze, and she lived quietly there until she died at the age of eighty-three.

The spark that had made Rosina shine in her youth had been snuffed out that tragic day, and, although they remained friends, Jessica was never able to get close to Rosina again.

They took to calling one another by their last names, when they did chance to meet, much like the older women in the community.

Rosina faired well financially, as Gus Menzies had been a shrewd businessman. Mary was packed off to Toronto to school and returned seldom, and soon, never. Jessica received the odd note from her Godchild at Christmas or on her birthday, but there was none of the closeness and love that Jessica had hoped for when she had held wee Mary in her arms at her baptism.

Doctor Evans aged quickly. It was that same autumn that he sustained a serious injury while treating a patient. He tried to subdue a drunken Indian and was stabbed in the chest. He was taken to North Bay where he underwent surgery, but he seemed not to be the same man after that.

His deep affection and admiration for Jessica did not dim, though, and he continued to keep in touch with her after he left Cobalt.

Jessica — well — Jessica just stayed on. She was clever, hard-working, unselfish, and it was only her dry English wit that kept her from seeming too saint-like.

George Dickerson came and went. And finally came and stayed.

"Evening, Ma'am," he said one night, popping around to Jessica's lodgings as he so often did.

"Hello, Mr. Dickerson," answered Jessica, not bothering to look up. She was counting stitches on a needle and that required her concentration.

Finally she raised her head and smiled. "Why, Mr. Dickerson, you've shaved your beard off!" He'd grown one on his last trip to the far north.

He grinned and nodded. "Yes, I did. It served its purpose well. It kept me warm on those cold nights up north. But now . . ." he paused, obviously wanting her reaction to his next sentence. "No — well — I'm hoping to travel less — sort of settle down. Let the younger men, the boys, do the leg work. I've decided to spend more time here in Cobalt, in my office."

If there was any special acknowledgement in Jessica's eyes, it was hard to distinguish, as she quickly looked back to the sock on her lap.

"I was knitting you a pair of socks, Mr. Dickerson — heavy ones, the kind of work sock a man wears into the North." She held the unfinished article up for him to see. "And I've had your tent laundered," she added. They both laughed.

"Will you marry me?" he asked so suddenly that she had no time to mask the feeling in her black eyes. They sat staring at one another for a short while, and finally she spoke.

"Yes, Mr. Dickerson . . . George, I'll marry you." There was no great passion in her voice, nor was there resignation. It was just something that was destined to be from their very first meeting on the train, when their eyes first met. George knew it then. And perhaps Jessica had known it too.

They were married at the little Anglican Church on the hill. It was a small ceremony. Doctor Evans gave the bride away.

It was a good marriage. They had their troubles, as does anyone who says "I do", but they saw them all through together.

And they had six sons. They watched with pride as Cobalt and their boys grew to maturity.

THE END